I0631238

Pelham Edgar

A Study of Shelley

with special reference to his nature poetry

Pelham Edgar

A Study of Shelley
with special reference to his nature poetry

ISBN/EAN: 9783337391065

Printed in Europe, USA, Canada, Australia, Japan

Cover: Foto ©Andreas Hilbeck / pixelio.de

More available books at **www.hansebooks.com**

A STUDY OF SHELLEY

With Special Reference to His Nature Poetry.

DISSERTATION

PRESENTED TO THE BOARD OF UNIVERSITY STUDIES
OF THE JOHNS HOPKINS UNIVERSITY FOR THE
DEGREE OF DOCTOR OF PHILOSOPHY.

BY

PELHAM EDGAR,

ASSOCIATE-PROFESSOR OF FRENCH IN VICTORIA UNIVERSITY.

TORONTO:
WILLIAM BRIGGS.
WESLEY BUILDINGS.
1899

With Special Reference to His Nature Poetry.

DISSERTATION

PRESENTED TO THE BOARD OF UNIVERSITY STUDIES
OF THE JOHNS HOPKINS UNIVERSITY FOR THE
DEGREE OF DOCTOR OF PHILOSOPHY.

BY

PELHAM EDGAR,

ASSOCIATE-PROFESSOR OF FRENCH IN VICTORIA UNIVERSITY

TORONTO:
WILLIAM BRIGGS.
WESLEY BUILDINGS.
1899

PREFATORY NOTE.

THE pages which follow are an initial contribution to the study of Shelley's Nature poetry. In establishing the existing criticism on the subject, I have refrained from comment except with reference to the question of idealization. An extension of this criticism in any thorough sense would have carried me much beyond the ordinary limits of an investigation of this kind. It was, therefore, possible merely to indicate the direction which the study will take (page 20), and to state my intention of publishing the results at some future date. I need make no apology for the importance which I have attached to Shelley's similes as throwing light upon his poetic methods of treating Nature; and in this connection I take the welcome opportunity of thanking Professor Bright for many valuable suggestions and much kindly aid.

TABLE OF CONTENTS.

PART I.—EXTANT CRITICISM.

	PAGE
Growth of love for Nature (Dowden, "Life of Shelley," 165*f*) . . .	7
Tendency to Idealization (Stephen, in *Cornhill*, XXXIX. ; Whipple, *Essays and Reviews*)	8
Love of Indefiniteness and Change (Brooke, in *Macmillan*, XLII.) . .	9
" " " (Sweet, in "Shelley Society Papers," I., Part II.	13
Power to Isolate Nature (Brooke)	10
Subtleness of Observation (Brooke)	10
" " (Scudder, in *Atlantic Monthly*, LXX.) . .	17
Primitive Quality or Mythopœic Power (Brooke)	11
" " " " (Sweet)	13, 15
Pathetic Fallacy (Brooke ; *Quarterly Review*, CLXIV. ; Roden Noel, in *British Quarterly*, LXXXII.)	12
Place in Development of Nature Poetry (Sweet). .	13
Shelley and Wordsworth (Sweet) . .	14
Objectivity (Sweet) . . .	14
Cosmic Sympathies (Sweet) . .	14
Vastness of Landscape (Sweet) . .	14
" " (Scudder)	18
Colour Sense, Analysis of (Sweet) . .	16
" " (Scudder) . .	17
Shelley and Coleridge (Sweet) . .	17
Shelley and Keats (Scudder)	17
Power to Vitalize Abstractions (Palgrave, "Landscape in Poetry") .	18
Lack of Human Feeling (Palgrave)	18

PART II.

1. Analysis of Similes	19, 21 32
2. Extension of Existing Criticism .	. 20
Arrangement of Similes . . .	33–155

I.

EXTANT CRITICISM ON SHELLEY'S NATURE POETRY.

Growth of his Love for Nature.

Professor Dowden, in his "Life of Shelley," refers to Shelley's early indifference for natural beauty.

In the midst of the mountains of Cwm Elan, in 1811, Shelley writes to his friend Hogg, "'This is most divine scenery, but all very dull, stale, flat, and unprofitable; indeed, the place is a very great bore.' The poet in Shelley at this time was trammelled and taken in the toils by the psychologist and metaphysician." ("Life of Shelley," I. 165.)

"In the summer of 1811 his delight in mountain and vale and stream was tracked and hunted down and done to death by his passion for psychological analysis. 'This country of Wales' (writing to Miss Hitchener) 'is exceedingly grand; rocks piled on each other to tremendous heights, rivers formed into cataracts by their projections, and valleys clothed with woods, present an appearance of enchantment. But why do they enchant? Why is it more affecting than a plain? It cannot be innate; is it acquired? Thus does knowledge lose all the pleasure which involuntarily arises by attempting to arrest the fleeting phantom as it passes. Vain attempt; like the chemist's ether, it evaporates under our observation; it flies from all but the slaves of passion and sickly sensibility who will not analyze a feeling.' And again, 'Nature is here marked with the most impressive characters of loveliness and grandeur. Once I was tremulously alive to tones and scenes; the habit of analyzing feelings, I fear, does not agree with this. It is spontaneous, and when it becomes subject to consideration, ceases to exist.'" ("Life of Shelley," I. 167.)

"'I am more astonished at the grandeur of the scenery' (letter to Hogg) 'than I expected. I do not *now* much regard it. I have other things to think of.'" ("Life of Shelley," I. 168.)

Contrast with these letters those which he wrote from Keswick after his marriage. (Letters of Nov. and Dec., 1811.) Here at last we begin to see the genuine Shelley.

Again, in 1812 we have evidence of the opposite excess of meaningless and delirious rapture, as in the letter to Miss Hitchener when her morality had been put in question.

"You are to my fancy as a thunder-riven pinnacle of rock, firm amid the rushing tempest and the boiling surge. Ay, stand forever firm, and when our ship anchors close to thee, the crew will cover thee with flowers."

Tendency to Excessive Idealization.

This forms the substance of LESLIE STEPHEN's contribution to the *Cornhill Magazine*, XXXIX. Compare *Quarterly Review*, LXIV., and SHAIRP in *Fraser's Magazine*, N. S. 20. To exemplify their extreme position I quote from Mr. Leslie Stephen. "The materials with which he works are impalpable abstractions, where other poets use concrete images. . . . When he speaks of natural scenery the solid earth seems to be dissolved, and we are in presence of nothing but the shifting phantasmagoria of cloudland, the glow of moonlight on eternal snow, or the 'golden lightning of the setting sun.'"

While admitting that the general temper of Shelley's poetry is distinctly ideal, it is necessary to make a protest against that partial view which removes his work entirely from the sphere of human interest, and regards it merely as the meteoric display of an overcharged imagination which has never fed upon the concrete realities of life.

WHIPPLE (*Essays and Reviews*) makes the following plea on Shelley's behalf against the charges of unreality and lack of human sympathy: "The predominance of his spiritual over his animal nature; the velocity with which his mind, loosed from the 'grasp of gravitation,' darted upwards into regions whither slower-pacing imaginations could not follow; the amazing fertility with which he poured out crowds of magnificent images, and the profuse flood of dazzling radiance, blinding the eye with excess of light, which they shed over his compositions, his love of idealizing the world of sense, until it became instinct with thought, and infusing into things dull and lifeless to the sight and touch the qualities of individual existence; the marvellous keenness of insight with which he pierced beneath even the refinements of thought, and evolved new materials of wonder and delight from a seemingly exhausted subject—all these, to a superficial observer, carry with them the appearance of unreality."

It is important to adjust ourselves aright towards this question of idealism in Shelley's poetry. We must frankly admit at the outset that the tendency towards idealism exists in a very marked manner in the poems. We find, therefore, that criticism ranges itself into two opposing camps. On the one hand, positive common-sense opinion, as represented by Leslie Stephen, will find that Shelley nourished his imagination with substance too rare and immaterial to form the food which a healthy and robust mind should crave as its natural diet. On the other hand, more enthusiastic critics like Whipple or Roden Noel (see p. 12) assert that his idealism constitutes the chief and enduring charm of his poetry. It is well here to hold a middle position. We may congratulate ourselves as lovers of English literature that our poetry with Shelley's advent received an imaginative impulse into ethereal regions where wing of poet never beat before. But is he, therefore, the "beautiful and ineffectual angel, beating in the void his luminous wings in vain," of Matthew Arnold's perverse creating? Shelley's burning zeal for humanity would of itself forbid the acceptance of that view in its sweeping entirety. In the poet's youth we must admit that his conception of humanity is visionary and false, and that his shadowy portraits are evasively delusive and vague in outline. But with growing years the concrete elements of his poetry gathered strength, and qualities of firmness and precision began to show themselves in such abundance as to afford the assurance in his future work of a more harmonious and equable relation between the ideal and the real world. In October, 1821, Shelley wrote to Mr. Gisborne, referring to the most idealistic of his poems: "'The Epipsychidion' is a mystery; as to real flesh and blood, you know that I do not deal in those articles; you might as well go to a gin-shop for a leg of mutton, as expect anything human or earthly from me." But let us first eliminate the sportive fun from this statement, and remember that within the less than two years that remained to him of life, he had produced those admirably human poems, "To Jane," and conceived and in part written a play upon the thoroughly human subject of "Charles I." In conclusion, we must bear in mind that in a large measure the impression of excessive idealism arises from the subtle character of the poetic imagery which Shelley employs to light up hidden affinities between human emotion and processes of beauty in the natural world. In this regard Shelley does not sin alone, and might shelter himself, did he require refuge from criticism, behind the accepted names of Lamartine or Victor Hugo, whose splendid imagery is conceived in a similar spirit, and employed for a similar end.

Love of Indefiniteness and Change (*cf. infra* SWEET).

REV. STOPFORD BROOKE. *Macmillan*, XLII.

To the love of indefiniteness and the love of change, qualities embedded in Shelley's temperament, STOPFORD BROOKE attributes the leading characteristics of his Nature poetry. "His love of that which is indefinite and changeful made him enjoy and describe better than any other English poet that scenery of the clouds and sky which is indefinite owing to infinite change of appearance. The incessant forming and unforming of the vapours which he describes in the last verse of 'The Cloud,' is that which he most cared to paint. Words-worth often draws, and with great force, the aspect of the sky, and twice, with great elaboration, in 'The Excursion'; but it is only a momentary aspect, and it is mixed up with illustrations taken from the works of men, with the landscape of the earth below where men are moving, with his own feelings about the scene, and with moral or imaginative lessons. Shelley, when he is at work on the sky, troubles it with none of these human matters,* and he describes not only the momentary aspect, but also the change and progress of the sunset or the storm. And he does this with the greatest care, and with a characteristic attention to those delicate tones and half-tones of colour which resemble the subtle imaginations and feelings he liked to discover in human nature, and to which he gave form in poetry."

Power to isolate Nature.

There follow references in detail to the more celebrated cloud studies at dawn or sunset or during storm to be found in the poems. Of the dawn in the opening of " Prometheus, II.," he says : "The changes of colour, as the light increases in the spaces of pure sky and in the clouds, are watched and described with precise truth ; the slow progress of the dawn, during a long time, is noted down line by line, and all the move-ment of the mists and of the clouds 'shepherded by the slow, unwilling wind.' Nor is that minuteness of observation want-ing which is the proof of careful love. Shelley's imaginative study of beauty is revealed in the way the growth of the dawn is set before us by the waxing and waning of the light of the star, as the vapours rise and melt before the morn. The storms are even better than the sunsets and dawns. . . . Criticism has no voice when it thinks that no other poet has ever attempted to render, with the same absolute loss of himself, the successive changes, minute by minute, of such an hour of tempest and of sunrise. We are alone with Nature ; I might even say, we see Nature alone with herself." Then follows an enthusiastic analysis of the "Ode to the West Wind."

Subtle Observa-tion.

Also, to his love of the indefinite and changeful, Stopford Brooke attributes Shelley's power of describing vast landscapes (e.g., "Euganean Hills," 90ff; "Alastor," 550ff), and his delight in the intricacy of forest scenery (" Recollection," 9ff, " Alastor," 420ff, " Rosalind," 95ff, " Prometheus," II. ii. and IV. 194ff.

Power to Isolate Nature (cf. infra SWEET).

Stopford Brooke proceeds to discuss Shelley's treatment of Nature in as far as it was affected by his lack of a definite idea concerning the source of Nature. "Again, just because Shelley had no wish to

* *Vide* Sweet. "Shelley Society Papers," I. Pt. II.

conceive of Nature as involved in one definite thought, he had the power of conceiving the life of separate things in Nature with astonishing individuality. When he wrote of the Cloud, or of Arethusa, or of the Moon, or of the Earth, as distinct existences, he was not led away from their solitary personality by any universal existence in which they were merged, or by the necessity of adding to these any tinge of humanity, any elements of thought or love, such as the Pantheist is almost sure to add. His imagination was free to realize pure Nature, and the power by which he does this, as well as the work done, are quite unique in modern poetry. Theology, with its one Creator of the universe; Pantheism, with its 'one spirit's plastic stress'; Science, with its one Energy, forbid the modern poet, whose mind is settled into any one of these three views, to see anything in Nature as having a separate life of its own. He cannot, as a Greek could do, divide the life of the air from that of the earth, of the cloud from that of the stream. But Shelley, able to loosen himself from all these modern conceptions which unite the various universe, could and did, when he pleased, divide and subdivide the life of Nature in the same way as a Greek. And this is the cause why, even in the midst of wholly modern imagery and a modern manner, one is conscious of a Greek note in many passages of his poetry of Nature. The following little poem on the Dawn might be conceived by a primitive Aryan. It is a Nature myth.

> " ' The pale stars are gone !
> For the sun, their swift shepherd,
> To their folds them compelling,
> In the depths of the dawn,
> Hastes, in meteor-eclipsing array, and they flee
> Beyond his blue dwelling
> * As fawns flee the leopard.'

Primitive Quality.

" But Shelley's conceptions of the life of these natural things are less human than even the Homeric Greek or early Indian poet would have made them. They describe the work of nature in terms of human act. Shelley's spirits of the earth and moon are utterly apart from our world of thought and from our life. Of this class of poems, 'The Cloud' is the most perfect example. It describes the life of the Cloud as it might have been a million years before man came on earth. The 'sanguine sunrise' and the 'orbèd maiden,' the moon, who are the playmates of the cloud, are pure elemental beings. . . . In Wordsworth's poems we touch the human heart of flowers and birds. In Shelley's, we touch 'Shapes that haunt Thought's wildernesses.' Yet it is quite possible, though we cannot feel affection for Shelley's Cloud or Bird, that they are both

---

* Compare also Sweet's consideration of Shelley in his myth making capacity ("Shelley Society Papers," I. Pt. II., *vide infra*), and see *Quarterly Review*, CLXIV.

truer to the actual fact of things than Wordsworth made his birds
and clouds.* Strip off the imaginative clothing from 'The Cloud,'
and science will support every word of it. Let the sky-lark sing,
let the flowers grow, for their own joy alone. In truth, what sympathy have they, what sympathy has nature with man?

The Pathetic Fallacy.

"The other side of Shelley's relation to nature is a remarkable
contrast to this statement. When he was absorbed in his own
being, and writing poems which concerned himself alone, he makes
nature the mere image of his own feelings, the creature of his mood."

In this connection reference must be made to the *Quarterly Review*, CLXIV., and to the *British Quarterly*, LXXXII. (Hon. Roden
Noel).

Quarterly Review, CLXIV. :

His own moods . . . formed no permanent essential part of
himself; he could, without effort, transfer them to Nature. . . .
The identity of feeling, which he thus establishes between himself
and Nature, is as fascinating as it is peculiar. Yet it is certainly a
sign of weakness. In "Alastor," for instance, he reads into his surroundings his own pensive and melancholy life. Autumn sighs in
the sere woods, the grass shivers at the touch of the poet's foot;
his own hair sings dirges in the wind. No man whose personality is
strongly marked, can thus transfer himself to the natural world.
In Shelley, the sense of personality was dimmed by the absence of
will. He never learned to distinguish between his own feelings and
those of others; but in his later poetry he shakes off the excessive
morbidity of "Alastor," . . . and no longer reads his own misery
into the aerial merriment of the wind, the wave and the bird. The
contrast offers a significant proof of the steady development of the
stronger sides of his character.

British Quarterly, LXXXII. (Hon. Roden Noel) :

Proceeding from the assertion that, in order to arrive at a satis-
factory idea of nature, science and poetry are alike necessary, the
essayist continues to oppose Ruskin's effort "to distinguish the
representation of Nature as she is, which he ascribes to Homer and
to Scott among ourselves, and the representation of her as she only
appears to our distorting emotions. That seems to me a misleading
distinction, because what Nature in herself, apart from our minds is,
we do not accurately know; we can see her only as she appears to
us by virtue of the constitution of our faculties, senses, understanding, emotion, and imagination. Therefore, I cannot admit that
there is a true nature, which the man of science and the land-sur-
veyor see, but a false nature, which the person of delicate suscepti-

---

* *Vide infra* (p. 12) Roden Noel on the distinction between scientific and
poetic truth.

bilities and the poet suppose themselves to see. . . . There is no more reason why those higher faculties should be excluded from their share and function in the revelation of truth than there is why the senses and the understanding should be excluded. . . . Hence, I cannot enter into Mr. Ruskin's preference of Scott over Shelley as a poet, which is founded on this distinction between them.* . . . What would Shelley's 'Alastor' be without the magnificent scenery of mountain and stream amid which he moves onward to the close? They are one. They have joined hands and interpret one another. The result of the poet's meditation is neither man alone, nor nature alone, but some fair spiritual child of their espousals. This, I maintain, is somewhat distinctively new and precious added to our intellectual and emotional treasure."

SWEET. "Shelley Society Papers," I. Pt. II.

This is the most elaborate study of Shelley's nature poetry that has hitherto appeared.

Shelley's Place in the Development of Nature Poetry.

The author briefly surveys the wide field of world literatures where the nature idea finds its inception and development. The **The Vedas.** Vedic nature poetry is important in connection with Shelley's mythology; "nor in a consideration of Shelley's attitude towards nature must we disregard the Teutonic and the Celtic elements in his poetry. To the former we **Teutonic and Celtic Elements.** relate his feeling for mystery, and to the latter we refer the extraordinary keenness of his colour faculty. Shelley's description of the imagined ruins of Venice in the 'Euganean Hills,' with the sea-mew flying above, and the palace-gate 'toppling o'er the abandoned sea,' recalls . . . that aspect of Old English lyric poetry represented by 'The Wanderer,' and the impressive fragment known as 'The Ruin.' . . . Shelley heightens the effect, almost as in 'Beowulf,' by

> " 'The fisher on his watery way,
>   Wandering at the close of day,'

hastening to pass the gloomy shore

> " 'Lest thy dead should, from their sleep
>   Bursting o'er the starlight deep,
>   Lead a rapid masque of death
>   O'er the waters of his path ! '

"The 'natural magic' of such a description as this is, or, at least, might be, wholly English, wholly Teutonic—strange as such an assertion may seem to a critic like Mr. Arnold, whose ideas of the

---

* See Ruskin's "Modern Painters," Pt. IV., Vol. III.

Teutonic spirit are gained from a one-sided contemplation of modern German literature at a period when it was still struggling for the mastery of the rudiments of style and technique, lost in the barbarism of the Thirty Years' War.

"Shelley's poem 'The Question,' is . . . as purely Celtic both in its colour-pictures, . . . and its ethereal unreality and delicate, fanciful sentiment. It need hardly be said that this 'Celtic note' in Shelley no more proves Celtic race-influence than the 'Greek note' in Keats proves that Keats was of Greek descent. Shelley looks at nature with the same eyes as an old Celtic poet, because both were inspired by the same sky and earth, both loved the same flowers, fields and forests."

After tracing English nature poetry to the first truly modern conception in Milton, the writer swiftly passes the intervening period and proceeds to a discussion of Shelley's work in closer detail.

Shelley and Wordsworth.

"Shelley's real sympathies are with inanimate nature. Here he is at home. Here he is unique and supreme. He is indeed 'the poet of nature' in a truer sense than Wordsworth is. Wordsworth is really the poet of the homely, the common-place in nature as in man. Whatever in nature harmonizes with his own narrow sympathies he assimilates and reproduces with a power all his own. . . . Shelley, on the other hand, seeks to penetrate into the very heart of nature in all her manifestations, without regard to their association with human feeling. While in his treatment of man he is all subjectivity, in his
Objectivity. treatment of nature he is often purely objective. In such a poem as 'The Cloud' there is not only no trace of Wordsworthian egotism, but the whole description . . . is as remote from human feeling as it could well be, consistent with the poetic necessity for personification."*

Cosmic and Elemental Sympathies.†

"The range of Shelley's sympathies is bounded only by the universe itself. He combines forests, mountains, rivers and seas
Vastness of into vast ideal landscapes ; he dives into the depths of
Landscape. the earth, soars among clouds and storms, and communes 'with the sphere of sun and moon.'"

Love of Indefiniteness and Change.‡

"Shelley's love of the changing and fleeting aspects of nature — the interest with which he watched the formation of mist and cloud

---

* *Cf. supra*, Stopford Brooke.
† See also Brandes' "Hauptströmungen," IV., pp. 248*f*, and Chevrillon in *Revue de Paris*, June 1st, 1898.
‡ *Cf. supra*, Stopford Brooke.

and the shifting hues of dawn and sunset- -is, like his sense of structure, a natural result of the half-scientific spirit with which he regarded nature, for it is in the changing phenomena of nature that real life lies. According to Mr. Brooke, Shelley's love for the changeful in nature is the result of the inherent changefulness of his temperament. But of this I can see but little in his life. He was impulsive enough —for without impulsiveness he would hardly have been a poet—but not fickle or undecided in his feelings and principles.

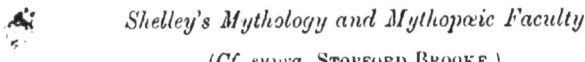

Shelley's Mythology and Mythopœic Faculty.

(Cf. supra, STOFFORD BROOKE.)

"Shelley's love of natural phenomena sometimes shows itself in naive expressions of delight, and simple comparisons which remind us of the nature-poetry of the Veda" (e.g., "Witch of Atlas," XXVII.)

After referring to the employment of a conventional mythology by other poets, the essayist notes it as a characteristic of Shelley that he is without a trace of that conventionalism. "He never brings in the figures of classical mythology incidentally, but only when they are the subject of his poetry, and his handling of them in such cases is always fresh and original, as in his 'Hymn to Apollo'—the most perfect reproduction of the spirit of Greek mythology that we have in modern literature. His conception of Jupiter in his 'Prometheus' is quite new and original—he makes him the personification of all that hinders the free development of the human mind, which latter is personified by Prometheus.

"We see, then, that even where Shelley is trammeled by traditional mythology, he reveals something of that myth-making faculty in which he stands alone among modern poets—the only one who at all approaches him in this respect being his contemporary, the Swedish poet, Stagnelius. When Shelley is free to follow his own fancy, he instinctively creates nature-myths of a strangely primitive type, unlike anything in Greek or the other fully-developed mythologies, but showing marked similarity to the personifications of Vedas. . . . It is not only Shelley critics who have been struck by this characteristic. Mr. Taylor, in his 'Anthropology' (page 290), after remarking that the modern poet 'still uses for picturesqueness the metaphors which to the barbarian were real helps to express his sense,' goes on to quote as an instance the opening lines of 'Queen Mab,' . . . and analyzes them as follows: 'Here the likeness of death and sleep is expressed by the metaphor of calling them brothers; the moon is brought in to illustrate the notion of paleness, the dawn of redness; while to convey the idea of dawn shining on the sea, the simile of its sitting on a throne is introduced, and its reddening is compared on the one hand to a rose, and on the other to blushing. Now, this is the very way in which early barbaric man, not for poetic affectation, but simply to find the plainest words to convey his thoughts, would talk in metaphors taken from nature.'"

"One of the best examples of Shelley's myth-making faculty is the little poem, 'The World's Wanderers' (IV. 51), . . . as remote as anything can well be from modern thought and sentiment. Its imagery and its strange unhuman pathos are alike primitive and elemental. The same sympathy with the heavenly bodies in their wanderings through space has been expressed by some of the older Greek lyric poets, but the conception of the star's rays as wings can hardly be paralleled outside of the 'Veda.'"

Cloud Mythology—See "Laon," II. v., and IX. xxxv.; "Cloud," 73; Prom. II. i. 145.

Cloud Comparisons—See "Summer and Winter"; "Hlleas," 957; "Witch," XLVIII., LII., LV.; Liberty, 5.

Shelley's Colour Sense.

(*Vide infra, Atlantic Monthly*, LXX.)

Quotations and references are made under a variety of rubrics.

Flashing and intermittent light.
"Prom." II. iii. 30 and IV. 182; "Epips." 546; "Dejection," II.; "Orpheus," 59.

Alternations of light and shade.
"Laon," II. xlix. and XII. xxxvi.; "Athanase," II. xiii. and II. l.; "Rosal." 102; "Prom." I. 27 and I. 678; "Sens. Plant," II. 25; "Alast." 310.

Atmospheric effects.
"Prom." I. 82, II. i. 10 and II. iii. 74; "Laon," III. iii.; "Rosal," 729; "Dejection," I.; "Witch," XXXVII.

Light seen through water.
"Witch," XXVIII.

Light seen through foliage.
"Laon," II. i., VII. xi., VIII. xxx. and XII. xviii.; 'Prom." II. ii. 75; "Sens. Plant," I. 23 and I. 43; "Epips." 502.

Transmitted light.
"Letter to Maria Gisborne," 123.

Refracted light.
"Alast." 334; "Laon," VII. 20.

Reflected light or colour.
"Alast." 352; "Laon," I. xx., III. xii. and XII. xviii; "Prom." I. 467, I. 743 and II. iii. 28; "Witch," XXV.; "Recollection," V.

Objects reflected in water.

"Alast." 200, 213, 406, 457, 494; "Laon," III. xi. and VI. xxxiii.; "Prom." III. iv. 78 and IV. 193; "Sens. Plant," I. 18; "West Wind," III. 33-35; "Invitation," 50; "Recollection," 53. Also compare "Prom." II. i. 17. with Wordsworth, "Peele Castle," and *cf.* Shelley, " Evening," III.; 'Liberty," VI; "Witch," LIX.

Colour Contrast.

"Alast." 137, 584; "Rosal." 782; "Prom." III. iii. 139; "Laon," I. xi.; "Witch," X.; "Marenghi," XIII.

Shelley and Coleridge.

"Coleridge's affinity to Shelley is shown especially in his descriptions of transmitted light and colour, . . . and in his elaborate pictures of reflection in water. . . . But Coleridge does not appear to have, any more than Wordsworth or Milton, any examples of reflected light or colour as distinguished from the reflection of definite objects: Shelley's picture of the 'lake-reflected sun' illumining the 'yellow bees in the ivy bloom' seems to be entirely his own. . . . The similarity between the two poets (Coleridge and S.) in their treatment of light does not seem to be the result of imitation on the part of the younger poet: the agreement is in spirit, not in detail. The love of light was instinctive in both, and was fostered by their surroundings. Coleridge learnt to observe and love the effects of transmitted and reflected light in the shady lanes, and by the rivulets and pools of his native Devon, while Shelley learnt the same lessons in the woods of Marlowe and in his boat on the Thames."

Colour Sense—(Continued).

An admirable study of Shelley's artistic use of colour is contained in *Atlantic Monthly*, LXX. (V. D. Scudder). The analysis follows.

Colour in Keats and Shelley.

It is only in the nineteenth century that the poets have become great colourists; and no one but Keats can in this respect rival the greatness of Shelley. If Keats has more force of colour, Shelley has more purity. Keats' colouring is opaque, though brilliant, like that of a butterfly's wing; Shelley's is translucent, like an opal. Ruskin tells us that nature always paints her loveliest hues on aqueous or crystalline matter; and the very law of nature seems to be the instinct of Shelley.

Colour in " Prometheus Unbound."

" But the colour in 'Prometheus Unbound' has a higher function than to vivify the detail of the poem, or to give us a series of exquisite vignettes. The drama, by the use of light and colour, is shaped to an organic whole. It shows the harmonious evolution

2

of a central theme; and this evolution is symbolically presented through the progress of the new cosmic day." The writer develops this thesis skilfully and at some length in the remainder of the essay. Referring in more general terms to Shelley's nature poetry— "It is in the treatment of nature that the distinctive powers of Shelley's poetry are most clearly seen. The 'Prometheus' is in one sense a nature-drama. The Soul of Nature is herself one of the personages. We are transported from the wildest mountain scenery to the luxuriance of tropical valleys. Sky-cleaving peaks, glaciers, precipices, vast rivers, lakes, forests, meet us on every page. We have a sense that the drama is for the most part enacted on the heights, where the air is pure from earthly taint, and heaven and earth seem to blend. The sky scenery, above all, with its pomp and gloom of storm, its sunrise and sunset, its 'flocks of clouds in spring's delight-ful weather,' is as great as can be found in English poetry; yet the

Vastness and Delicacy. bold outline work, the strong and broad treatment of the vaster aspects of nature, reveal the poet less than the renderings of delicate detail, of fleeting sights and sounds lost on a grosser perception.

See "Prom." I. 44-47; II. i. 83-86; II. v. 11-14; III. ii. 4-9; III. ii. 25-28; IV. 180-184; IV. 431-436.

The sensitiveness and passion for change which we have seen to be the notes of Shelley's temperament, are evident in every one of these passages. (*Cf. supra*, Stopford Brooke.) "It is doubtful whether any poet before our century, whatever his equipment, could so closely and finely have rendered the minutiæ of nature."

The latest systematic presentation in English criticism of Shelley's nature poetry is contained in Francis Palgrave's 'Landscape in Poetry,' Macmillan & Co., 1897. The treatment is sketchy and unsatisfactory, and, if anything, hostile in tone. He objects that Shelley's landscape "is inevitably limited and dyed by the colours of his mind; . . . that no true poet of any age has left us so gigantic a mass of wasted effort, exuberance so Asiatic, such oceans (to speak out) of fluent, well-intended platitude." His shorter and chiefly his later lyrics show him to the best advantage. "Yet even here at times the matter is attenuated as the film of the soap-bubble, gaining through its very thinness its marvellous iridescent beauty. 'Shelley seems to go up and burst,' was Tennyson's remark on a passage of this character.

Vivifying Power. "In his best moods, where he has focussed his eye on his subject, it has that strange power of vitalizing abstractions and things of nature on which Macaulay has commented in his brilliant manner.

Lack of Human Feeling. "We must not look in his landscape for human feeling interfused as in Coleridge's, for the chord of true passion, or of the humanly pathetic, Shelley could scarcely strike; nor again for Nature moralized and spiritualized, as by

Wordsworth ; Shelley's landscape is essentially descriptive, but raised to a life of its own by an imaginative power of perhaps unsurpassed pure vividness, and that personifying habit which we have just noticed."

Literal truth and fidelity of description is accorded to the landscape in the "Euganean Hills," and to a few passages from his later lyrics.

II.

I have now given the substance of the most important studies on the subject of Shelley's nature poetry, and in the course of this presentation have found it necessary to combat only the extreme views which obtain with reference to the poet's idealistic tendencies. To obtain a satisfactorily complete idea of Shelley's nature poetry, the existing criticism has to be extended and supplemented in many directions. With this end in view, I have endeavoured

1. To bring to bear upon the problem an entirely new method of examination (namely, the study of the Similes).

2. To supplement investigations such as Sweet's, whose only fault lies in their incompleteness.

1. A STUDY OF SHELLEY'S SIMILES.

I here advance a large amount of material, arranged in such a manner as to throw abundant light upon Shelley's treatment of beauty in the external world, to illustrate his preferences and the individual peculiarities of his genius, and to exhibit his marvellous skill in adapting the world of nature to the elucidation of subtle intellectual states.

The wealth of Shelley's figurative language, and the extraordinary range of his similes have stirred the wonder of critics, and led them to affirm in his poetry a brilliancy that blinds and dazzles with excess. I wish, on the contrary, to affirm their artistic perfection, as constantly subordinated to some defined and conscious æsthetic impulse.

Shelley's own opinion of the nature of his powers will serve as a valuable initial commentary upon this portion of my work. "And in this I have long believed that my power consists in sympathy, and that part of the imagination which relates to sympathy and contemplation. I am formed, if for anything not in common with the herd of mankind, *to apprehend minute and remote distinctions of feeling, whether relative to external nature or the living beings which surround us,* and to communicate the conceptions which result from considering either the moral or the material universe as a whole."— *Letter to Godwin,* December 11th, 1817.

It is clear, then, that we have in a systematic presentation of the similes an important factor which has never entered into the consideration of Shelley's Nature poetry; and in the light of his figurative language we may read the subtler operations of his mind, and see the paths upon which it was prone to run, in as far as human limitations grant us such an insight.

2. EXTENSION OF EXISTING CRITICISM.*

The following investigations are extended :

(a) *Love of Indefiniteness and the Love of Change.*

In these characteristics of Shelley's genius, Stopford Brooke assumes to discover the key to his philosophy of Nature. The analysis is skilfully conducted, and it is impossible to dispute the fact that Shelley's changeful temperament is mirrored faithfully in his poetry. But while not actually challenging these results, it is possible to show that they are misapplied. It seemed necessary, therefore, to investigate afresh Shelley's philosophy of Nature, to connect it with his theory of Beauty, and to point at least to some permanent and abiding ideas which give character and solidity to Shelley's work in this direction.

(b) *Shelley's Place in the Development of Nature Poetry.*

Sweet has made a general approach to this subject. In connection with Shelley's philosophy of Nature, more special reference than in Dr. Sweet's essay must be made to Shelley in his relation to Wordsworth, and in a lesser degree to Coleridge, Scott, Byron, and Keats.

(c) *Colour in Shelley's Poetry.*

This has already received treatment in Section I. It only remains, after the analysis of the colour similes given below, to supplement the categories which Sweet has established.

---

* NOTE.—This second section of the study, comprising II. 2 (a), (b), and (c), will be shortly published.

1. ANALYSIS OF THE SIMILES.

The total number of similes in Shelley's poetry is 1989. The above collection contains 1720, all of which have a bearing upon appearances of the external world, whether developed for the sake of their own beauty or subordinated to the illumination of subtle mental operations. This fact is in itself significant.

I now pass to a consideration of the various classes of simile in some detail. The basis of arrangement is not a merely artificial classification, but is founded upon the most prominent characteristic in every case ; though all are broadly included within the generic title of Nature Similes.

(1) Similes of Colour.*

The similes in which colour is the most prominent feature number 425, whereas colour as a more subdued element may be observed in many more. Comparing this result proportionately with the similes arising from other senses than that of sight, we find that Similes of Sound amount to 210, while Similes of Odour naturally sink to 12. Examining the Similes of Colour more closely they fall into various natural subdivisions.

(a) Cloud Colour.

It satisfies our preconceived idea of Shelley's poetry to discover that 59 similes involve more or less careful and beautiful cloud descriptions (always bearing in mind that many admirable cloud similes occur in other categories). By reference to 2, 3, 4, 9, 11, 13, 52, 59, we gain an insight into Shelley's habitual **Descriptions of men and women.** method of describing human (or spiritual) forms. Here his tendency to idealization mars the concrete presentation of form and feature. His women are filmy shapes of diaphanous vapour, and even his men are effeminate creations entirely wanting in masculine vigour, and impelled alone by the fierce unrest of the spiritual flame within. To confirm this statement further reference should be made to the following passages in the poems.

Descriptions of Women.

See "Alastor," 175*f*; "Laon," II. xxiii.,'II. xxix., V. xxiii*f*, V. xliv.

Descriptions of Men (or male spirits).

"Laon," I. xlii., I. lvii., IV. xxix. ; "Rosalind," 909*ff*, 1009*f*; "Prince Ath." *passim.*

Shelley's descriptions of men are certainly vitiated by this excessive idealism. Contrast, for example, the brawn and muscle of Goethe's "Prometheus," or of Tennyson's "Geraint"—

---

* The analysis which follows is in part an extension of Sweet's categories (see pp. 16, 17).

> " Who, moving, cast the coverlet aside,
> And bared the knotted column of his throat,
> The massive square of his heroic breast,
> And arms on which the standing muscle sloped,
> As slopes a wild brook o'er a little stone,
> Running too vehemently to break upon it.
> And Enid woke and sat beside the couch,
> Admiring him, and thought within herself,
> Was ever man so grandly made as he?"—

or Kipling's unconscious heroes with honest sweat of toil on their begrimed faces. The modern world has done with men, however eloquent their eyes and gestures, who weep and faint with weariness. They are a survival of seventeenth century French sentimentality, utterly alien to the English temperament, and as happily buried in the past as the Satanism of Byron's breed of destiny-branded heroes.

Idealism, which was the weakness of Shelley's masculine figures, is an element that intensifies the beauty of his women. They are not wholly abstractions of cloud and vapour. The general impression which their description conveys may be bewildering, but only because the images which denote it are merged in the Ideal of Beauty,—

> " Till they are lost, and in that Beauty furled
> Which penetrates and clasps and fills the world,
> Scarce visible from extreme loveliness."

Clouds in repose or slow-moving (or vapours).

1, 3, 16, 17, 23, 30; *cf.* also in other categories 225, 1290, 1296, 1363, 1695.

Clouds in swift motion (or vapours).

9, 13, 18, 31, 36, 37, 39, 47, 53; *cf.* also 1364, 1373, 1477, 1485, 1487, 1491, 1497, 1534, 1567, 1578, 1706.

A pregnant contrast between Shelley and Wordsworth is afforded by their respective descriptions of clouds, Shelley preferring habitually to revel in their swiftness, and Wordsworth to rejoice in their deep repose. The strenuous palpitating swiftness of Shelley is certainly never attained by the elder poet, though he has his moments of keen participation in the ardours of rapid motion, as witness his noble poem, " To the Clouds."

The love of speed was rooted in Shelley's temperament (as the similes of swiftness attest), and the clouds he paints are suffused also with an intensity and purity of colour which no English poet has ever approached.

Intensity of Colour in Cloud Similes.

5, 18, 19, 26, 36, 43, 50.

Colour Contrast, 5, 12, 13, 21.

Transmitted Light, 33, 34, 38, 40, 45, 46, 51, 55.

(*b*) WATER COLOUR—36 similes.

Transmitted Light, 65, 71 ; *Reflected,* 71, 95 ; *Intensity,* 61, 90 ; *Contrast,* 61, 63, 74, 91.

(*c*) THE SUN—31 similes.

Transmitted, 124 ; *Intensity,* 100, 118, 120, 121 ; *Contrast,* 113.

(*d*) THE MOON—22 similes.

Transmitted, 135, 136, 141, 148 ; *Reflected,* 129, 142 ; *Intensity,* 133, 139, 145 ; *Contrast,* 128.

(*e*) THE STARS—37 similes, and see under (*j*).

Transmitted, 159, 167, 168 ; *Reflected,* 149, 154 ; *Intensity,* 158 (in context), 161, 162, 176 ; *Contrast,* 168 ; *Motion,* 173.

178 deserves attention, where the light of a star is compared to the scent of a jonquil. One sense interpreted by another.

(*f*) LIGHTNING—11 similes.

Transmitted, 187 ; *Reflected,* 192 ; *Contrast,* 187, 194.

(*g*) METEORS, COMETS—14 similes.

(*h*) THE SKY—19 similes.

Reflected, 227 ; *Intensity,* 215.

(*i*) FIRE—23 similes.

Intensity, 237, 239, 244, 247, 248.

(*j*) EYES—30 similes.

Basis of comparison :
Fire, 253 ; Stars, 254, 255, 258, 263, 264 (N.B.), 276, 277, 282 ; *Meteors,* 256 ; *Moon* (-light), 257, 275 ; *Sunset,* 267 ; *Dawn,* 262 ; *Night,* 271, 278 ; *Lightning,* 259 ; *Sky,* 265, 273 ; *Dove,* 266 ; *Sleep,* 260 ; *Death,* 261.
Intensity, 267 (N.B.) ; *Contrast,* 263, 267.

(*k*) DARKNESS, SHADOW—32 similes.

Note especially for their boldness, 295 and 297.

(*l*) WHITE LIGHT—18 similes.

Basis of comparison :
Snow, 315, 316, 317, 318, 321, 324, 329, 331.
Silver, 319 ; *Frost,* 322.
Gruesome in character, 323, 327.

(*m*) GENERAL COLOUR SIMILES—93 similes.

Transmitted or *Suffused* colours, 352, 359, 361, 391, 393, 395, 407, 412, 417. In other categories, 548.
Reflected, 334, 362 ; *Intensity,* 413 (N.B.)
Contrast, 335, 338, 347, 365, 377, 412, 413 (N.B.)
Light expressed in terms of music, 357 (*cf. supra,* 178).

(2) SIMILES OF SOUND—210 similes.

Many points of interest arise in this category to admirably illustrate the range of Shelley's sympathies. As Sweet in his suggestive study observes : "The range of Shelley's sympathies is bounded only by the universe itself. He combines forests, mountains, rivers, and seas into vast ideal landscapes ; he dives into the depths of the earth, soars among clouds and storms, and communes with the sphere of sun and moon." So here we find a Byronic exultation in the stormy symphonies which are the voice of nature's unrest, and a subtle penetrating sympathy, to which Byron's coarser-fibred spirit was not attuned, for the delicate eddies of sound that steal upon the sense in an hour of calm.

Thunder affords the basis of comparison in three unremarkable similes, 460, 462, 539.

Earthquake, 439, 476, and 474, where the hush between two earthquakes symbolizes the awed silence of a multitude.

Volcano. The cry of a multitude bursts like a volcano's voice in 464.

Tempest ; and wild outbursts of sound are compared in 564 to a tempestuous wind tearing the sluggish clouds, and less successfully in 430 (from an early poem) to the weird notes of a wind among the trees. 440, 466, 634, describe the silence in the pauses of tempest.

Human Voice. The similes descriptive of the *human voice* abound in delicate perception. The bases of comparison for the human voice are as follows : *Bird*, 436, 602 ; *Wind in trees*, 438, (446) ; *Wind among flowers*, 481 ; *Dying Wind*, 458, 471 ; *Wind on water*, 427 ; *Wind in ruins*, 429, 612, 626, (*cf.* 873) ; *Wind*, 428 ; *Flame*, 482 ; (*Words = Fire*, 563 ; *Embers*, 572) ; *Ice*, 470 ; *Stream*, 454, 455, 457 ; *Waves on sand*, 480 ; *Music*, 434, 452, 483, 484, 505, 506, 587 ; *Waterfalls*, 433 ; *Light*, 619 ; *Shout = Sea*, 477 ; *Sound = Sea*, 478.

The characteristic manner, already illustrated, of expressing one sense in terms of another is illustrated as follows : *Sound = Sight*, with generally bright light superadded, 441, 449, 533, 548, 549, 557, 574, 575, and see above where *Voice* = Flame, Fire, Light, etc. *Sound* = Odours, 467, 488 (N.B.), 536 (N.B.) ; *Gruesome*, 444, 450, 620, 622.

(3) SIMILES OF ODOUR—12 similes.

The sense of smell, as lower on the intellectual plane, contains naturally few similes. A few additional ones are contained in the preceding category.

641 and 642 are more luxuriantly sensuous in character than is usual with Shelley, and remind one rather of Keats, or of Tennyson in his studiously sensuous mood as in the "Lotos Eaters."

(4) Simile and Metaphor—184 similes.

In this category simile and metaphor are combined with high poetic effect, the simile, as a rule, rising out of the body of the metaphor. This gives to the figurative expression, as a whole, a volume of sustained power, which is frequently lacking in the lighter individual similes. Occasionally, as in 649, the simile seems to inspire the metaphor which follows as its natural completion. So also 704, 712-13, 714, 716, 717, 825.

Examples of the reverse process where the metaphor is completed by a simile:

653. Hope *clings* like ice. (In cases like this it is, however, almost impossible to say whether the metaphorical idea of "hope clinging" came first into the poet's mind, and the simile expression "like ice" came as a natural complement to the idea, or whether, as the order of words in the original suggests, the simile inspired the metaphor. The former would be the more natural poetic sequence of ideas.)

660. Agony is *worn* like a robe.

661. In the *wilderness* of years her memory appears like a green home.

Noteworthy similes in this category.

690-1. (Imitated from "Calderon." See Shelley's note.) Here a condition in Nature is elucidated and amplified by human analogy. This reversal of the natural process of simile (from human to natural) is not uncommon in Shelley, though rare in other poets.

Observe, as representing many others, the magnificent similes, 712-3.

Other fine similes in this category are 717, 718, 719, 731, 732, 745, 746, 751, 761-2 (note the vigour and intensity, and also the element of colour), 765 (cloud imagery), 766, 785, 791 (cloud imagery). 813 contains the gruesome element so common in Shelley.

The similes in this category almost all repay study for the penetrating insight which they reveal into beautiful processes in nature, presented not alone for their own sake, but as revealing the significance of human conditions.

In 738 the simile and metaphor are not in harmony—'a blot upon the page of fame' being likened to a 'serpent's path.' The analogy is too remote to be successful.

(5) Double Similes—183 similes.

It will at once be evident that some of these partake of the characteristics of other categories, as for example, 885, 887, which might have been classified under *Simile and Metaphor.*

But taking even a doubtful example like 885, it will be seen that there is a certain parallelism of structure which justifies its insertion among double similes. "As a golden chalice catches the bright wine which else had sunk into the thirsty dust, so is my overflowing love gathered into thee." (as) Asia : chalice (so) I : the wine.

This parallelism or double-thread of simile will be revealed by an analysis of any simile under this rubric. Some examples, as 839, 879, etc., are much condensed, and a very few, as 841, 962, are obscure from mere crudeness.

Gruesome Similes, 836, 850, 939.

Accumulative Similes, 859*f*, 881*f*, 919*f*, 983*f*, 989*f*, 998*f*.

These similes are very characteristic of Shelley. Readers of "Trelawny's Record" will remember his interesting relation of the poet's own account of his methods of composition. "When my brain gets heated with thought it soon boils, and throws off images and words faster than I can skim them off. In the morning, when cooled down, out of the rude sketch, as you justly call it, I shall attempt a drawing." This swift succession of imagery is also found apart from the double similes; e.g., 76*f*, 176*f* (and indeed throughout the "Triumph of Life," which is a vast succession of accumulated similes), 290*f*, 297*f*, 318*f*, 513*f* (this is of the type Double Simile, but included under Similes of Sound), 545*f*, 603*f*. Also see "Hymn to Intellectual Beauty," I. ; and as a remoter instance of the same rush of figurative thought, observe the accumulated metaphors in "Epipsychidion," 21*ff*.

(6) HOMERIC SIMILES—49 similes.

These are merely double similes of a more extended and pictorial character. As in the Homeric simile proper, the analogy is not maintained through every detail of the comparison. On the contrary, there need be only one essential point of contact, but the artistic impulse continues to develop a sustained poetic image, wrought out seemingly for the sake of its own beauty, and rather as an imaginative than as an intellectual stimulus. The type is a familiar one to the student of the classical poets, or even of our own classically minded poets, Milton, Tennyson, Arnold. *E.g.*, "Iliad," IV. : "As when on the echoing beach the sea wave lifteth itself up in serried array before the driving west wind ; out on the mid deep doth it first raise its head, and then breaketh upon the land, and roareth aloud, and goeth with arched crest around the promontories, and speweth afar the foaming brine ; even thus in close array moved the hosts of the Greeks without pause to battle."

As an example of finely-wrought similes of this order in Shelley's poetry, reference should be made to 1015, 1036, 1050, 1058, 1059, 1060.

These are very successful similes in their kind, though not fashioned so carefully after the classical model, as certain famous examples in Milton, Tennyson, or Arnold. Some, as 1018, might easily have been classified as *Double Similes*.

Gruesome, 1060.

(7) Human to Natural—145 similes.

"The imagery which I have employed will be found, in many instances, to have been drawn from the operations of the human mind, or from those external actions by which they are expressed. This is unusual in modern poetry, although Dante and Shakespeare are full of instances of the same kind : Dante indeed more than any other poet, and with greater success. But the Greek poets, as writers to whom no resource of awakening the sympathy of their contemporaries was unknown, were in the habitual use of this power ; and it is the study of their works (since a higher merit would probably be denied me), to which I am willing that my readers should impute this singularity." (*Shelley, Preface to "Prometheus Unbound."*)

The similes in this category require no special comment.

(8) Human to Human—112 similes.

Of these I reserve only seven as containing an element of Nature description.

(9) Human to Animal (or the reverse)—72 similes.

Romanticism implies for English poetry primarily a vast widening of the sympathies which embrace now not only man in all the hidden recesses of his nature, but extend to a compassionate pity for the dumb creation, and an emotional love for the inanimate world of natural beauty. In all these respects Shakespeare had foreshadowed the modern attitude of mind, but after his death until Thomson, or even until Cowper, we do not find these qualities again united.

Shelley's treatment of the animal world is not entirely sympathetic. His attitude of compassion or the reverse is determined by the one significant fact as to whether the animal in question is carnivorous or not. This fact in itself expresses Shelley's deep-rooted disgust for flesh-eating in man or beast.

Thus he speaks of *dogs* habitually in a tone of loathing, and makes them the symbol of a base and treacherous character, *e.g.*, 1223, 1229, 1255, 1271.

Even in 1251, 1282, where his sympathies for the oppressed in any form might have influenced him, he abates nothing of his habitual loathing for the friend of man. A reference to Ellis' "Concordance" will give other examples of Shelley's antipathetic feeling for dogs. (See also *Hounds.*) The only notable exception occurs in "Rosalind," 1069*f.*

This same reason for his hatred of dogs inspires his sentiments towards the fiercer wild animals, *e.g.*, *Wolves*, 1226, 1457, (see Ellis), *Tigers*, (see Ellis). This hostile treatment of beasts of prey need not, however, astonish us. It is only within the last few years that the splendid creatures of the jungle or the desert have entered as an element of beauty into artistic creation, and Leconte de Lisle and

Rudyard Kipling have alone sought to enter sympathetically into the meaning that lurks within their savage and unshaped intelligence.

With *Fish* the same principle holds. *Shark, Dog-fish,* 1279.

Serpents. Here the symbolical idea attaching to the serpent intervenes, and by a capricious reversal of Biblical teaching, Shelley identifies in "Laon and Cythna" the Serpent with the Spirit of Good. On the whole, however, he regards the serpent as inspiring loathing or disgust, *e.g.,* 1215, 1218, 1220, 1221, 1227, 1281.

Turning now to animals for which Shelley manifests compassion or affection, we find that *The Horse* is never harshly mentioned. In 1240 and 1260 a sympathetic feeling for the horse suffering oppression is shown (contrast Dogs above), and readers of "Laon and Cythna" will not forget the vigorous description of the Tartarean horse that bears Cythna and her lover to a refuge from the disastrous battle. ("L. & C." VI. xix*f.*)

Antelopes, Deer, Fawns, etc. These animals as representing at once the claims of grace and swiftness, and innocency trembling beneath the harsh oppression of the strong, are treated by the poet with compassionate sympathy. 1244, 1246, (and see Ellis).

Birds. Here only the more grossly carnivorous are subjects of aversion.

Vultures. 1233, 1252, 1255, 1284, (and *Ravens*).

Eagles. The Eagle is saved by his very sublimity, as evident from 1248, 1272, 1273.

But in "Laon and Cythna" he is regarded as the symbol of the Evil Spirit, and other passages in the poems refer to him in his rapacious character, *e.g.,* "Arethusa," III. 16; "Hellas," 307; "Laon and Cythna," VII. xxvii. 4.

(10) HUMAN TO ABSTRACTIONS, ETC.—40 similes.

Of these three only are retained. 1288 and 1289 are subtly imaginative, and reveal Shelley's primitive tendency to create living essences, as it were the presiding spirits or divinities of beautiful places.

(11) NATURAL to NATURAL—119 similes.

Gruesome, 1336.

Reflected Light, 1346; *Reflected Form,* 1378.

Colour, 1382, 1383.

Cloud or Vapour Imagery, 1290, 1292, 1293, 1296, 1305, 1342, 1347, 1348, 1349, 1363, 1364, 1373, 1403.

(12) Natural to Human or Natural Phenomena to Mental Phenomena, Spirits, etc.—40 similes.

Shairp insisted that Shelley was incapable of direct forcible description, because, while contemplating a landscape, his thoughts evaporated into fantastic and unreal conceptions.

"So entirely at home is he in this abstract shadowy world of his own making, that when he would describe common visible things he does so by likening them to those phantoms of the brain, as though with these last alone he was familiar. Virgil likens the ghosts by the banks of Styx to falling leaves—Shelley likens falling leaves to ghosts : The dead leaves ' Are driven like ghosts from an enchanter fleeing.' We see thus that nature as it actually exists has little place in Shelley's poetry." (Shairp in *Fraser's*, N. S., XX.)

This is weak and insipid criticism with but a grain of truth in it. The similes, for example, wherein Shelley expresses nature in terms of the human or spiritual world, are rare indeed by comparison with those in which human conditions are illustrated by a reference to the external world. Descriptions of the last-named kind prove, moreover, that Shelley could write when he would with his "eye upon the object"; and many detailed descriptions besides would attest his powers of a concrete and definite presentation of beauty. Bearing this reservation in mind, we may admit that the *Quarterly Review*, Vol. CLXIV., makes a nearer hit at the truth. " Except in the distinct descriptions contained in ' Julian and Maddalo,' or the distinct studies of atmospheric effects, everything is allegorized and idealized. Substance fades when the characteristics of nature change with his moods, and the ' orbèd maiden with white fire laden ' becomes a ' dying lady, lean and pale.' Shelley, with his quivering sensibility, his fresh imagination, his intense and simple nature, treats stream and fountain cloud and bird, in the true spirit of a mythological poet. He associates inanimate matter with the attributes of sentient mind ; endows it with his own passions ; tinges it with the hues of his own life. His pictures are so charged with supernatural life that he seems unable to observe without personifying. . . ."

In point of fact, Shelley in this figurative type merely conforms to the usage of the great idealistic poets. He represents Nature as a living symbol. And whereas the majority of poets materialize their ideas by images drawn from the external world, Shelley spiritualizes inanimate nature by a vivid symbolical interpretation of natural phenomena translated into the language of the intellect. Lamartine, the great idealist in French literature, as Shelley in English literature, affords innumerable examples of this faculty.

He speaks of a white corolla—

" Elle est pâle comme une joue
Dont l'amour a bu les couleurs."

Or again

> " De l'astre de la nuit un rayon solitaire,
> A travers les vitraux du sombre sanctuaire,
> Glissait comme l'espoir à travers le malheur,
> Ou dans la nuit de l'âme un regard du Seigneur."

Gruesome Similes. Shelley's inevitable tendency to revel in gruesome ideas in the midst of beauty (*cf.* Hugo's employment of the grotesque) shows itself in the following similes : 1426, 1428, 1430, 1432.

(13) NATURAL TO ANIMAL—27 similes.

Gruesome, 1497.

Number 1474, and the whole poem from which it is taken, admirably reveal Shelley's mythopœic power.

(14) SIMILES OF SWIFTNESS AND EVANESCENCE—45 similes.

These similes are of great value for the characteristic expression which they give to an important side of Shelley's genius. Endowed with faculties of perception attuned to the highest pitch of intensity, and with emotional desires ever fleeting beyond the reach of attainment, his poetry vibrates with an eager vehemence of speed, incomparable surely within the range of literature ; and there is always present amid all the ardours of emotional pursuit an ineffable sense of loss or unattained desire, poignantly expressed again and again by the confession of the transiency of earthly joys, and by the evanescence of those insecure delights which crumble in the hand stretched out to seize them. I have therefore classed together the similes of speed and of evanescence as representing two closely related expressions of the same qualities of mind.

In his similes of swiftness Shelley stands alone. His similes of evanescences are at one with the traditions of poetry in all ages and in every land. No great poet has ever been blind to the fleeting character of earthly beauty, nor to the perilous tenure by which we hold the transient gifts of time. Isaiah was not the first to give utterance to this confession of human impotence in that splendid passage in the thirty-fourth chapter :

> " And all the host of heaven shall waste away :
> And the heavens shall be rolled up like a scroll ;
> And all their host shall wither ;
> As the withered leaf falleth from the vine,
> And as the blighted fig from the fig-tree ; "

and while poetry exists there will be heard this human cry voicing the dumb protest of the world against the relentless march of change.

An analysis of these similes will show us Shelley's favourite comparisons.

Swiftness represented by

Cloud(s), 1477, 1485, 1491, 1497, 1519, 1520, 1534, 1545, 1556, 1567, 1578, 1596.

Shadow(s), 1516, 1552, 1571, 1579, 1584, 1587, 1621.

Thought(s), 1504, 1521, 1541, 1543, 1560, 1592; *Wind*, 1538, 1573, 1583.

Whirlwind, 1503; *Tempest-vapour*, 1502, 1542.

Storm, 1572, 1601; *Leaves in tempest*, 1487; *Insects in gale*, 1493.

Mist, 1621; *Volcano-smoke*, 1490; *Earthquake*, 1599.

River-foam, 1479 : *Foam from ship*, 1550; *Gossamer*, 1517.

Light, 1518, 1605; *Morning*, 1515; *Fire*, 1537, 1611.

Moon, 1523; *Meteor*, 1561; *Star*, 1580; *Dream*, 1563, 1590.

Eagle, 1498, 1505, 1581; *Antelope*, 1597; *Tiger*, 1582; *Horse*, 1602.

Evanescence represented by

Cloud(s), 1482, 1485, 1508, 1509, 1528, 1553, 1558, 1564, 1613.

Dew, 1481, 1488, 1536, 1546, 1566, 1576, 1609.

Mist, 1495, 1510, 1531, 1542, 1595, 1614.

Shadow(s), 1499, 1506, 1511, 1514, 1539, 1565, 1575.

Smoke, 1486, 1507, 1512; *Foam*, 1588; *Ware*, 1615.

River (in Sand), 1501, 1549, 1570. *Bubbles on River*, 1562.

Spray, 1540. *Wind*, 1513, 1620, 1593. *Taper*, 1554.

Dream, 1569, 1574. *Moonlight*, 1594. *Embers*, 1604.

Corpse, 1591. *Dust*, 1577. *Insect*, 1555.

Child's Legend in Sand, 1585 (and *cf.* 1589).

(15) SIMILES OF LOVE.—55 similes.

Of these, 41 bear upon Nature, and are retained. Shelley usually approaches love after the manner of the mystics, regarding it as the vital creative principle and the indissoluble band which knits the universe. Love and beauty in Shelley's half formless philosophy are so merged one in the other, that it is frequently difficult to dissociate them, and a discussion of the one topic would involve an investigation of the other. Here it need only be observed as a matter of curiosity that Love for the most part is figuratively expressed by an image of *Light*, *e.g.*, 1623, 1624, 1625, 1626, 1627, 1630, 1632, 1637, 1646, 1649, 1650.

Is this a reflection of the Neo-Platonic philosophy? Plotinus, it will be remembered, attached mystical significance to light.

(16) SIMILES OF DREAM—51 similes.

(Five retained.)

(17) SIMILES OF THOUGHT—30 similes.
(Twenty retained.)
Compared to *Shadows*, 1668, 1671, 1672. *Light*, 1673, 1676.

(18) SIMILES OF NUMBER—25 similes.
(To denote a multitude.)
Basis of Comparison.

Leaves, 1688, 1689, 1699, 1704, 1705, 1711. (Note the difference in presentation in each case.)

Sand, 1690, 1693. *Waves*, 1691, 1692, 1702. *Clouds*, 1695, 1697, 1706. *Summer flies*, 1700, 1709. *Gnats*, 1701, 1703, 1708. *Ants*, 1712. *Mist*, 1721.

This category on examination will show how Shelley's originality enabled him to escape the bounds of conventionality. For no class of similes has such an artificial array of examples established by literary tradition, since Homer first numbered the hosts of well-greaved Achaians.

"So stood they in the flowery Scamandrian plain, unnumbered as are leaves and flowers in their season. Even as the many tribes of thick flies that hover about a herdsman's steading in the spring season, when milk drencheth the pails, even in like number stood the flowing-haired Achaians upon the plain in face of the Trojans, eager to rend them asunder" . . . or the following,—"Of a truth have I oft ere now entered into battles of the warriors, yet have I never seen so goodly a host, and so great ; for in the very likeness of the leaves of the forest or the sands of the sea, are they marching along the plain to fight against the city." The Bible also is a treasure-house for such similes, and the danger of conventional usage is therefore evident. The following only may be considered conventional, 1688, 1689, 1690, 1691, 1693, 1699, 1700, 1703 ; whereas in the other examples the poet's subtle powers of perception are exercised to derive the appropriate imagery from the field of Nature.

FLOWER SIMILES.

It only now remains to refer to the numerous flower similes or references that are scattered through the various categories. Many of these are extremely careful and delicate studies.

Flowers in General,—15, 75, 132, 164, 165, 169, 174, 190, 243, 333, 353, 378, 391, 396, 400, 401-2-3-4, 559, 593, 636, 639, 640, 643, 683, 684, 747, 754, 825, 852, 906, 908, 968, 980, 986, 1006, 1016, 1020, 1022, 1031, 1042, 1065, 1075, 1103, 1109, 1112, 1114, 1130, 1135, 1148, 1149, 1195, 1312, 1392, 1401, 1405, 1424, 1436, 1444, 1649.

Roses, 33, 341, 362, 370, 397, 605, 646, 753, 1089, 1090, 1423. *Lilies*, 352, 393, 729, 1178, 1332, 1422. *Hyacinth*, 536, 554, 886. *Violet*, 624, 637, 638, 1023. *Snowdrop*, 638. *Daisy*, 1333. *Lemonflower*, 641. *Magnolia*, 1380. *Sensitive Plant*, 1454.

SIMILES OF COLOUR AND LIGHT.

(a) CLOUD COLOUR (AND MIST).

1   The pyramids
Of the tall cedar overarching, frame
Most solemn domes within, and far below,
Like clouds suspended in an emerald sky,
The ash and the acacia floating hang
Tremulous and pale.   —*Alast.* 433*ff.*

2 Even as a vapour fed with golden beams
That ministered on sunlight, ere the west
Eclipses it, was now that wondrous frame—   —*Alast.* 633*ff.*

3 Its shape reposed within : slight as some cloud
That catches but the palest tinge of day
     When evening yields to night,
Bright as that fibrous woof when stars indue
 • Its transitory robe.   —*D. W.* 59.

4   Human eye hath ne'er beheld
A shape so wild, so bright, so beautiful,
As that which o'er the maiden's charmèd sleep,
     Waving a starry wand,
Hung like a mist of light   —*D. W.* 70.

5 Thou must have marked the billowy mountain clouds,
Edged with intolerable radiancy,
      Towering like rocks of jet
      Above the burning deep   —*D. W.* 197.

6   And yet there is a moment

When those far clouds of feathery purple gleam
Like fairy lands girt by some heavenly sea :   —*D. W.* 201.

7 And walked as free as light the clouds among,   —*L. & C.* Ded.

8 Even like the dayspring, poured on vapours dank,
The beams of that one Star did shoot and quiver
Thro' my benighted mind—and were extinguished never.
                     —*L. & C.* I. 41.

9   at night, methought in dream
A Shape of speechless beauty did appear :
It stood like light on a careering stream
Of golden clouds which shook the atmosphere ;
                  —*L. & C.* I. 42.

3

10   and as the vapours lie
Bright in the outspread morning's radiancy,
So were these thoughts invested with the light
Of language   —*L. & C.* II. 16.

11 She moved upon this earth a shape of brightness,
A power that from its objects scarcely drew
One impulse of her being—in her lightness
Most like some radiant cloud of morning dew
Which wanders thro' the waste air's pathless blue,
To nourish some far desert   —*L. & C.* II. 23.

12   the twilight's gloom
Lay like a charnel's mist within the radiant dome.
         —*L. & C.* V. 22.

13 She stood beside me like a rainbow braided
Within some storm, when scarce its shadows vast
From the blue paths of the swift sun have faded,
         — *L. & C.* V. 24.

14   for now
A power, a thirst, a knowledge, which below
All thoughts, like light beyond the atmosphere,
Clothing its clouds with grace, doth ever flow,
Came on us as we sat in silence there,
Beneath the golden stars of the clear azure air.
        —*L. & C.* VI. 30.

15   as an autumnal blossom
Which spreads its shrunk leaves in the sunny air,
After cold showers, like rainbows woven there,
Thus in her lips and cheeks the vital spirit
Mantled, and in her eyes, an atmosphere
Of health and hope ;   —*L. & C.* VI. 55.

16 And the white clouds of noon which oft were sleeping,
In the blue heaven so beautiful and fair,
Like hosts of ghastly shadows hovering there ;
        —*L. & C.* VII. 15.

17 My eye and voice grew firm, calm was my mind,
And piercing, like the morn, now it has darted
Its lustre on all hidden things, behind
Yon dim and fading clouds which load the weary wind.
        —*L. & C.* VII. 30.

18   the day was dying :—
Sudden, the sun shone forth, its beams were lying
Like boiling gold on Ocean, strange to see,
And on the shattered vapours, which defying
The power of light in vain, tossed restlessly
In the red Heaven, like wrecks in a tempestuous sea.
        —*L. & C.* XI. 2.

19 It was a stream of living beams, whose bank
On either side by the cloud's cleft was made,
And where its chasms that flood of glory drank,
Its waves gushed forth like fire, —*L. & C.* XI. 3.

20   when bright, like dawning day,
The Spectre of the Plague before me flew. —*L. & C.* XII. 25.

21   and hope and peace
On all who heard him did abide,
Raining like dew from his sweet talk,
As where the evening star may walk,
Along the brink of the gloomy seas,
Liquid mists of splendour quiver.   —*R. & H.* 641.

22 And in that dark and evil day
Did all desires and thoughts, that claim
Men's care, ambition, friendship, fame,
Love, hope, though hope was now despair—
Indue the colors of this change,
As from the all-surrounding air
The earth takes hues obscure and strange,
When storm and earthquake linger there. — *R. & H.* 724.

23 On my faint eyes and limbs did dwell
That spirit as it passed, till soon
As a frail cloud wandering o'er the moon,
Beneath its light invisible,
Is seen when it folds its grey wings again
To alight on midnight's dusky plain,
I lived and saw, and the gathering soul,
Passed from beneath that strong control, —*R. & H.* 1039.

24 There is no lament for him
Like a sunless vapour, dim
Who once clothed with life and thought
What now moves nor murmurs not. -- *Eng. H.* 61.

25 Gathering round with wings all hoar,
Thro' the dewy mist they soar
Like grey shades, till the Eastern heaven
26 Bursts, and then, as clouds of even,
Flecked with fire and azure, lie
In the unfathomable sky,
So their plumes of purple grain,
Starred with drops of golden rain,
Gleam above the sunlight woods,
As in silent multitudes
On the morning's fitful gale
Thro' the broken mist they sail,
And the vapours cloven and gleaming
Follow down the dark steep streaming,
Till all is bright, and clear, and still,
Round the solitary hill. —*Eng. H.* 74.

27 From the sea a mist has spread,
And the beams of morn lie dead
On the towers of Venice now,
Like its glory long ago, —*Eng. H.* 210.

28 Noon descends around me now :
'Tis the noon of autumn's glow,
When a soft and purple mist
Like a vaporous amethyst,

29 Or an air-dissolvèd star
   Mingling light and fragrance   —*Eng. II.* 285.

30 The awful shadow of some unseen Power
   Floats tho' unseen amongst us—

   Like clouds in starlight widely spread.   —*II. I. B. I.*

31 Spirit of Beauty   . . .

   Thy light alone like mist o'er mountains driven

   Gives grace and truth to life's unquiet dream.   —*II. I. B.* III.

32 Look, sister, ere the vapour dim thy brain:
   Beneath is a wide plain of billowy mist,
   As a lake, paving in the morning sky,
   With azure waves which burst in silver light,
   Some Indian vale.   —*Prom.* II. iii. 18.

                     and the light
33 Which fills this vapour, as the aerial hue
   Of fountain-gazing roses fills the water,
   Flows from thy mighty sister   —*Prom.* II. v. 11.

34 Child of Light ! thy limbs are burning
   Thro' the veil which seems to hide them ;
   As the radiant lines of morning
      Thro' the clouds ere they divide them ;
   And this atmosphere divinest
   Shrouds thee wheresoe'er thou shinest.   —*Prom.* II. v. 54.

35 The elements obey me not. I sink
   Dizzily down, ever, for ever, down.
   And, like a cloud, mine enemy above
   Darkens my fall with victory.   —*Prom.* III. ii. 80.

36 Its wheels are solid clouds, azure and gold,
   Such as the genii of the thunder storm
   Pile on the floor of the illumined sea
   When the sun rushes under it ; they roll
   And move and grow as with an inward wind ;
                   —*Prom.* IV. 214.

37 The joy, the triumph, the delight, the madness !
   The boundless, overflowing, bursting gladness,
   The vaporous exultation not to be confined !
      Ha ! ha ! the animation of delight
      Which wraps me, like an atmosphere of light,
   And bears me as a cloud is borne by its own wind.
                  —*Prom.* IV. 319.

38   Drinking from thy sense and sight
     Beauty, majesty, and might

     As a grey and watery mist
     Glows like solid amethyst
   Athwart the western mountain it enfolds,
     When the sunset sleeps
       Upon its snow   —*Prom.* IV. 481.

39 The wrecks of the tempest, like vapours of gold,
    Are consuming in sunrise   —*Vis. of Sea*, 127.

40   Thou bearer of the quiver,
    Whose sunlike shafts pierce tempest-wingèd Error,
    As light may pierce the clouds when they dissever
    In the calm regions of the orient day   —*Ode to Lib.* X.

41   I hear the pennons of her car
    Self-moving, like cloud charioted by flame ;
                  —*Ode to Lib.* XVIII.

42 How glorious it will be to see her Majesty
    Flying above our heads, her petticoats
    Streaming like .   .   .   .   .
    .   .   .   .
    Or like a cloud dyed in the dying day
    Unravelled on the blast from a white mountain ;
                  —*Œd. Tyr.* 95.

43   one intense
    Diffusion, one serene Omnipresence
    Whose flowing outlines mingle in their flowing
    Around her cheeks and utmost fingers glowing
    With the unintermitted blood, which there
    Quivers (as in a fleece of snow-like air
    The crimson pulse of living morning quiver)   —*Epips.* 94.

44   the moving pomp might seem
    Like pageantry of mist on an autumnal stream.   —*Adon.* XIII.

45 His cold pale limbs and pulseless arteries
    Are like the fibres of a cloud instinct
    With light,   —*Hell.* 142.

46   A mortal shape to him
        Was like the vapour dim
    Which the orient planet animates with light ;   —*Hell.* 215

47 The Anarchies of Africa unleash
    Their tempest-wingèd cities of the sea,
    To speak in thunder to the rebel world.
    Like sulphurous clouds, half shattered by the storm,
    They sweep the pale Ægean,   —*Hell.* 299.

48 In the death hues of agony
    Lambently flashing from a fish,
    Now Peter felt amused to see
    Shades like a rainbow's rise and flee,
        Mixed with a certain hungry wish.   —*P. B.* XXVI.

49   the thunder smoke
    Is gathering on the mountains, like a cloak
    Folded across their shoulders broad and bare ;
                  —*Lett. to M. G.* 116.

50   Such clouds as flit,
    Like splendour-wingèd moths about a taper,
    Round the red west when the sun dies in it   —*Witch,* III.

51   and on the water for her tread
A tapestry of fleece-like mist was strewn,
Dyed in the beams of the ascending moon   — *Witch*. LIII.

52 Its shape was such as summer melody
Of the south wind in spicy vales might give
To some light cloud bound from the golden dawn
To fairy isles of evening,   —*Fragm. of Dram.* 215.

53   See those thronging chariots
Rolling like painted clouds before the wind
Behind their solemn steeds   —*Chas. I.*, I. 136.

54 Oh, light us to the isles of the evening land !
Like floating Edens cradled in the glimmer
Of sunset, through the distant mist of years
Touched by departing hope, they gleam !   —*Chas. I.*, IV. 22.

55   and the sense
Of hope through her fine texture did suffuse
Such varying glow, as summer evening casts
On undulating clouds and deepening lakes.   —*D. W.* 36.

56 Let us laugh and make our mirth,
At the shadows of the earth,
As dogs bay the moonlight clouds,
Which like spectres wrapt in shrouds,
Pass o'er night in multitudes   --*Inroc. to Mis.* XII.

57   From that Typhaen mount, Inarime,
There streamed a sunlight vapour, like the standard
Of some ætherial host ;   —*Ode to Nap.* 44.

58 On one side of this jagged and shapeless hill
There is a cave, from which there eddies up
A pale mist like aerial gossamer,   —*Orph.* 18.

59 The Fairy's frame was slight, yon fibrous cloud,
That catches but the palest tinge of even
And which the straining eye can hardly seize
When melting into eastern twilight's shadow.
Were scarce so thin, so slight   —*Q. M.* 94.

(*b*) Water Colour.

60 With the sun's cloudless orb,
Whose rays of rapid light
Parted around the chariot's swifter course,
And fell like ocean's feathery spray
Dashed from the boiling surge
Before a vessel's prow.   —*D. W.* 153.

61 For where the irresistible storm had cloven
That fearful darkness the blue sky was seen
Fretted with many a fair cloud interwoven
Most delicately, and the ocean green,
Beneath that opening spot of blue serene,
Quivered like burning emerald :   —*L. & C.* I. 4.

62 Only 'twas strange to see the red commotion
　　Of waves like mountains o'er the sinking sphere
　　Of sunset sweep,　　　　　　　　　　—*L. & C.* I. 15.

63 Beside that Image then I sate, while she
　　Stood, mid the throngs which ever ebbed and flowed
　　Like light amid the shadows of the sea
　　Cast from one cloudless star,　　　—*L. & C.* V. 51

64　　　　　　　　　　while tears pursued
　　Each other down her fair and listening cheek
　　Fast as the thoughts that fed them, like a flood
　　From sunbright dales ;　　　　　—*L. & C.* VII. 2.

65 And in that roof of crags a space was riven
　　Thro' which there shone the emerald beams of heaven,
　　Shot thro' the lines of many waves inwoven,
　　Like sunlight thro' acacia woods at even,　—*L. & C.* VII. 11.

66 Below the fountain's brink was richly paven
　　With the deep's wealth, coral and pearl, and sand
　　Like spangling gold,　　　　　　—*L. & C.* VII. 13.

67 When the summer wind faint odours brought
　　From mountain flowers, even as it passed
　　His cheek would change, as the noon-day sea
　　Which the dying breeze sweeps fitfully.　—*R. & H.* 1015.

68 Beneath is spread like a green sea
　　The waveless plain of Lombardy,
　　Bounded by the vaporous air,
　　Islanded by cities fair ;　　　　—*Eug. H.* 90.

69 And far on high the keen sky-cleaving mountains
　　From icy spires of sun-like radiance fling
　　The dawn, as lifted Ocean's dazzling spray,
　　From some Atlantic islet scattered up,
70 Spangles the wind with lamp-like water drops,
　　　　　　　　　　　　—*Prom.* II. iii. 78.

71　　　　　　　　　　I hid myself
　　Within a fountain in the public square,
　　Where I lay like a reflex of the moon
　　Seen in a wave under green leaves ;　—*Prom.* III. iv. 61.

72 With mighty whirl the multitudinous orb
　　Grinds the bright brook into an azure mist
　　Of elemental subtlety, like light :　— *Prom.* IV. 253.

73 The plumèd insects swift and free,
　　Like golden boats on a sunny sea.　—*Sens. P.* I. 82.

74 And wherever her airy footsteps trod,
　　Her trailing hair from the grassy sod
　　Erased its light vestige, with shadowy sweep,
　　Like a sunny storm o'er the dark green deep.　—*Sens. P.* II. 25.

75 Three days the flowers of the garden fair,
　　Like stars when the moon is awakened, were,
　　Or the waves of Baiæ, ere luminous
　　She floats up through the smoke of Vesuvius.　—*Sens. P.* III. I.

76 While the surf like a chaos of stars, like a rout
77, 78 Of death-flames, like whirlpools of fire-flowing iron
    With splendour and terror the black ship environ,
79 Or like sulphur-flakes hurled from a mine of pale fire
    In fountains spout o'er it.   *—Vision of Sea*, 13.

80 And I was laid asleep, spirit and limb,
    And all my being became bright or dim
    As the moon's image in a summer sea,
    According as she smiled or frowned on me ;   *—Epips.* 295.

81 And many a fountain, rivulet, and pond,
    As clear as elemental diamond,
82 Or serene morning air ;   *—Epips.* 436.

83 Let there be Light ! said Liberty,
    And like sunrise from the sea
    Athens arose !   *—Hell.* 682.

84   I see the waves upon the shore,
    Like light dissolved in star-showers, thrown :
            —Stanzas near Nap. II.

85 This quicksilver no gnome has drunk—within
    The walnut bowl it lies, veinèd and thin,
    In colour like the wake of light that stains
    The Tuscan deep, when from the moist moon rains
    The inmost shower of its white fire—the breeze
    Is still, blue heaven smiles o'er the pale seas.
            —Letter to M. G. 66.

86 The ripe corn under the undulating air
    Undulates like an ocean ;   *—Letter to M. G.* 119.

87 And down the earthquaking cataracts which shiver
    Their snow-like waters into golden air,   *— Witch*, XLII.

88 The water flashed like sunlight by the prow
    Of a noon-wandering meteor flung to Heaven ;
            — Witch, XLVI.

89 To glide adown old Nilus, where he threads
    Egypt and Æthiopia, from the steep
        Of utmost Axumé, until he spreads,
    Like a calm flock of silver-fleeced sheep,   *— Witch*, LVII.
    His waters on the plain

90 And the sun's image radiantly intense
.   .   .   .
    Burned on the waters of the well that glowed
    Like gold, and threaded all the forest's maze
    With winding paths of emerald fire ;   *—Tr. of L.* 345.

91   Like a gloomy stain
    On the emerald main   *—Areth.* III.
    Alpheus rushed behind,

92   And under the caves,
    Where the shadowy waves
    Are as green as the forest's night :   *—Areth.* IV.

93   Great spirit, deepest Love

.   .   .   .
Or, with thy harmonizing ardours fill
And raise thy sons, as o'er the prone horizon
Thy lamp feeds every twilight wave with fire.   *—Ode to N.* 165.

94 Now all the tree-tops lay asleep
    Like green waves on the sea,   *—To June,* 29.

95 O'er the thin texture of its frame
    The varying periods painted changing glows,
        As on a summer evening,
    When soul-enfolding music floats around,
    The stainless mirror of the lake
    Re-images the eastern gloom
    Mingling convulsively its purple lines
        With sunset's burnished gold   *—Q. M.* 3.

(c) The Sun.

96 The moon arose: and lo, the ætherial cliffs
    Of Caucasus, whose icy summits shone
    Among the stars like sunlight,   *— Alast.* 352.

97 A speck, a cloud, a shape, approaching grew,
    Like a great ship in the sun's sinking sphere
    Beheld afar at sea, and swift it came anear   *—L. & C.* I. 6.

98 And oft in cycles since, when darkness gave
    New weapons to thy foe, their sun-like fame
    Upon the combat shone—   *—L. & C.* I. 32.

99 Day after day the burning sun rolled on
    Over the death-polluted land—it came
    Out of the east like fire,   *—L. & C.* X. 13.

100   the day was dying :—
Sudden the sun shone forth, its beams were lying
Like boiling gold on Ocean, strange to see,
And on the shattered vapours, which defying
The power of light in vain, tossed restlessly
In the red Heaven, like wrecks in a tempestuous sea.
                      —L. & C. XI. 2.

101 And as the meteor's midnight flame
    Startles the dreamer, sun-like truth
    Flashed on his visionary youth.   *—R. & H.* 617.

102 And the light which flushed through his waxen cheek
    Grew faint, as the rose-like hues which flow
    From sunset o'er the Alpine snow :   *—R. & H.* 1009.

103 And that eternal honour which should live
    Sun-like, above the reek of mortal fame.   *—Cenci,* V. iii. 31.

104 Pity the self-despising slaves of Heaven,
    Not me, within whose mind sits peace serene
    As light in the sun, throned :   *—Prom.* I. 429.

105 And far on high the keen sky-cleaving mountains
From icy spires of sun-like radiance fling
The dawn,   —*Prom.* II. iii. 28.

106 Vast beams like spokes of some invisible wheel
Which whirl as the orb whirls, swifter than thought,
Filling the abyss with sun-like lightnings.   —*Prom.* IV. 274.

107   thou bearer of the quiver,
Whose sun-like shafts pierce tempest-wingèd Error.
                                             —*Ode to Lib.* X.

108 When like heaven's sun girt by the exhalation
Of its own glorious light, thou didst arise,
Chasing thy foes from nation unto nation
Like shadows.   —*Ode to Lib.* XI.

109   Thou Mirror
In whom, as in the splendour of the sun,
All shapes look glorious which thou gazest on !   — *Epips.* 30.

110 Imagination ! which from earth and sky,
And from the depths of human phantasy,
As from a thousand prisms and mirrors, fills
The Universe with glorious beams, and kills
Error, the worm, with many a sun-like arrow
Of its reverberated lightning.   —*Epips.* 164.

111 Soft as an Incarnation of the Sun,
When light is changed to love, this glorious One
Floated into the cavern where I lay,   —*Epips.* 335.

112 Another Athens shall arise
And to remoter time
Bequeath, like sunset to the skies,
The splendour of its prime ;   —*Hell.* 1084.

113 Like wingèd stars the fire-flies flash and glance
Pale in the open moonshine, but each one
Under the dark trees seems a little sun. —*Letter to M. G.* 281.

114 And she saw princes couched under the glow
Of sun-like gems ;]   —*Witch,* LXIV.

115 And on the right hand of the sun-like throne.
                                             —*Witch,* LXXIV.

116 For he seemed stormy, and would often seem
A quenchless sun masked in portentous clouds.
                                             —*Fragm. of Dram.* 107.

117 This Charles the First
Rose like the equinoctial sun (engirt)
By vapours   —*Chas. I.* 46.

118 And a cold glare, intenser than the noon,
But icy cold, obscured with blinding light
The sun, as he the stars.   —*Tr. of L.* 77.

119   I arose, and for a space
The scene of woods and waters seemed to keep
Though it was now broad day, a gentle trace
Of light diviner than the common sun
Sheds on the common earth,   —*Tr. of L.* 335.

120   there stood
    Amid the sun, as he amid the blaze
    Of his own glory, on the vibrating
    Floor of the fountain, paved with flashing rays,
    A shape all light.   *—Tr. of L.* 348.

121 And many a fresh Spring-morn would he awaken
    While yet the unrisen sun made glow, like iron
    Quivering in crimson fire, the peaks unshaken
    Of mountains and blue isles which did environ
    With air-clad crags that plain of land and sea—   *—Mar.* XXII.

122   And under the water
        The Earth's white daughter
        Fled like a sunny beam ;   *—Areth.* III.

123 And leaving noblest things vacant and chidden,
    Cold as a corpse after the spirit's flight,
    Blank as the sun after the birth of night.   *—Zucca,* IV.

124 There lay the glade and neighbouring lawn,
    And through the dark green wood
    The white sun twinkling like the dawn
    Out of a speckled cloud.   *—Recoll.* 65.

125   The sun's unclouded orb
        Rolled through the black concave :
        Its rays of rapid light
    Parted around the chariot's swifter course,
    And fell, like ocean's feathery spray
        Dashed from the boiling surge
        Before a vessel's prow.   *—Q. M.* 242.

126 And countless spheres diffused
        An ever-varying glory.

  .   .   .   .
    Some shone like suns, and as the chariot passed,
        Eclipsed all other light.   *—Q. M.* 255.

(*d*) The Moon.

127   How wonderful is Death,
        Death and his brother Sleep !
    One pale as yonder wan and hornèd moon,
        With lips of lurid blue,   *—D. W.* 1.

128 And countless spheres diffused
        An ever-varying glory.
    It was a sight of wonder, some were hornèd,
    And, like the moon's argentine crescent hung
    In the dark dome of heaven,   *—D. W.* 162.

129 And that strange boat, like the moon's shade did sway
    Amid reflected stars that in the waters lay.   *—L. & C.* 1. 22.

130   from that night
    She fled ; like those illusions clear and bright,
    Which dwell in lakes, when the red moon on high
    Pause ere it wakens tempest ;   *—L. & C.* VII. 22.

131   Behold !
The sinking moon is like a watch-tower blazing
Over the mountains yet ;   —*L. & C.* VIII. 1.

132   high above was spread
The emerald heaven of trees of unknown kind,
Whose moonlike blooms and bright fruit overhead
A shadow, which was light, upon the waters shed
            —*L. & C.* XII. 18.

133   the prow and stern did curl
Hornèd on high, like the young moon supine,
When o'er dim twilight mountains dark with pine,
It floats upon the sunset's sea of beams,
Whose golden waves in many a purple line
Fade fast, till borne on sunlight's ebbing streams,
Dilating, on earth's verge the sunken meteor gleams.
            —*L. & C.* XII. 21.

134   for thro' the sky
The spherèd lamps of day and night, revealing
New changes and new glories, rolled on high,
Sun, moon, and moon-like lamps, the progeny
Of a diviner Heaven, serene and fair :   —*L. & C.* XII. 38.

135   yet his countenance
Raised upward, burned with radiance
Of spirit-piercing joy, whose light,
Like the moon struggling through the night
Of whirlwind-rifted clouds, did break
With beams that might not be confined.   —*R. & H.* 1154.

The awful shadow of some unseen Power
     Floats though unseen among us, visiting
     This various world with as inconstant wing
As summer winds that creep from flower to flower
136 Like moonbeams that behind some piny mountain shower,
     It visits with inconstant glance
     Each human heart and countenance ;   —*H. I B.* I.

Spirit of Beauty.   .   .
.   .   .   .
Thy light alone—like mist o'er mountains driven,
     Or music by the night wind sent
     Thro' strings of some strange instrument,
137   Or moonlight on a midnight stream,
Gives grace and truth to life's unquiet dream.   —*H. I. B.* III.

138   'tis He, arrayed
In the soft light of his own smiles, which spread
Like radiance from the cloud-surrounded moon.
            —*Prom.* II. i. 120.

139   and from their glassy thrones
Blue Proteus and his humid nymphs shall mark
The shadow of fair ships, as mortals see
The floating bark of the light-laden moon
With that white star, its sightless pilot's crest,
Borne down the rapid sunset's ebbing sea ;
            —*Prom.* III. ii. 23.

140 And where my moon-like car will stand within
    A temple, gazed upon by Phidian forms   —*Prom.* III. iv. 111

141   the brightness
    Of her divinest presence trembles through
    Her limbs, as underneath a cloud of dew
    Embodied in the windless heaven of June
    Amid the splendour-wingèd stars, the moon
    Burns, inextinguishably beautiful :   —*Epips.* 77.

142   Thine eyes glowed in the glare
        Of the moon's dying light ;
    As a fenfire's beam on a sluggish stream,
    Gleams dimly, so the moon shone there,   — *Lines*, III.

143 But Peter's verse was clear, and came
. . . .
   Or like the sudden moon, that stains
   Some gloomy chamber's window panes
     With a broad light like day.   —*Peter B.* XIV.

144   and now she grew
    Pale as that moon, lost in the watery night.   — *Witch*, LIV.

145   Like the young moon
    When on the sunlit limits of the night
    Her white shell trembles amid crimson air,
    And whilst the sleeping tempest gathers might
    Doth, as the herald of its coming, bear
    The ghost of its dead mother, whose dim form
    Bends in dark ether from her infant's chair,
    So came a chariot on the silent storm
    Of its own rushing splendour,   —*Tr. of L.* 79

146 And so she moved under the bridal veil,
    Which made the paleness of her cheek more pale,
    And deepened the faint crimson of her mouth,
    And darkened her dark locks, as moonlight doth,   —*Gin.* 13.

147 A moonbeam in the shadow of a cloud
    Was less heavenly fair—   —*Gin.* 21.

148   Those lines of rainbow light
    Are like the moonbeams when they fall
    Through some cathedral window,   —*Q. M.* 54.
                    (*Note change in D. W.*)

(e) THE STARS.

149 And countless spheres diffused
      An ever-varying glory
  . . . . .
              some did shed
    A clear mild beam like Hesperus, while the sea
    Yet glows with fading sunlight.   —*D. W.* 164.

. . . .
150   others dashed
    Athwart the night with trains of bickering fire,
    Like sphered worlds to death and ruin driven,   —*D. W.* 170.

151 Some shone like stars, and as the chariot passed
    Bedimmed all other light   —*D. W.* 173.

152   And yet there is a moment
    When the sun's highest point
    Peers like a star o'er ocean's western edge,   —*D. W.* 201.

153 The city's moonlight spires and myriad lamps
    Like stars in a sublunar sky did glow   —*L. & C.* V. 1.

154 The shadow of the lingering waves did wear
    Light, as from starry beams: —*L. & C.* XII. 20.

155 And where melodious falls did burst and shiver
    Among rocks clad with flowers, the foam and spray
    Sparkled like stars upon the sunny river,   —*L. & C.* XII. 34.

156 That ivory dome, whose azure night
    With golden stars, like heaven, was bright   —*R. & H.* 1094.

157 More yet come, one by one; the air around them
    Looks radiant as the air around a star.   —*Prom.* I. 692.

158 Their beauty gives me voice. See how they float
    On their sustaining wings of skiey grain
    Orange and azure deepening into gold :
    Their soft smiles light the air like a star's fire.
        —*Prom.* 1. 759.

159 Or when some star of many a one
    That climbs and wanders thro' steep night,
    Has found the cleft thro' which alone
    Beams fall from high those depths upon,
    Ere it is borne away, away,
    By the swift heavens that cannot stay,
    It scatters drops of golden light,
    Like lines of rain that ne'er unite.   —*Prom.* II. ii. 14.

160 Sister, it is not earthly : how it glides
    Under the leaves ! how on its head there burns
    A light like a green star, whose emerald beams
    Are twined with its fair hair ! how, as it moves,
    The splendour drops in flakes upon the grass !
        —*Prom.* III. iv. 1.

161 And from a star upon its forehead, shoot,
162 Like swords of azure fire, or golden spears
    With tyrant-quelling myrtle overtwined,
    Embleming heaven and earth united now,
163 Vast beams like spokes of some invisible wheel
    Which whirl as the orb whirls, swifter than thought,
    Filling the abyss with sun-like lightnings,
        —*Prom.* IV. 270.

164 Three days the flowers of the garden fair,
    Like stars when the moon is awakened, were,
        —*Sens. Pl.* III. 1.

165 The leprous corpse touched by this spirit tender
    Exhales itself in flowers of gentle breath ;
    Like incarnations of the stars, when splendour
    Is changed to fragrance, they illumine death,
    And mock the merry worm that wakes beneath ;   —*Adon.* XX.

166 Whilst burning through the inmost veil of Heaven,
    The soul of Adonais like a star,
    Beacons from the abode where the eternal are.   - *Adon.* LV.

167 Though in his eyes a cloud and burthen lay,
    Through which his soul, like Vesper's serene beam
    Piercing the chasms of ever-rising clouds,
    Shone softly burning ;   —*Prince Ath.* I. 60.

168 The Balearic fisher, driven from shore,
    Hanging upon the peakèd wave afar,
    Then saw their lamp from Laian's turret gleam,
    Piercing the stormy darkness like a star,
    Which pours beyond the sea one steadfast beam.
    Whilst all the constellations of the sky
    Seemed reeling through the storm.   —*Prince Ath.* II. 24.

169   The hoary grove
    Waxed green and flowers burst forth like starry beams
               —*Prince Ath.* III. 8.

170 Let the horsemen's scymitars
    Wheel and flash like sphereless stars
    Thirsting to eclipse their burning
    In a sea of death and mourning.   —*Mask of A.* LXXVIII.

171 Beyond, the surface of the unsickled corn
    Trembles not in the slumbering air, and borne
    In circles quaint, and ever-changing dance,
    Like wingèd stars the fire-flies flash and glance,
    Pale in the open moonshine, but each one
    Under the dark trees seems a little sun,
172 A meteor tamed : a fixed star gone astray
    From the silver regions of the Milky Way ;
               —*Letter to M. G.* 278.

173 Through the green splendour of the water deep
    She saw the constellations reel and dance
    Like fire-flies   —*Witch,* XXVIII.

174 Until the golden eye of the bright flower,
    Through the dark lashes of those veinèd lids,
    Disencumbered of their silent sleep,
    Gazed like a star into the morning light
               —*Fragm. of Dram.* 168.

175   And thou
    Fair star, whose beam lies on the wide Atlantic,
    Athwart its zones of tempest and of calm,
    Bright as the path to a belovèd home,
    Oh, light us to the isles of the evening land !
               —*Chas I.* IV. 18.

176   so on my sight
Burst a new vision, never seen before,
And the fair shape waned in the coming light,
As veil by veil the silent splendour drops
From Lucifer, amid the chrysolite
Of sunrise, ere it tinge the mountain tops ;
177 And as the presence of that fairest planet,
Although unseen, is felt by one who hopes
That his day's path may end as he began it
178 In that star's smile, whose light is like the scent
Of a jonquil when evening breezes fan it,
179 Or the soft note in which his dear lament
180 The Brescian Shepherd breathes, or the caress
That turned his weary slumber to content ;   —*Tr. of L.* 410.

181 The golden gates of Sleep unbar
Where Strength and Beauty met together,
Kindle their image like a star
In a sea of glassy weather   —*Bridal S.* 1*f.* 12*f.* 23*f.*

182 And the smile thou wearest
Wraps thee like a star
Is wrapt in light   ···*Fragm. of Hell.* 184.

183 Thou, whom seen nowhere, I feel everywhere,
From Heaven and Earth and all that in them are,
Veiled art thou, like a   .   .   .   star   —*Zucc.* III.

184   but the fair star
That gems the glittering coronet of morn,
Sheds not a light so mild, so powerful,
As that which bursting form the Fairy's form,
Spread a purpureal halo round the scene,   —*Q. M.* 98,

185 The vast and fiery globes that rolled
Around the Fairy's palace-gate
Lessened by slow degrees and soon appeared
Such tiny twinklers as the planet orbs
That there attendant on the solar power
With borrowed light pursued their narrower way —*Q. M.* 220.

(*f*) Lightning.

186   Not the strong impulse hid
In those flushed cheeks, bent eyes, and shadowy frame
Had yet performed its ministry : it hung
Upon his life, as lightning in a cloud
Gleams, hovering ere it vanish, ere the floods
Of night close over it   —*Alast.* 415.

187   awful scene
Where power in likeness of the Arve comes down
From the ice gulphs that gird his secret throne,
Bursting through these dark mountains like the flame
Of lightning through the tempest ;   —*Mont. B.* 15.

188 Or when free thoughts like lightnings are alive ;
                         —*L. & C.* I. 33.

189 When mid soft looks of pity, there would dart
A glance as keen as is the lightning's stroke
When it doth rive the knots of some ancestral oak.
　　　　　　　　　　　　　　　—*L. & C.* IV. 6.

190 And smiles—as when the lightning's blast
Has parched some heaven-delighting oak,
The next spring shows leaves pale and rare,
But like flowers delicate and fair,
On its rent boughs,—again arrayed
His countenance in tender light :　　　—*R. & H.* 787.

191 　　Like veiled lightning asleep
. . . .
A spell is treasured but for thee alone　　—*Prom.* II. iii. 83.

192 　　Luther caught thy wakening glance,
　　Like lightning from his leaden lance
Reflected, it dissolved the visions of the trance
In which as in a tomb the nations lay :　　—*Ode to Lib.* X.

193 Aye, even the dim words which obscure thee now
Flash, lightning-like, with unaccustomed glow　　—*Epips.* 33.

194 If Bacon's eagle spirit had not leapt
Like lightning out of darkness　　　　—*Tr. of L.* 269

195 But keener thy gaze than the lightning's glare,　　—*Liberty*, III.

196 　　Fairest of the Destinies,
　　Disarray thy dazzling eyes :
　　Keener far thy lightnings are
Than the wingèd (bolts) thou bearest　　—*Fragm. Hell.* 180.

(*g*) Meteors, Comets.

197 A lurid earth-star, which dropped many a spark
From its blue train, and spreading widely, clung
To their wild hair, like mist the topmost pines among
　　　　　　　　　　　　　　—*L. & C.* XI. 12.

198 And as the meteor's midnight flame
Startles the dreamer, sun-like truth
Flashed on his visionary youth,　　　　—*R. & H.* 615.

199 In thine halls the lamp of learning,
Padua, now no more is burning,
Like a meteor, whose wild way
Is lost over the grave of day,
It gleams betrayed and to betray ;　　　—*Eng. Hills*, 256.

200 I have heard those more skilled in spirits say,
The bubbles, which the enchantment of the sun
Sucks from the pale faint water-flowers that pave
The oozy bottom of clear lakes and pools,
Are the pavilions where such dwell and float
Under the green and golden atmosphere
Which noon-tide kindles thro' the woven leaves ;
And when these burst, and the thin fiery air,
The which they breathed within those lucent domes,

4

Ascends to flow like meteors thro' the night,
They ride on them, and rein their headlong speed,
And bow their burning crests, and glide in fire
Under the waters of the earth again.   *—Prom.* II. ii. 70.

201   Their bright locks
Stream like a comet's flashing hair: they all
Sweep onward.   *—Prom.* II. iv. 138.

202   the bright visions,
Wherein the singing spirits rode and shone,
Gleam like pale meteors through a watery night.
                                  —Prom. IV. 514.

203 And the meteors of that sublunar heaven,
    Like the lamps of the air when night walks forth,
    Laughed round her footsteps up from the earth!
                                  —Sens. Pl. II. 10.

204   Death, Fear,
Love, Beauty are mixed in the atmosphere;
Which trembles and burns with the fervour of dread
Around her wild eyes, her bright hand, and her head,
Like a meteor of light o'er the waters!   *— Vision of Sea,* 161.

205   her petticoats streaming
   .   .   .   .
Or like a meteor, or a war-steed's mane,   *— Œd. Tyr.* 95.

206 Another splendour on his mouth alit,
   .   .   .   .
And as a dying meteor stains a wreath
Of moonlight vapour, which the cold night clips,
It flashed through his pale limbs, and pass'd to its eclipse
                                  —Adon. XII.

207 Like winged stars the fire-flies flash and glance,
    Pale in the open moonshine, but each one
    Under the dark trees seems a little sun,
    A meteor tamed;   *—Letter to M. G.* 281.

208 And the marsh meteors, like tame beasts, at night
    Came licking with blue tongues his veined feet;   *—Mar.* XX.

209 And the marsh meteors   .   .   .
   .   .   .   .
And he would watch them, as, like spirits bright,
In many entangled figures quaint and sweet
To some enchanted music they would dance,   *—Mar.* XX.

210 From Prospero's enchanted cell,
    As the mighty verses tell,
    To the throne of Naples, he
    Lit you o'er the trackless sea
    Flitting on, your prow before,
    Like a living meteor.   *— With a Guitar,* 17.

(*h*) THE SKY.

211 The other glowing like the vital morn,
    When throned on ocean's wave
    It breathes over the world: *—D. W.* 5.

212 Yet likest evening's vault that faery hall,
213 As heaven low resting on the wave it spread
  Its floors of flashing light,
  Its vast and azure dome ;   —*D. W.* 221.

214   unfathomable deeps
Blue as the overhanging heaven, that spread
And wind among the accumulated steeps ; *Mont. B.* 64.

215 It was a temple, such as mortal hand
Has never built, nor ecstasy, nor dream,
Reared in the cities of enchanted land ;
'Twas likest heaven, ere yet day's purple stream
Ebbs o'er the western forest, while the gleam
Of the unrisen moon among the clouds
Is gathering, when with many a golden beam
The thronging constellations rush in crowds,
Paving with fire the sky and the marmoreal floods.
         —*L. & C.* I. 49.

216 His eyes were dark and deep, and the clear brow
Which shadowed them was like the morning sky,
The cloudless heaven of Spring, when in their flow
Thro' the bright air, the soft winds as they blow
Wake the green world   —*L. & C.* I. 59.

217 Her looks were sweet as Heaven's when loveliest
In Autumn eves   —*L. & C.* V. 50.

218   alas ! from many spirits
The wisdom that had waked that cry, was fled,
Like the brief glory which dark Heaven inherits
From the false dawn, which fades ere it is spread,
Upon the night's devouring darkness shed :
         —*L. & C.* IX. 5.

219 The awful shadow of some unseen Power
  Floats tho' unseen among us,—
 . . . .
 Like hues and harmonies of evening —*H. I. B.* I.

220 And we breathe, and sicken not,
The atmosphere of human thought ;
Be it dim and dark and grey,
Like a storm-extinguished day,
Travelled o'er by dying gleams ;
Be it bright as all between
Cloudless skies and windless streams,
Silent, liquid, and serene   —*Prom.* I. 675.

221 And women, too, frank, beautiful, and kind
As the free heaven which rains fresh light and dew
On the wide earth, past : —*Prom.* III. iv. 153.

222 Drinking from thy sense and sight
Beauty, majesty, and might,
 . . . .
As a violet's gentle eye
Gazes on the azure sky
Until its hue grows like what it beholds —*Prom.* IV. 485.

223   At the helm sits a woman more fair
Than heaven, when unbinding its star-braided hair,
It sinks with the sun on the earth and the sea.
         —*Vis. of Sea*, 66.

224 The cares we waste upon our heavy crown
Would make it light and glorious as a wreath
Of heaven's beams for his dear innocent brow.
         —*Chas. I.* 491.

225 When the north wind congregates in crowds
The floating mountains of the silver clouds
From the horizon—and the stainless sky
Opens beyond them like eternity,   —*Summer and W.* 3.

226 From every point of the Infinite
Like a thousand dawns on a single night
  The splendours rise and spread   —*Prol. Hell.* 62.

227 We paused beside the pools that lie
  Under the forest bough,
Each seemed as 'twere a little sky
Gulphed in a world below ;   —*To Jane Recoll.* V.

228 A firmament of purple light
  Which in the dark earth lay
More boundless than the depth of night
And purer than the day.   —*To Jane Recoll.* V.

229   Heaven's ebon vault
Studded with stars unutterably bright,
Through which the moon's unclouded grandeur rolls,
Seems like a canopy which love had spread
To curtain her sleeping world.   —*Q. M.* 4.

(i) Fire.

230 Thou too, aerial Pile ! whose pinnacles
Point from one shrine like pyramids of fire —*Summer Eve*, 13.

231 One seat was vacant in the midst, a throne,
Reared on a pyramid like sculptured flame,
Distinct with circling steps which rested on
Their own deep fire—   —*L. & C. I.* 55.

232   And fires blazed far amid the scattered camps,
Like springs of flame, which burst where'er swift Earthquake stamps
         —*L. & C. V.* 1.

233 The misery of a madness slow and creeping,
Which made the earth seem fire, —*L. & C. VII.* 15.

234 Yet soon bright day will burst—even like a chasm
Of fire, to burn the shrouds outworn and dead,
Which wrap the world :   —*L. & C. IX.* 5.

235 Aloft, her flowing hair like strings of flame did quiver.
         —*L. & C. XI.* 3.

236   towers far and near
     Pierce like reposing flames the tremulous atmosphere
                                    —*L. & C.* XII. 5.

237 Yet, yet, one brief relapse, like the last beam
     Of dying flames, the stainless air around
     Hung silent and serene—a blood-red gleam
     Burst upwards, hurling fiercely from the ground
     The globèd smoke,—   —*L. & C.* XII. 16.

238   And before that chasm of light,
          As within a furnace bright,
          Column, tower, and dome, and spire,
239   Shine like obelisks of fire,
          Pointing with inconstant motion
          From the altar of dark ocean
          To the sapphire-tinted skies:
240   As the flames of sacrifice
          From the marble shrines did rise,
          As to pierce the dome of gold
          Where Apollo spoke of old.   —*Eug. Hills*, 104.

241 Hither the sound has borne us—to the realm
     Of Demogorgon, and the mighty portal,
     Like a volcano's meteor-breathing chasm,   —*Prom.* II. iii. 1.

242 Pour forth heaven's wine, Idalian Ganymede,
     And let it fill the Daedal cups like fire.   —*Prom.* III. i. 25.

243 The unseen clouds of the dew, which lie
     Like fire in the flowers till the sun rides high. —*Sens. P.* I. 86

244 And the green lizard, and the golden snake,
     Like unimprisoned flames, out of their trance awake.
                                 Adon. XVIII.

245 And grey walls moulder round on which dull Time
     Feeds, like slow fire upon a hoary brand;
     And one keen pyramid with edge sublime,
     Pavilioning the dust of him who planned
     This refuge for his memory, doth stand
246 Like flame transformed to marble: —*Adon.* L.

247 And then—as if the earth and sea had been
     Dissolved into one lake of fire, were seen
248 Those mountains towering as from waves of flame,
     Around the vaporous sun, from which there came
     The inmost purple spirit of light, and made
     Their very peaks transparent   —*Jul. & M.* 80.

249 Men scarcely know how beautiful fire is—
     Each flame of it is as a precious stone
     Dissolved in ever-moving light,   —*Witch*, XXVII.

250 In thy dark eyes a power like light doth lie
     . . . .
     Within thy breath, and on thy hair, like odour it is yet
     And from thy touch like fire doth leap   —*Const.* I.

251 There must have lived within Marenghi's heart
That fire, more warm and bright than life or hope,
—*Mar.* XVIII.

252   When memory came
(For years gone by leave each a deepening shade),
His spirit basked in its internal flame,
As when the black storm hurries round at night
The fisher basks beside his red firelight   —*Mar.* XXV.

(*j*) EYES.

253 Life, and the lustre that consumed it, shone
As in a furnace burning secretly
From his dark eyes alone.   *Alast.* 252.

254   O ! there are spirits of the air,
    And genii of the evening breeze,
   And gentle ghosts, with eyes as fair
    As star-beams among twilight trees :   —*To Coler.* 1.

255 Then she arose, and smiled on me with eyes
Serene yet sorrowing, like that planet fair,
While yet the daylight lingereth in the skies
Which cleaves with arrowy beams the dark red air,
        —*L. & C.* I. 21.

256 Small serpent eyes trailing from side to side,
Like meteors on a river's grassy shore,   —*L. & C.* I. 56.

257   an eye of blue
Looked into mine, like moonlight, soothingly :
        —*L. & C.* I. 58.

258   her dark and deepening eyes,
Which, as twin phantoms of one star that lies
O'er a dim well, move, though the star reposes,
Swam in our mute and liquid ecstasies,   —*L. & C.* VI. 33.

259 A voiceless thought of evil, which did spread
With the quick glance of eyes, like withered lightnings shed.
        —*L. & C.* X. 16.

260   her dark and intricate eyes
261 Orb within orb deeper than sleep or death,
Absorbed the glories of the burning skies,
Which, mingling with her heart's deep ecstasies,
Burst from her looks and gestures :   —*L. & C.* XI. 5.

262   his eyes are mild
And calm, and like the morn about to break,
Smile on mankind—   —*L. & C.* XII. 3.

263   And his keen eyes glittering through mine,
   Filled me with the flame divine,
   Which in their orbs was burning far,
   Like the light of an unmeasured star.
   In the sky of midnight dark and deep :   —*R. & H.* 1134.

264   I feel, I see
Those eyes which burn thro' smiles that fade in tears,
Like stars half quenched in mists of silver dew.
* —Prom.* II. i. 27.

265 Thine eyes are like the deep, blue, boundless heaven
Contracted to two circles underneath
Their long, fine lashes ; dark, far, measureless,
Orb within orb, and line thro' line inwoven.
* —Prom.* II. i. 114.

266   the young spirit
That guides it has the dovelike eyes of hope ;
* —Prom.* II. iv. 159.

267 The terrors of his eye illumined heaven
With sanguine light, through the thick ragged skirts
Of the victorious darkness as he fell ;
Like the last glare of day's red agony,
Which, from a rent among the fiery clouds,
Burns far along the tempest-wrinkled deep   *—Prom.* III. ii. 4.

268 And your eyes are as love which is veiled not ?
* —Prom.* IV. 92.

269   Be your wounds like eyes
To weep for the dead.   *—Ode* 3.

270 With those clear drops, which start like sacred dew
From the twin lights thy sweet soul darkens through,
* —Epips.* 142.

271 And then came one of sweet and earnest looks,
Whose soft smiles to his dark and night-like eyes
272 Were as the clear and ever-living brooks
Are to the obscure fountains whence they rise
Showing how pure they are ;   *—Canc. Adon.* 1.

273   Oh, speak not of her eyes ! which seem
Twin mirrors of Italian heaven, yet gleam
With such deep meaning, as we never see
But in the human countenance ;   *—Jul. & M.* 147.

274   and eyes whose arrowy light
Shone like the reflex of a thousand minds.
* —Prince Ath.* II. i. 4.

275 Her hair was brown, her sphered eyes were brown,
And in their dark and liquid moisture swam,
Like the dim orb of the eclipsed moon,
* —Fragm. Prince Ath.* 1.

276 Yet when the spirit flashed beneath, there came
The light from them, as when tears of delight
Double the western planet's serene flame.
* —Fragm. Prince Ath.* 4.

277 When Peter heard of his promotion,
His eyes grew like two stars for bliss ;   *—Peter B.* VII. vii.

278   deep her eyes, as are
Two openings of unfathomable night
Seen through a temple's cloven roof—   *—Witch*, V.

279 In thy dark eyes a power like light doth lie,
Even though the sounds which were thy voice, which burn
Between thy lips, are laid to sleep ;
280 Within thy breath, and on thy hair, like odour it is yet,
281 And from thy touch like fire doth leap.   *—Const.* I.

282   Thrills with her lovely eyes,
Which like two stars amid the heaving main
Sparkle through liquid bliss.   *Q. M.* 38.

(*k*) DARKNESS, SHADOW.

283 Below, the smoke of roofs involved in flame
Rested like night,   *—L. & C.* III. 16.

284 I watched, unt 1 the shades of evening wrapt
Earth like an exhalation   *—L. & C.* III. 18.

285   confusion, then despair
Descends like night   *—L. & C.* V. 7.

286 O Spirit vast and deep as Night and Heaven !
     —L. & C. V. 51, 2.

287   her dark hair was dispread
Like the pine's locks upon the lingering blast,
Over mine eyes its shadowy strings it spread &
Fitfully,   *—L. & C.* VI. 21.

288 The pitchy smoke of the departed fire
Still hung in many a hollow dome and spire
Above the towers like night :   *—L. & C.* XII. 26.

289 Sometimes through forests, deep like night, we glode,
     —L. & C. XII. 35.

290   I bear a darker, deadlier gloom
291 Than the earth's shade, or interlunar air,
292 Or constellations quenched in murkiest cloud,
     —Cenci, II. i. 189.

293 When its wound was closed, there stood
Darkness o'er the day like blood. *—Prom.* I. 101.

294 Sister, 1 hear the thunder of new wings

. . . .

    their shadows make
The space within my plumes more black than night.
     —Prom. I. 521.

295   1 see a mighty darkness
Filling the seat of power, and rays of gloom
Dart round, as light from the meridian sun,
Ungazed upon and shapeless. *—Prom.* II. iv. 2.

296   That terrible shadow floats
Up from its throne, as may the lurid smoke
Of earthquake-ruined cities o'er the sea. —*Prom.* II. iv. 150.

297 Peace ! peace ! A mighty Power which is as darkness,
Is rising out of Earth, and from the sky
298 Is showered like night, and from within the air
299 Bursts, like eclipse which had been gathered up
Into the pores of sunlight :   —*Prom.* IV. 510.

300 To forgive wrongs darker than death or night ;
        —*Prom.* IV. 571.

301   Six the thunder has smitten,
And they lie back as mummies on which Time has written
His scorn of the embalmer ;   — *Vision of S.* 61.

302 Black as a cormorant the screaming blast — *Vision of S.* 105.

303   armies mingled in obscure array,
Like clouds with clouds, darkening the sacred bowers
Of serene heaven   —*Ode to Lib.* XII.

304 The future looks as black as death, a cloud,
305 Dark as the frown of Hell hangs over it— —*Œd. Tyr.* 96.

306 And others said that such mysterious grief
From God's displeasures like a darkness, fell
On souls like his which owned no higher law
Than love ;   —*Prince Ath.* I. 93.

307   but o'er the visage wan
Of Athanase, a ruffling atmosphere
Of dark emotion. a swift shadow ran,
Like wind upon some forest-bosomed lake,
Glassy and dark,—   —*Prince Ath.* II. ii. 47.

308   the flagging wing
Of the roused cormorant in the lightning flash
Looked like the wreck of some wind-wandering
Fragment of inky thunder-smoke - *Witch*, L.

309 And o'er what seemed the head a cloud-like crane
Was bent, a dim and faint ætherial gloom
Tempering the light.   —*Tr. of L.* 91.

310 And Gregory and John and men divine
 . . . .
Who rose like shadows between man and God —*Tr. of L.* 288.

311 And tyrants and slaves are like shadows of night
In the van of the morning light   —*Lib.* IV.

312 A portal as of shadowy adamant
Stands yawning on the highway of the life
Which we all tread, a cavern huge and gaunt ;
Around it rages an unceasing strife
313 Of shadows, like the restless clouds that haunt
The gap of some cleft mountain, lifted high
Into the whirlwinds of the upper sky. —*Alley.* 1.

314   A firmament of purple light
       Which in the dark earth lay
       More boundless than the depth of night,
       And purer than the day.   *—To Jane Rec.* 57.

(*l*) White Light, Pallor.

              some, whose white hair shone
315 Like mountain snow   *—L. & C.* I. 54.

316 Let tortures strain the truth till it be white
       As snow thrice sifted by the frozen wind   *—Cenci*, V. ii. 170.

                    Cities then
317 Were built, and through their snow-like columns flowed
       The warm winds   *—Prom.* II. iv. 94.

318 From its curved roof the mountain's frozen tears
319 Like snow, or silver, or long diamond spires,
320 Hung downwards, raising forth a doubtful light.
                        —Prom. III. iii. 15.

321 Within it sits a wingèd infant, white
       Its countenance, like the whiteness of bright snow ;
322 Its plumes are as the feathers of sunny frost,
       Its limbs gleam white, through the wind-flowing folds
       Of its white robe, woof of ætherial pearl.
       Its hair is white, the brightness of white light
       Scattered in strings, yet its two eyes are heavens
       Of liquid darkness,   *—Prom.* IV. 219.

323 The lilies were drooping, and white, and wan
       Like the head and the skin of a dying man   *—Sens. Pl.* III. 28.

                his hair and beard
324 Are whiter than the tempest-sifted snow.   *—Hell.* 140.

325 O pallid as Death's dedicated bride,
       Thou mockery which art sitting by my side,
       Am I not wan like thee ?   *—Jul. and Madd.* 384.

326   Last came Anarchy : he rode
         On a white horse splashed with blood ;
         He was pale even to the lips
         Like Death in the Apocalypse   *—Mask.* VIII.

327   From the workhouse and the prison,
         Where pale as corpses newly risen,
         Women, children, young and old,
         Groan for pain and weep for cold.   *—Mask*, LXVIII.

328 Her lips and cheeks were like things dead, so pale   *—Sunset.*

329 His hands were clasped, veined and pale as snow.   *—Tass.* 22.

330 And their mothers look pale, like the white shore
       Of Albion free no more   *—Lines*, Vol. IV. i. 16.

331 The wreaths of stony myrtle, ivy and pine,
       Like winter leaves o'ergrown by moulded snow
                      —Ode to Nap. 17.

when the prow

332 Made the invisible water white as snow.   —*Ode to Nap.* 42.

(*m*) GENERAL.

333   Like restless serpents, clothed
In rainbows and in fire, the parasites,
Starred with ten thousand blossoms, flow around
The grey trunks.   —*Alast.* 438.

334 Hither the poet came, his eyes beheld
Their own wan light through the reflected lines
Of his thin hair, distinct in the dark depth
Of that still fountain ; as the human heart
Gazing in dreams over the gloomy grave,
Sees its own treacherous likeness there.   —*Alast.* 469.

335   Must that divinest form

.   .   .   .   .   .
              whose azure veins
Steal like dark streams along a field of snow,
336 Whose outline is as fair as marble clothed
In light of some divinest mind, decay ?   —*D. W.* 12.

337 Ardent and pure as day thou burnest   —*D. W.* 92.

338   bright scales did leap
Where'er the Eagle s talons made their way,
Like sparks into the darkness   —*L. & C.* I. 11.

339   Their sun-like form
Upon the combat shone—a light to save
Like Paradise spread forth beyond the shadowy grave
                 —*L. & C.* I. 32.

340 Mountains of ice, like sapphire, piled on high
Hemming the horizon round, in silence lay
On the still waters   —*L. & C.* I. 47.

341 The radiance of whose limbs rose-like and warm
Flowed forth   —*L. & C.* I. 57.

342   did my spirit wake
From sleep, as many-coloured as the snake
That girds eternity ?   —*L. & C.* IV. 4.

343 As thus the old man spoke, his countenance
Gleamed on me like a spirit's   —*L. & C.* IV. 16.

344 A glorious pageant, more magnificent
Than kingly slaves arrayed in gold and blood,
When they return from carnage,   —*L. & C.* V. 14.

345   the King with gathered brow, and lips
Wreathed by long scorn, did inly sneer and frown
With hue like that when some great painter dips
His pencil in the gloom of earthquake and eclipse.
              —*L. & C.* V. 23.

346 As I approached, the morning's golden mist,
    Which now the wonder-stricken breezes kist
    With their cold lips, fled, and the summit shone
    Like Athos seen from Samothracia, drest
    In earliest light by vintagers,   *—L. & C.* V. 43.

347 She, like a spirit through the darkness shining,
                           —L. & C. V. 52.

348 Thro' which, his way the diver having cloven,
    Past like a spark sent up out of a burning oven.
                         —L. & C. VII. 11.

349   as a friend whose smile
    Like light and rest at morn and even is sought,
    That wild bird was to me,   *—L. & C.* VII. 14.

350, 351 And brows as bright as spring or morning, ere
    Dark time had there its evil legend wrought
    In characters of cloud which wither not   *—L. & C.* VIII. 29.

352 But one was mute, her cheeks and lips most fair
    Changing their hues like lilies newly blown,
    Beneath a bright acacia's shadowy hair,
    Waved by the wind amid the sunny noon,
    Showed that her soul was quivering ;   *—L. & C.* VIII. 30.

353   Thy mother Autumn, for whose grave thou bearest
    Fresh flowers, and beams like flowers, with gentle feet,
    Disturbing not the leaves which are her winding-sheet.
                         —L. & C. IX. 22.

354 The light of such a joy as makes the stare
    Of hungry snakes like living emeralds glow,
    Shone in a hundred human eyes—   *L. & C.* XI. 25.

355   A woman sits thereon,
    Fairer it seems than aught that earth can breed,
    Calm, radiant, like the phantom of the dawn,
    A spirit from the caves of daylight wandering gone
                        —L. & C. XII. 8.

356 Now with a bitter smile, whose light did shine
    Like a fiend's hope upon his lips and eyne,
                         —L. & C. XII. 11.

357 And in quick smiles whose light would come and go,
    Like music o'er wide waves,   *—L. & C.* XII. 37.

358 And down my cheeks the quick tears ran
    Like twinkling rain-drops from the eaves.
    When warm Spring showers are passing o'er ;   *—R. & H.* 366.

359 For his cheek became, not pale, but fair,
    As rose-o'ershadowed lilies are :   *—R. & H.* 819.

    Thy light alone like mist o'er mountains driven,
360   Or music by the night wind sent
    Thro' strings of some strange instrument,

 .   .   .   .
    Gives grace and truth to life's unquiet dream   *—H. I. B.* III.

361 With golden-sandalled feet, that glow
Under plumes of purple dye
Like rose-ensanguined ivory   —*Prom.* I. 319.

362 As from the rose which the pale priestess kneels
To gather for the festal crown of flowers
The aerial crimson falls, flushing her cheek,
So from our victim's destined agony
The shade which is our form invests us round,
Else we are shapeless as our mother Night.   *Prom.* I. 467.

363   and thro' yon peaks of cloud-like snow
The roseate sunlight quivers   —*Prom.* II. i. 24.

364 Like the spark nursed in embers

365 Like a diamond, which shines
On the dark wealth of mines,
A spell is treasured but for thee alone.
           —*Prom.* II. iii. 84.

366 How its soft smiles attract the soul ! as light
Lures wingèd insects through the lampless air.
           —*Prom.* II. v. 161.

367   *Ione.*
          Yet feel you no delight
From the past sweetness?
        Panthea.
         As the bare green hill
When some soft cloud vanishes into rain,
Laughs with a thousand drops of sunny water
To the unpavilioned sky !   —*Prom.* IV. 181.

368 Some Spirit is darted like a beam from thee,
Which penetrates my frozen frame,   —*Prom.* IV. 327.

369 But the bee and the beam-like ephemeris
Whose path is the lightning's,   —*Sens. P.* II. 49.

370 The rose leaves, like flakes of crimson snow
Paved the turf and moss below   —*Sens. P.* III. 26.

371   a leech
Fit to suck blood, with lubricous round rings,
Capaciously expatiative, which make
His little body like a red balloon,   —*Œd. Tyr.* 184.

372 When, like a noon-day dawn, there shone again
Deliverance.   —*Epips.* 276.

373 Athwart that wintry wilderness of thorns
Flashed from her motion splendour like the Morn's
           —*Epips.* 379.

374 And, as those married lights, which from the towers
Of Heaven look forth, and fold the wandering globe
In liquid sleep and splendour, as a robe ;   —*Epips.* 355.

375 It is an isle, 'twixt Heaven, Air, Earth, and Sea,
Cradled and hung in clear tranquillity ;
Bright as that wandering Eden Lucifer,
Washed by the soft blue oceans of young air.   —*Epips.* 457.

376 She rose like an autumnal Night, that springs
    Out of the East and follows wild and drear
    The golden Day,   —*Adon.* XXIII.

377   the dead live there
    And move like winds of light on dark and stormy air.
                        —*Adon.* XLIV.

378 Pass till the Spirit of the spot shall lead
    Thy footsteps to a slope of green access,
    Where, like an infant's smile over the dead,
    A light of laughing flowers along the grass is spread.
                        —*Adon.* XLIX.

379 Thermopylæ and Marathon
    Caught, like mountains beacon-lighted,
        The springing fire.   —*Hell.* 54.

380   her hoary ruins glow
    Like Orient mountains lost in day :   —*Hell.* 84.

381 To-morrow and to-morrow are as lamps
    Set in our path to light us to the edge   —*Hell.* 644.

382 Athens arose !—around her born,
    Shone like mountains in the morn
    Glorious states :—   —*Hell.* 684.

383   and when the earth is fair
    The shadow of thy moving wings imbue
    Its deserts and its mountains, till they wear
    Beauty like some bright robe ;—   —*Prince Ath.* II. iv. 8.

384 Clothed with the Bible, as with light,   —*Mask.* VI.

385 For with pomp to meet him came
    Clothed in arms like blood and flame,
    The hired murderers,   — *Mask.* XV.

386   a Shape arrayed in mail
    Brighter than the viper's scale,
    And upborne on wings whose grain
387 Was as the light of sunny rain.   —*Mask.* XXVIII.

388 And those plumes the light rained thro'
    Like a shower of crimson dew,   —*Mask.* XXIX.

389 But Peter's verse was clear .   .

    .   .   .   .   .   .
    Like gentle rains, on the dark plains,
    Making that green which late was grey,   —*Peter B.* V. xiv.

390 When lamp-like Spain, who now relumes her fire
    On Freedom's hearth, grew dim with Empire :—
                     —*Letter to M. G.* 33.

391 Carved lamps and chalices, and vials which shone
    In their own golden beams each like a flower,
    Out of whose depth a fire-fly shakes his light
    Under a cypress in a starlight night.   — *Witch*, XX.

392 The silver moon into that winding dell,
   With slanted beam athwart the forest tops,
   Tempered like golden evening, feebly fell ;
393   A green and glowing light like that which drops
   From folded lilies in which glow-worms dwell
   When earth over her face night's mantle wraps :
                            — *Witch*, XXXIX.

394 And it unfurled its heaven-coloured pinions,
   With stars of fire spotting the stream below ;
   And from above into the Sun's dominions
   Flinging a glory, like the golden glow
   In which Spring clothes her emerald-wingèd minions,
   All interwoven with fine feathery snow
   And moonlight splendour of intensest rime,
   With which frost paints the pines in winter time.
                            — *Witch*, XLIV.

395 And all the forms in which those spirits lay
   Were to her sight like the diaphanous
   Veils, in which those sweet ladies oft array
   Their delicate limbs,   — *Witch*, LXV.

396   and the grave
   Of such, when death oppressed the weary soul,
   Was as a green and overarching bower
   Lit by the gems of many a starry flower.   — *Witch*, LXIX.

397 While the musk-rose leaves, like flakes of crimson snow
   Showered on us,   — *Fragm. of Drama*, 67.

398 And poured upon the earth within the vase
   The element with which it overflowed,
399 Brighter than morning light, and purer than
   The waters of the Springs of Himalah.
                     — *Fragm. of Drama*, 147.

400 And day by day, green as a gourd in June,
   The plant grew fresh and thick.   — *Fragm. of Drama*, 161.

401   its stem and tendrils seemed
   Like emerald snakes, mottled and diamonded,
   With azure mail and streaks of woven silver ;
                   — *Fragm. of Drama*, 163.

402 And all the sheaves that folded the soft buds
   Rose like the crest of cobra-di-capel.   — *Fragm. of Drama*, 166.

403   You almost saw
   The pulses
   With which the purple velvet flower was fed
   To overflow, and like a poet's heart
   Changing bright fancy to sweet sentiment,
   Changed half the light to fragrance.   — *Fragm. of Drama*, 172.

404   and it seemed
   In hue and form that it had been a mirror
   Of all the hues and forms around it.   — *Fragm. of Drama*, 218.

405 What thinkest thou of this quaint mask which turns,
   Like morning from the shadow of the night,
   The night to day,   — *Chas. I.* I. 2.

406 Until Heaven's kingdom shall descend on Earth,
Or Earth be like a shadow in the light
Of Heaven absorbed.   *—Chas. I.* III. 28.

407   for the shade it spread
Was so transparent, that the scene came through
As clear as when a veil of light is drawn
O'er evening hills they glimmer ;   *— Tr. of L.* 30.

408 And a cold glare, intenser than the noon,
But icy cold, obscured with blinding light
The sun,   *—Tr. of L.* 77.

409   like day she came
Making the night a dream :   *—Tr. of L.* 389.

410   the crew
Seemed in that light, like atomies to dance
Within a sunbeam   *—Tr. of L.* 445.

411 And others, like discoloured flakes of snow
On fairest bosoms and the sunniest hair,
Fell,   *—Tr. of L.* 511.

412 The eddy whirled her round and round
Before a gorgeous gate which stood
Piercing the clouds of smoke which bound
Its very arch with light like blood ;   *— Mar. Dream,* XVIII.

413 And, when he saw beneath the sunset's planet
A black ship walk over the crimson ocean,
Its pennants streaming on the blasts that fan it,
Its sails and ropes all tense and without motion,
Like the dark ghost of the unburied even
Striding across the orange-coloured heaven.   *—Mar.* XXVII.

414 Upon its lips and eyelids seems to lie
Loveliness like a shadow.   *—Medus.* I.

415   A light such
As sleepers wear, lulled by the voice they love,   *– Fiord.* 38.

416   The Giant Powers move,
Gloomy or bright as the thrones they fill.   *—Prol. Hell.* 69.

417   Haste thou and fill the waning crescent
With beams as keen as those which pierced the shadow
Of Christian night rolled back upon the West *—Prol. Hell.* 169.

418   but the weary glare
Lay like a chaos of unwelcome light
Vexing the sense with gorgeous undelight,   *—Giner.* 18.

419 Glow-worms went out on the river's brim,
Like lamps which a student forgets to trim.   *—Serch.* 22.

420 Where mighty shapes—pyramid, dome, and tower—
Gleamed like a pile of crags.   *— Frag. of Dream,* v. 4.

421 Tears pure as Heaven's rain,   *—Zucc.* X.

422 Its light within the gloomy breast
Spreads like a second youth again.   *—Magn. Lady, IV.*

423 Best and brightest, come away!
Fairer far than this fair Day,   *—To June, 1.*

424 Now the last of many days,
All beautiful and bright as thou,   *-To Jane, Recoll. 1.*

425 There was a little lawny islet
By anemone and violet,
Like mosaic, paven   *—The Isle, 1.*

SIMILES OF SOUND.

MUSIC—WORDS—SILENCE.

426 Her voice was like the voice of his own soul
Heard in the calm of thought; its music long,
427 Like woven sounds of streams and breezes, held
His inmost sense suspended in its web
Of many-coloured woof and shifting hues.   *—Alast. 53.*

428   Yet, a little, ere it fled,
Did he resign his high and holy soul
To images of the majestic past,
That paused within his passive being now,
Like winds that bear sweet music, when they breathe
Through some dim lattice chamber.   *--Alast. 627.*

429 Hark! whence that wondrous sound?
      'Tis like a wondrous strain that sweeps
      Around a lonely ruin
When west winds sigh and evening waves respond
      In whispers from the shore.   *—D. W. 48.*

430   Hark! whence that rushing sound?
  . . . .
'Tis wilder than the unmeasured notes
Which from the unseen lyres of dells and groves
      The genii of the breezes sweep.   *—D. W. 53.*

431 Such sounds as breathed around like odorous winds
      Of wakening spring arose,   *—D. W. 75.*

432   whence from secret springs
The source of human thought its tribute brings
Of waters —with a sound but half its own,
Such as a feeble brook will oft assume
In the wild woods, among the mountains lone,
Where waterfalls around it leap for ever,
Where woods and winds contend, and a vast river
Over its rocks ceaselessly bursts and raves.   *—Mont. B. 4.*

433 Or where with sound like many voices sweet,
Waterfalls leap among wild islands green, *—Ded. L. & C.* II.

434 One voice came forth from many a mighty spirit,
Which was the echo of three thousand years ;
And the tumultuous world stood mute to hear it,
As some lone man who in a desert hears
The music of his home : *—Ded. L. & C.* XIII.

435 Her voice was like the wildest saddest tone
Yet sweet, of some loved voice heard long ago. *—L. & C.* I. 22.

436   suddenly
She would arise, and like the secret bird
Whom sunset wakens, fill the shore and sky
With her sweet accents—a wild melody ! *—L. & C.* II. 28.

437 Triumphant strains which, like a spirit's tongue,
To the enchanted waves that child of glory sung.
                        —L. & C. II. 28.

438 When from that stony gloom a voice arose,
Solemn and sweet as when low winds attune
The midnight pines ; *—L. & C.* III. 28.

439   the chain, with sound
Like earthquake, through the chasm of that steep stair did bound,
                        —L. & C. III. 29.

440   a trance which awes
The thoughts of men with hope—as when the sound
Of whirlwind, whose fierce blasts the waves and clouds confound,
Dies suddenly, the mariner in fear
Feels silence sink upon his heart—thus bound
The conquerors pause, *—L. & C.* IV. 27.

441 Like a bright ghost from Heaven that shout did scare
The slaves, *—L. & C.* V. 7.

442 As we approached a shout of joyance sprung
At once from all the crowd, as if the vast
And peopled Earth its boundless skies among
The sudden clamour of delight had cast,
When from before its face some general wreck had past.
                        —L. & C. V. 15.

443   like a tomb
Its sculptured walls vacantly to the strokes
Of footfalls answered, *—L. & C.* V. 22.

444   It was a tone
Such as sick fancies in a new-made grave
Might hear. *— L. & C.* V. 27.

445   like the rush of showers
Of hail in spring, pattering along the ground,
Their many footsteps fell, else came no sound
From the wide multitude : *—L. & C.* V. 29

446 Slowly the silence of the multitudes
Past, as when far is heard in some lone dell
The gathering of a wind among the woods— *—L. & C.* V. 31.

447 To hear the restless multitude forever
    Around the base of that great Altar flow,
    As on some islet burst and shiver
    Atlantic waves ;   —*L. & C.* V. 41.

448 To feel the dream-like music, which did swim
449 Like beams thro' floating clouds on waves below,
    Falling in pauses from that Altar dim,
    As silver-sounding tongues breathed an aerial hymn.
                             —*L. & C.* V. 41.

                        but blind
450 And silent, as a breathing corpse did fare
451 Leaning upon my friend, till like a wind
    To fevered cheeks, a voice flowed o'er my troubled mind.
                      —*L. & C.* V. 45.

452 Like music of some minstrel heavenly-gifted
    To one whom friends enthral, this voice to me :
                        —*L. & C.* V. 46.

    She like a spirit through the darkness shining
    In tones whose sweetness silence did prolong,
453 As if to lingering winds they did belong,
    Poured forth her inmost soul :   —*L. & C.* V. 52.

454 Her voice was as a mountain stream which sweeps
    The withered leaves of autumn to the lake,
    And in some deep and narrow bay then sleeps
    In the shadow of the stones ;   —*L. & C.* V. 53.

455 And heard her musical pants, like the sweet source
    Of waters in the desert,   —*L. & C.* VI. 20.

456   the sound as of a Spirit's tongue.
                        —*L. & C.* VI. 32.

457 The tones of Cythna's voice like echoes were
    Of those far-murmuring streams.   —*L. & C.* VI. 42.

458 The Tyrant heard her singing to her lute
    A wild, and sad, and spirit-thrilling lay,
    Like winds that die in wastes—   *L. & C.* VII. 4.

459   and they began to breathe
    Deep curses, like the voice of flames far underneath
                      —*L. & C.* VII. 7.

460   a sound arose like thunder.
                      —*L. & C.* VII. 10.

461   from your hearts
    I feel an echo ; thro' my inmost frame
    Like sweetest sound, seeking its mate, it darts
                  —*L. & C.* VIII. 17.

462 The very darkness shook, as with a blast
    Of subterranean thunder at the cry ;   —*L. & C.* VIII. 28.

463   they heard the startling cry,
    Like earth's own voice lifted unconquerably
    To all her children,   —*L. & C.* IX. 3.

464 So from that cry over the boundless hills
Sudden was caught one universal sound.
Like a volcano's voice, whose thunder fills
Remotest skies—   —*L. & C.* IX. 4.

465 And like a subterranean wind that stirs
Some forest among caves, the hopes and fears
From every human soul, a murmur strange
Made as I past ;   —*L. & C.* IX. 6.

466 A pause of hope and awe the city bound
Which, like the silence of a tempest's birth
When in its awful shadow it has wound
The sun, the wind, the ocean, and the earth,
Hung terrible, ere yet the lightnings have leapt forth
                                             —*L. & C.* IX. 11.

467   thine own wild songs which in the air
Like homeless odours floated,   —*L. & C.* IX. 12.

468   from many a dale
The antelopes who flocked for food have spoken
With happy sounds, and motions, that avail
Like man's own speech ;   —*L. & C.* X. 2.

469 For, from the utmost realms of earth, came pouring
The banded slaves whom every despot sent
At that throned traitor's summons, like the roaring
Of fire, whose floods the wild deer circumvent
In the scorched pastures of the South, so bent
The armies of the leaguèd kings around
Their files of steel and flames ;—   —*L. & C.* X. 4.

470   when from beneath a cowl
A voice came forth, which pierced like ice thro' every soul,
                                             —*L. & C.* X. 31.

471 His voice was like a blast that burst the portal
Of fabled hell ;   —*L. & C.* X. 40.

472   some kissed their marble feet, with moan
Like love, and died,   —*L. & C.* X. 48.

473 When the last echo of those terrible cries
Came from a distant street like agonies
Stifled afar.—   —*L. & C.* XI. 13.

474 There was such silence through the host, as when
An earthquake trampling on some populous town
Has crushed ten thousand with one tread, and men
Expect the second ;   —*L. & C.* XII. 6.

475   in that dread pause, he lay
As in a quiet dream—   —*L. & C.* XII. 7.

476   they hear
The tramp of hoofs like earthquake,   —*L. & C.* XII. 8.

477   a gathering shout
Bursts like one sound from the ten thousand streams
Of a tempestuous sea :—   —*L. & C.* XII. 10.

478   a blood-red gleam
Burst upwards, hurling fiercely from the ground
The globèd smoke, I heard the mighty sound
Of its uprise, like a tempestuous ocean ; —*L. & C.* XII. 16.

479   slowly there is heard
The music of a breath-suspending song,
Which, like the kiss of love when life is young,
Steeps the faint eyes in darkness sweet and deep ;
With ever-changing notes it floats along,
Till on my passive soul there seemed to creep
480 A melody, like waves on wrinkled sands that leap.
      —*L. & C.* XII. 17.

481 Like the autumn wind, when it unbinds
The tangled locks of the nightshade's hair,
Which is twined in the sultry summer air
Round the walls of an outworn sepulchre,
Did the voice of Helen, sad and sweet,
And the sound of her heart that ever beat,
As with sighs and words she breathed on her,
Unbind the knots of her friend's despair
Till her thoughts were free to float and flow ;
And from her labouring bosom now,
482 Like the bursting of a prisoned flame,
The voice of a long-pent sorrow came. — *R. & H.* 207.

483   his words could bind
Like music the lulled crowd,   —*R. & H.* 636.

484 And said, with voice that made them shiver,
And clung like music in my brain, —*R. & H.* 890.

485 And light and sound ebbed from the earth,
Like the tide of the full and weary sea
To the depths of its own tranquillity —*R. & H.* 970.

486   till new emotions came,
Which seemed to make each mortal frame
One soul of interwoven flame,
A life in life, a second birth
In worlds diviner far than earth,
Which, like two strains of harmony
That mingle in the silent sky,
Then slowly disunite, passed by
And left the tenderness of tears,
The soft oblivion of all fears,
A sweet sleep :   —*R. & H.* 977.

487 The melody of an old air
Softer than sleep.   —*R. & H.* 1098.

488 Daylight on its last purple cloud
Was lingering grey : and soon her strain
The nightingale began, now loud,
Climbing in circles the windless sky,
Now dying music ; suddenly
'Tis scattered in a thousand notes,
And now to the hushed ear it floats
Like field smells known in infancy,
Then failing, soothes the air again. —*R. & H.* 1103.

489   like spirit his words went
Through all my limbs with the speed of fire ;   —*R. & H.* 1132.

490 Or the whirlwind up and down
Howling, like a slaughtered town,   —*Eug. Hills,* 56.

491   and Ocean
Welcomed him with such emotion
That its joy grew his, and sprung
From his lips like music flung
O'er a mighty thunder-fit
Chastening terror :   —*Eug. Hills,* 178.

492 The awful shadow of some unseen Power
Floats, though unseen, among us

     .   .   .   .   .   .
            Like memory of music fled   —*H. I. B.* 1.

493 There shall be lamentation heard in Heaven
As o'er an angel fallen   —*Cenci,* IV. i. 185.

494 Hark, 'tis the castle horn ; my God, it sounds
Like the last trump   —*Cenci,* IV. iii. 57.

495 Brother, lie down with me upon the rack,
And let us each be silent as a corpse ;   —*Cenci,* V. iii. 48.

496 Ha, what an awful whisper rises up !
'Tis scarce like sound ; it tingles thro' the frame
As lightning tingles, hovering ere it strike. —*Prom.* I. 132.

497 These solid mountains quiver with the sound
Even as the tremulous air   —*Prom.* I. 522.

498   Your call was as a wingèd car
Driven on whirlwinds fast and far ;   —*Prom.* I. 525.

499   His words outlived him, like swift poison
Withering up truth, peace and pity   —*Prom.* I. 548.

500 Hark, sister ! what a low yet dreadful groan
Quite unsuppressed is tearing up the heart
Of the good Titan, as storms tear the deep,
501 And beasts hear the sea moan in inland caves -*Prom.* I. 578.

502 Thy words are like a cloud of wingèd snakes : —*Prom.* I. 632.

503   Only a sense
Remains of them, like the Omnipotence
Of music, when the inspired voice and lute
Languish, ere yet the responses are mute,
Which thro' the deep and labyrinthine soul,
504 Like echoes thro' long caverns, wind and roll. -*Prom.* I. 801

505   and his voice fell
Like music which makes giddy the dim brain,
Faint with intoxication of keen joy.   —*Prom.* II. i. 65.

506   I could hear
His voice, whose accents lingered ere they died
Like footsteps of weak melody :   —*Prom.* II. i. 87.

507   Thou speakest, but thy words
Are as the air ; I feel them not.   *—Prom.* II. i. 108.

508 A wind arose among the pines ; it shook
The clinging music from their boughs, and then
Low, sweet, faint sounds, like the farewell of ghosts
Were heard :   *—Prom.* II. i. 156.

509 When there is heard thro' the dim air
The rush of wings, and rising there
Like many a lake-surrounded flute
Sounds overflow the listener's brain
So sweet that joy is almost pain.   *—Prom.* II. ii. 36.

510 There those enchanted eddies play
Of echoes, music-tongued, which draw,
By Demogorgon's mighty law,
With melting rapture or sweet awe,
All spirits on that secret way ;
As inland boats are driven to Ocean
Down streams made strong with mountain thaw.
                               —Prom. II. ii. 41.

511 The storm of sound is driven along,
Sucked up and hurrying ; as they fleet
Behind, its gathering billows meet
And to the fatal mountain bear
Like clouds amid the yielding air.   *—Prom.* II. ii. 59.

512 The vale is girdled with their walls.   A howl
Of cataracts from their thaw-cloven ravines,
Satiates the listening wind, continuous, vast,
Awful as silence.   *—Prom.* II. iii. 33.

    While the sound whirls around,
        Down, down !
513 As the fawn draws the hound,
514 As the lightning the vapour,
515 As a weak moth the taper :
516, 517 Death, despair ; love, sorrow :
518, 519 Time both : to-day, to-morrow :
520 As steel obeys the spirit of the stone,
        Down, down !   *—Prom.* II. iii. 63.

521 But thy voice sounds low and tender
Like the fairest, for it folds thee
    From the sight, that liquid splendour   *—Prom.* II. V. 61.

522 And from the flower-inwoven soil divine
Ye all-triumphant harmonies arise,
As dew from earth under the twilight stars ;
Drink ! be the nectar circling thro' your veins
The soul of joy, ye ever-living Gods,
Till exultation burst in one wide voice
523 Like music from Elysian winds.   *—Prom.* III. i. 27.

524 And we will search, with looks and words of love,
For hidden thoughts, each lovelier than the last,
Our unexhausted spirits ; and like lutes
Touched by the skill of the enamoured wind ;

Weave harmonies divine, yet ever new,
From difference sweet where discord cannot be.
And hither come, sped on the charmèd winds ;
525 Which meet from all the points of heaven, as bees
From every flower aerial Enna feeds,
At their known island-homes in Himera,
The echoes of the human world,   —*Prom.* III. iii. 34.

526   this is the mystic shell ;
See the pale azure fading into silver
Lining it with a soft yet glowing light ;
Looks it not like lulled music sleeping there ?
                                   —*Prom.* III. iii. 70.

527 Thou breathe into the many-folded shell,
Loosening its mighty music ; it shall be
As thunder mingled with clear echoes ;   —*Prom.* III, iii. 80.

528   The pine boughs are singing
                Old songs with new gladness,
                The billows and fountains
                Fresh music are flinging
Like the notes of a spirit from land and from sea :
                                   —*Prom.* IV. 48.

529 See, where the Spirits of the human mind
Wrapt in sweet sounds, as in bright veils, approach.
                                   —*Prom.* IV. 81.

530   Listen too,
How every pause is filled with under-notes,
Clear, silver, icy, keen awakening tones,
Which pierce the sense, and live within the soul,
As the sharp stars pierce winter's crystal air
And gaze upon themselves within the sea.   — *Prom.* IV. 188.

531 Two visions of strange radiance float upon
The ocean-like enchantment of strong sound,
Which flows intenser, keener, deeper yet
Under the ground and through the windless air.
                                   —*Prom.* IV. 202.

532   which as they roll
Over the grass, and flowers, and waves, wake sounds
Sweet as a singing rain of silver dew.   —*Prom.* IV. 233.

533 Oh, gentle Moon, the voice of thy delight
Falls on me like thy clear and tender light
Soothing the seaman borne the summer night
        Through isles forever calm ;   — *Prom.* IV. 495.

534 I rise as from a bath of sparkling water,
A bath of azure light, among dark rocks,
Out of the stream of sound.   · *Prom.* IV. 503.

535   Ah, me ! sweet sister,
The stream of sound has ebbed away from us,
And you pretend to rise out of its wave,
Because your words fall like the clear, soft dew
Shaken from a bathing wood-nymph's limbs and hair.
                                   —*Prom.* IV. 505.

536 And the hyacinth purple, and white, and blue,
 Which flung from its bells a sweet peal anew
 Of music so delicate, soft, and intense,
 It was felt like an odour within the sense. —*Sens. P.* I. 25.

 The quivering vapours of dim noon-tide,
 Which like a sea o'er the warm earth glide,
 In which every sound, and odour, and beam,
537 Move, as reeds in a single stream : —*Sens. P.* I. 90.

538 He had torn the cataracts from the hills,
 And they clanked at his girdle like manacles : —*Sens. P.* III. 92.

539   a loud, long, hoarse cry
 Bursts at once from their vitals tremendously,
 And 'tis borne down the mountainous vale of the wave,
 Rebounding like thunder, from crag to cave, — *Vis. of Sea*, 94.

540   the whirl and the splash
 As of some hideous engine whose brazen teeth smash
 The thin winds and soft waves into thunder ; the screams
 And hissings crawl fast o'er the smooth ocean streams,
541 Each sound like a centipede. — *Vis. of Sea.* 144.

542 Thou art unseen, but yet I hear thy shrill delight,

    Keen as are the arrows
    Of that silver sphere,
   Whose intense lamp narrows
    In the white dawn clear,
 Until we hardly see, we feel that it is there.

543   All the earth and air
     With thy voice is loud,
    As, when night is bare,
     From one lonely cloud
 The moon rains out her beams, and heaven is overflowed.

544   From rainbow clouds there flow not
     Drops so bright to see,
 As from thy presence showers a rain of melody.

545   Like a poet hidden
     In the light of thought,
    Singing hymns unbidden,
     Till the world is wrought
 To sympathy with hopes and fears it heeded not :

546   Like a high-born maiden
     In a palace-tower,
    Soothing her love-laden
     Soul in secret hour
547 With music sweet as love, which overflows her bower :

548   Like a glow-worm golden
     In a dell of dew,
    Scattering unbeholden
     Its aerial hue
 Among the flowers and grass, which screen it from the view :

549   Like a rose embowered
          In its own green leaves,
        By warm winds deflowered,
          Till the scent it gives
Makes faint with too much sweet these heavy-wingèd thieves.
                        —Skylark, 33.

550 My song, its pinions disarrayed of night,
    Drooped ; o'er it closed the echoes far away
Of the great voice which did its flight sustain
    As waves which lately paved his watery way
Hiss round a drowner's head in their tempestuous play.
                        —Ode to Lib. XIX.

551   The beast
Has a loud trumpet like the Scarabee,   *—Œd. Tyr.* 156.

552 Dinging and singing,
    From slumber I rung her,
    Loud as the clank of an iron-monger ;   *—Œd. Tyr.* 236.

553   and your cries
More dulcet and symphonious than the bells
Of village towers on sunshine holiday,   *— Œd. Tyr.* 122.

554 And from her lips, as from a hyacinth full
555 Of honey-dew, a liquid murmur drops,
    Killing the sense with passion ; sweet as stops
Of planetary music heard in trance.   *—Epips.* 83.

556 Such difference without discord, as can make
    Those sweetest sounds, in which all spirits shake
As trembling leaves in a continuous air ?   *—Epips.* 144.

557 And music from her respiration spread
    Like light,—   *—Epips.* 329.

558 And every motion, odour, beam, and tone
    With that deep music is in unison :
    Which is a soul within the soul—they seem
Like echoes of an ante-natal dream.   *—Epips.* 453.

559   Rekindled all the fading melodies,
      With which, like flowers that mock the corse beneath,
He had adorned and hid the coming bulk of death.
                        —Adon. II.

560 And love taught grief to fall like music from his tongue
                      —Adon. XXX.

    And ever as he went he swept a lyre
   .   .   .   .   .
561 Now like the . . . of impetuous fire
    Which shakes the forest with its murmurings,
562 Now like the rush of the aerial wings
    Of the enamoured wind among the treen
    Whispering unimaginable things,   *—Canc. Adon.* 1.

563   Breathe low, low
The words which, like secret fire, shall glow
Through the veins of the frozen earth—   *—Hell.* 31.

564 When the fierce shout of Allah-illa-Allah !
Rose like the war-cry of the northern wind
Which kills the sluggish clouds, and leaves a flock
Of wild swans struggling with the naked storm   —*Hell.* 290.

565   Through the city
Like birds before a storm, the Santons shriek,   – *Hell.* 590.

566   Thy words stream like a tempest
Of dazzling mist within my brain— they shake
567 The earth on which I stand, and hang like night
On Heaven above me—   —*Hell.* 786.

568 And crash of brazen mail as of the wreck
Of adamantine mountains—   —*Hell.* 821.

569 The sound of their oceans, the light of their sky,
The music and fragrance their solitudes breathe,
Burst, like morning on dream, or like heaven on death
     Through the walls of our prison ;   —*Hell.* 1055.

570 And, from the waves, sound like delight broke forth
Harmonizing with solitude,   —*Jul. & M.* 25.

571 And those are his sweet strains which charm the weight
From madmen's chains, and make this Hell appear
A Heaven of sacred silence hushed to hear.   *Jul. & M.* 259.

572   I do but hide
Under these words like embers, every spark
Of that which has consumed me.   —*Jul. & M.* 503.

573   their thousand voices rose,
They passed like aimless arrows from his ear.
                —*Prince A.* I. 52.

574   the sweet enthusiasm
Which overflows in notes of liquid gladness,
Filling the sky like light !   —*Prince A.* II. ii. 37.

575 Then Plato's words of light in thee and me
Lingered like moonlight in the moonless east,
               —*Prince A.* II. ii. 61.

576 The waterfalls were voiceless—for their fountains
Were changed to mines of sunless fountains now,
Or by the curdling winds, like brazen wings
Which clanged along the mountain's marble brow,
Warped into adamantine fretwork, hung
And filled with frozen light the chasm below.
             —*Prince A.* II. iii. 25.

577   Like many a voice of one delight
The winds, the birds, the ocean floods,
578 The City's voice itself is soft like Solitudes.—*Stanzas in Dej.* I.

579 With step as soft as wind it past   —*Mask.* XXX.

580 Lastly from the palaces
    Where the murmur of distress
    Echoes, like the distant sound
    Of a wind alive around
    Those prison halls,   —*Mask.* LXX.

581 Be your strong and simple words
    Keen to wound as sharpened swords,
582 And wide as targes let them be
    With their shade to cover ye.   —*Mask.* LXXIV.

583 Let the tyrants pour around
    With a quick and startling sound,
    Like the loosening of the sea
    Troops of armed emblazonry.   —*Mask.* LXXV.

584 And these words shall then become
    Like oppression's thundered doom
    Ringing through each heart and brain,   —*Mask.* XC.

585 And her low voice was heard like love,   — *Witch*, V.

585a   All familiar things he touched,
    All common words he spoke, became to me
    Like forms or signs of a diviner world.   —*Fragm. of Dram.* 55.

586 Your breath is like soft music, your words are
    The echoes of a voice which on my heart
587 Sleeps like a melody of early days.   —*Fragm. of Dram.* 100.

588 Soft melodies, as sweet as April rain
    On silent leaves   —*Fragm. of Dram.* 182.

589   his words, like arrows
    Which know no aim beyond the archer's wit,
    Strike sometimes what eludes philosophy.   —*Chas. I.* II. 105.

590   My word is as a wall
    Between thee and this world thine enemy—   —*Chas. I.* II. 204.

591   and that his words
    Sound like the echoes of our saddest fears?   —*Chas. I.* II. 461.

592 So did that shape its obscure tenour keep
    Beside my path, as silent as a ghost :   —*Tr. of L.* 432.

593 Upon my heart thy accents sweet
      Of peace and pity fell like dew
    On flowers half dead ;—   —*Lines to M. W. G.* IV.

594   thy voice is as the tone
    Of my heart's echo,   —*To* ——. 5.

595 And hark ! a rush as if the deep
    Had burst its bonds ;   --*M.'s Dream*, XIII.

596 A breathless awe, like the swift change
      Unseen, but felt in youthful slumbers,
    Wild, sweet, but incommunicably strange,
      Thou breathest now in fast ascending numbers.
                —*To Const.* II.

597 Whilst, like the world-surrounding air, thy song
   Flows on, and fills all things with melody.
    Now is thy voice a tempest swift and strong,
   On which, like one in trance upborne,
    Secure o'er rocks and waves I sweep,
   Rejoicing like a cloud of morn.   *To Const.* IV.

598 And heaps of fraud-accumulated gold
   Plead, loud as thunder, at Destruction's throne.
            —*To Lord Chest.* II,

599 A sweet and creeping sound
   Like the rushing of wings was heard around ; —*Fragm.* II.

600 Listen, listen, Mary mine,
   To the whisper of the Apennine,
   It bursts on the roof like the thunder's roar,
601 Or like the sea on a northern shore,
   Heard in its raging ebb and flow
   By the captives pent in the cave below. —*Pass. of Apenn.* 1.

602 And your sweet voice, like a bird
   Singing love to its lone mate
   In the ivy-bower disconsolate   —*To Mary*, 3.

603 And as a vale is watered by a flood,
604 Or as the moonlight fill the open sky
605 Struggling with darkness—as a tuberose
   Peoples some Indian dell with scents which lie
   Like clouds above the flower from which they rose,
   The singing of that happy nightingale
   In this sweet forest, from the golden close ·
   Of evening, till the star of dawn may fail,
   Was interfused upon the silentness : — *Woodm. & Night*, 6.

606 A silver spirit's form . . .

  . . . . . .
   It fades, with such a sigh, as sedge
   Breathes o'er the breezy streamlet's edge. —*Tasso.* III.

    Lips touched by seraphim
    Breathe out the choral hymn

  . . . . . .
607   Sweet as if angels sang,
608   Loud as that trumpet's clang
    Wakening the world's dead gang —*Nat. Anth.* VI.

609   Wrapt in sweet wild melodies
    Like an exhalation wreathing
    To the sound of air low breathing
    Thro' Æolian pines, which make
    A shade and shelter to the lake
    Where it rises soft and slow : —*Birth of Pleas.* 4.

610   She went, ever singing
   In murmurs as soft as sleep :   —*Areth.* I.

611 And heard the autumnal leaves like light footfalls
   Of spirits passing through the street : —*Ode to Nap.* 2.

612 What wondrous sound is that, mournful and faint,
But more melodious than the murmuring wind
Which through the columns of a temple glides? —*Orph.* 35.

613 But in their speed they bear along with them
The warning sound, scattering it like dew
Upon the startled sense. —*Orph.* 41.

614 As in a brook, fretted with little waves
By the light airs of spring—each riplet makes
A many-sided mirror for the sun,
While it flows musically thro' green banks,
Ceaseless and pauseless, ever clear and fresh,
So flowed his song, reflecting the deep joy
And tender love that fed those sweetest notes,
The heavenly offspring of ambrosial food —*Orph.* 59.

615 There rose to Heaven a sound of angry song.
'Tis as a mighty cataract that parts
Two sister rocks with waters swift and strong,
And casts itself with horrid roar and din
Adown a steep : from a perennial source
It ever flows and falls, and breaks the air
With loud and fierce, but most harmonious roar,
And as it falls casts up a vaporous spray
Which the sun clothes in hues of Iris light.
Thus the tempestuous torrent of his grief
Is clothed in sweetest sounds and varying words
Of poesy. —*Orph.* 72.

As I have seen
616 A fierce south blast tear through the darkened sky,
Driving along a rack of wingèd clouds,
Which may not pause, but ever hurry on,
As their wild shepherd wills them, while the stars,
Twinkling and dim, peep from between the plumes.
Anon the sky is cleared, and the high dome
Of serene Heaven, starred with fiery flowers,
Shuts in the shaken earth ; or the still moon
Swiftly, yet gracefully, begins her walk,
Rising all bright behind the eastern hills.
I talk of moon, and wind, and stars, and not
Of song ; but would I echo his high song
Nature must lend me words ne'er used before,
Or I must borrow from her perfect works,
To picture forth his perfect attributes. —*Orph.* 87.

617 Thy sweet child Sleep, the filmy-eyed,
Murmured like a noon-tide bee,
Shall I nestle by thy side ? —*To Night*, IV.

618 Sad Aziola ! many an eventide
Thy music I had heard
By wood and stream, meadow and mountain-side,
And fields and marshes wide,
Such as nor voice, nor lute, nor wind, nor bird,
The soul ever stirred : —*Aziola* II.

and then as one

619 Whose sleeping face is stricken by the sun
    With light like a harsh voice, which bids him rise
    And look upon his day of life with eyes
    Which weep in vain that they can dream no more.   *—Giner.* 50.

my knell

620 Will mix its music with that merry bell,
    Does it not sound as if they sweetly said,
    " We toll a corpse out of its marriage bed " ?   *— Giner.* 76.

621 A silence fell upon the guests,—a pause
    Of expectation, as when beauty awes
    All hearts with its approach, though unbeheld :   *—Giner.* 135.

622 And silence, and a sense that lifts the hair
    From the scalp to the ankles, as it were
    Corruption from the spirit passing forth,
    And giving all it shrouded to the earth.   *—Giner.* 152.

623 Pour forth the sound like enchanted wine   *—Music,* I.

624 The dissolving strain, through every vein
    Passes into my heart and brain.
    As the scent of a violet withered up,
        Which grew by the brink of a silver lake :
    When the hot noon has drained its dewy cup,
        And mist there was none its thirst to slake—
    And the violet lay dead while the odour flew
    On the wings of the wind o'er the waters blue.
625 As one who drinks from a charmèd cup
    Of foaming and sparkling and murmuring wine
    Whom a mighty enchantress filling up
    Invites to love with her kiss divine   *—Music,* III. & IV.

626   No song but sad dirges
    Like the wind through a ruined cell,
        Or the mournful surges
    That ring the dead seaman's knell.   *—Lines,* II.

628   Now all the tree-tops lay asleep

    As still as in the silent deep
    The ocean woods may be—   *—To Jane Recoll.* 29.

629   As the moon's soft splendour
    O'er the faint cold starlight of heaven
          Is thrown,
      So your voice most tender
    To the strings without soul had then given
          Its own.   *—To Jane,* II.

630 Thinking over every tone
    Which, though silent to the ear,
    The enchanted heart could hear,
    Like notes which die when born, but still
    Haunt the echoes of the hill ;   *—In Bay of Lerici,* 10.

631 Hark ! whence that rushing sound ?

    'Tis softer than the west wind's sigh ;   *—Q. M.* 45.

632 The long and lonely colonnades,
    Through which the ghost of Freedom stalks,
      Seem like a well-known tune,
    Which in some dear scene we have loved to hear,
      Remembered now in sadness.   —*Q. M.* II. 168.

633 How beautiful this night ! the balmiest sigh
    Which vernal zephyrs breathe in evening's ear,
    Were discord to the speaking quietude
    That wraps this moveless scene.   —*Q. M.* IV. 1.

634 All is deep silence, like the fearful calm
    That slumbers in the storm's portentous pause.—*Q. M.* IV. 53.

635   Then dulcet music swelled
Concordant with the life-strings of the soul :
It throbbed in sweet and languid beatings there,
Catching new life from transitory death,—
Like the vague sighings of a wind at even,
That wakes the wavelets of the slumbering sea
And dies on the creation of its breath,
And sinks and rises, fails and swells by fits : —*Q. M.* VIII. 19.

SIMILES OF ODOUR.

636   but my wings were faint
With the delights of a remembered dream
As are the noontide plumes of summer winds
Satiate with sweet flowers.   —*Prom.* II. i. 35.

637 Which breath now rises, as amongst tall weeds
    A violet's exhalation.   —*Prom.* III. iii. 131.

638 The snow-drop and then the violet,
    Arose from the ground with the warm rain wet,
    And their breath was mixed with fresh odour, sent
    From the turf, like the voice and the instrument
           —*Sens. Pl.* I. 13.

639 The sweetness seems to satiate the faint wind ;
    And in the soul a wild odour is felt,
    Beyond the sense, like fiery dews that melt
    Into the bosom of a frozen bud.   —*Epips.* 108.

640 The breath of her false mouth was like faint flowers,
           —*Epips.* 258.

641 The light clear element which the isle wears
    Is heavy with the scent of lemon-flowers,
    Which float like mist laden with unseen showers,
642 And falls upon the eye-lids like faint sleep ;   —*Epips.* 446.

643 The odour from the flower has gone
    Which like thy kisses breathed on me ;   —*Song,* 1.

644   and without whom
This world would smell like what it is—a tomb :
                                        — *Letter to M. G.* 210.

645 And odours in a kind of aviary
          Of ever-blooming Eden-trees she kept
Clipt in a floating net, a love-sick Fairy
          Had woven from dew-beams while the moon yet slept,
As bats at the wired window of a dairy,
          They beat their vans ;   —*Witch,* XVI.

646   as a tuberose
Peoples some Indian dell with scents which lie
Like clouds above the flower from which they rose,
                                        — *Woodm. & Night.* 8.

647   And the Champak's odours fail
Like sweet thoughts in a dream :   —*Ind. Seren.* II.

——————

SIMILE AND METAPHOR..

648   Till morning on his vacant mind
Flashed like strong inspiration.   —*Alast.* 126.

649   sleep,
Like a dark flood suspended in its course,
Rolled back its impulse on his vacant brain.   —*Alast.* 189.

650   and this love did sway
My spirit like a storm, contending there alway   —*L. & C.* I. 37.

651   So that when Hope's deep source in fullest flow,
          Like earthquake did uplift the stagnant ocean
Of human thoughts—mine shook beneath the wide emotion
                                        —*L. & C.* I. 38.

652 Till from that glorious intercourse, at last,
As from a mine of magic store, I drew
Words which were weapons ;   —*L. & C.* II. 20.

653 And baffled hope like ice still clung to me   —*L. & C.* II. 21.

654   Truth its radiant stamp
Has fixed, as an invulnerable charm
Upon her children's brow, dark Falsehood to disarm
                                        —*L. & C.* II. 44.

655   and his soul-subduing tongue
Were as a lance to quell the mailèd crest of wrong.
                                        —*L. & C.* IV. 17.

656   the murderer
Who slaked his thirsting soul as from a well
Of blood and tears with ruin !   —*L. & C.* V. 31.
6

657 A stormy night's serenest morrow,
   Whose showers are pity's gentle tears,
   Whose clouds are smiles of those that die
   Like infants without hopes or fears,
   And whose beams are joys which lie
   In blended hearts,   —*L. & C.* V. 50, 4.

658   while the stream
   Of life our bark doth on its whirlpools bear,
   Spreading swift wings as sails to the dim air ;
             —*L. & C.* VI. 29.

659 Where knowledge from its secret source enchants
   Young hearts with the fresh music of its springing,
   Ere yet its gathered flood feeds human wants
   As the great Nile feeds Egypt ; —*L. & C.* VI. 41.

660   thus all things were
   Transformed into the agony which I wore
   Even as a poisoned robe around my bosom's core
            —*L. & C.* VII. 15.

661   Yes, in the wilderness of years
   Her memory, aye, like a green home appears,
            —*L. & C.* VII. 19.

662 My mind became the book through which I grew
   Wise in all human wisdom, and its cave,
   Which like a mine I rifled through and through,
   To me the keeping of its secrets gave— —*L. & C.* VII. 31.

663 Thy songs were winds whereon I fled at will,
   As in a wingèd chariot, o'er the plain
   Of crystal youth ;   —*L. & C.* VII. 33.

664 And his red hell's undying snakes among
   Will bind the wretch on whom he fixed a stain,
   Which, like a plague, a burthen, and a bane,
   Clung to him while he lived ; —*L. & C.* VIII. 8.

665 Falsehood, and fear, and toil, like waves have worn
   Channels upon her cheek.   —*L. & C.* VIII. 15.

666 The flood of tyranny, whose sanguine waves
   Stagnate like ice at Faith,   —*L. & C.* IX. 23.

667, 668 And grey Priests triumph, and like blight or blast
   A shade of selfish care o'er human looks is cast.
            —*L. & C.* IX. 24.

669 Behold ! Spring comes, tho' we must pass, who made
   The promise of its birth, even as the shade
   Which from our death, as from a mountain, flings
   The future, a broad sunrise ; —*L. & C.* IX. 25.

670   thus arrayed
   As with the plumes of overshadowing wings,
671 From its dark gulph of chains, Earth like an eagle springs
            —*L. & C.* IX. 25.

672   Want and Pest
Were horrible, but one more fell doth rear,
As in a hydra's swarming lair, its crest
Eminent among these victims—even the Fear
Of Hell :   *L. & C.* XI. 7.

673 What were his thoughts linked in the morning sun,
Among those reptiles, stingless with delay,
Even like a tyrant's wrath ?   *—L. & C.* XII. 7.

674 Which that we have abandoned now,
Weighs on the heart like that remorse
Which altered friendship leaves. *—R. & H.* 27.

675 Walking beneath the night of life,
Whose hours extinguished, like slow rain
Falling forever, pain by pain,
The very hope of death's dear rest ; *—R. & H.* 332.

676 Pale with the quenchless thirst of gold,
Which, like fierce fever, left him weak : *—R. & H.* 424.

677   and hope and peace
On all who heard him did abide,
Raining like dew from his sweet talk, *—R. & H.* 641.

678   yet all men loved
Young Lionel, ...
All but the priests, whose hatred fell
Like the unseen blight of a smiling day.
The withering honey-dew, which clings
Under the bright green buds of May,
Whilst they unfold their emerald wings : *—R. & H.* 673.

679 Whose hope was like the life of youth
Within him, and when dead, became
A spirit of unresting flame, *—R. & H.* 732.

680 And wingèd hope, on which upborne,
His soul seemed hovering in his eyes,
Like some bright spirit newly born
Floating amid the sunny skies,
Sprang forth from his rent heart anew. *—R. & H.* 798.

681 And their swords and their sceptres I floating see,
Like wrecks in the surge of eternity. *—R. & H.* 900.

682 The truth flashed o'er me like quick madness *—R. & H.* 998.

683 Such flowers, as in the wintry memory bloom
Of one friend left, adorned that frozen tomb. *—R. & H.* 1310.

684   while like flowers
In the waste of years and hours,
From your dust new nations spring
With more kindly blossoming. *—Eug. Hills,* 163.

685   oh, rather say
Though thy sins and slaveries foul
Overcloud a sun-like soul *—Eug. Hills,* 191.

686   But a friend's bosom
Is as the inmost cave of our own mind
Where we sit shut from the wide gaze of day,
And from the all-communicating air. *—Cenci*, II. ii. 88.

687 If I must live day after day, and keep
These limbs, the unworthy temple of thy spirit,
As a foul den from which what thou abhorrest
May mock thee, unavenged—   *—Cenci*, III. i. 128.

688 Self-murder! no, that might be no escape,
For thy decree yawns like a Hell between
Our will and it :—   *—Cenci*, III. i. 132.

689 And, honoured lady, while I speak, I pray
That you put off, as garments overworn,
Forbearance and respect, remorse and fear, *—Cenci*, III. i. 207.

690 And in its depth there is a mighty rock,
Which has from unimaginable years,
Sustained itself with terror and with toil
Over a gulph, and with the agony
With which it clings seems slowly coming down ;
Even as a wretched soul hour after hour,
Clings to the mass of life ; yet clinging, leans ;
And leaning makes more dark the dread abyss
In which it fears to fall ; beneath this crag
691 Huge as despair, as if in weariness,
The melancholy mountain yawns.— *—Cenci*, III. i. 246.

692   That word parricide,
Although I am resolved, haunts me like fear.
           —Cenci, III. i. 340.

693   No, 'tis her stubborn will
Which by its own consent shall stoop as low
As that which drags it down.   *—Cenci*, IV. i. 10.

694   and make his youth
The sepulchre of hope, where evil thoughts
Shall grow like weeds on a neglected tomb *—Cenci*, IV. i. 52.

695   this devil
Which sprung from me as from a hell *—Cenci*, IV. i. 119.

696   aye, of the inmost soul,
Which weeps within tears as of burning gall *—Cenci*, V. iii. 66.

697 Plead with awakening earthquake, o'er whose couch
Even now a city stands, strong, fair, and free ;
Now stench and blackness yawn, like death.
        —Cenci, V. iv. 103.

698 How will thy soul, cloven to its depths with terror,
Gape like a hell within !   *—Prom.* I. 55.

699   Till thine Infinity shall be
    A robe of envenomed agony ;
And thine Omnipotence a crown of pain,
To cling like burning gold round thy dissolving brain.
        —Prom. I. 288.

700 The hope of torturing him smells like a heap
 Of corpses, to a death-bird after battle   -*Prom.* I. 339.

701   bend thy soul in prayer,
 And like a suppliant in some gorgeous fane,
 Let the will kneel within thy haughty heart :   —*Prom.* I. 376.

702 For what submission but that fatal word,
 The death-seal of mankind's captivity,
 Like the Sicilian's hair-suspended sword,
 Which trembles o'er his crown, whould he accept,
 Or could I yield ?   —*Prom.* I. 396.

703 That we will be dread thought beneath thy brain,
 And blood within thy labyrinthine veins
 Crawling like agony.   —*Prom.* I. 488.

704 Leave the hatred as in ashes
  Fire is left for future burning :
 It will burst in bloodier flashes
  When ye stir it soon returning   —*Prom.* I. 506.

       and the present is spread
705 Like a pillow of thorns for thy slumberless head.
           —*Prom.* I. 562.

706 I bid ascend those subtle and fair spirits,
 Whose homes are the dim caves of human thought,
 And who inhabit, as birds wing the wind,
 Its world-surrounding ether :   —*Prom.* I. 658.

707, 708 From all the blasts of heaven thou hast descended :
 Yes, like a spirit, like a thought, which makes
 Unwonted tears throng to the horny eyes,
 And beatings haunt the desolated heart,
 Which should have learnt repose : thou hast descended
 Cradled in tempests ; thou dost wake, O Spring !
 O child of many winds ! As suddenly
 Thou comest as the memory of a dream,
 Which now is sad because it hath been sweet ;
709, 710 Like genius, or like joy which riseth up
 As from the earth, clothing with golden clouds
 The desert of our life.   —*Prom.* II. i. 1.

711 How like death-worms the wingless moments crawl !
          Prom. II. i. 16.

712   Hark ! the rushing snow !
 The sun-awakened avalanche ! whose mass
 Thrice sifted by the storm, had gathered there
 Flake after flake, in heaven-defying minds
 As thought by thought is piled, till some great truth
 Is loosened, and the nations echo round,
 Shaken to their roots, as do the mountains now
         —*Prom.* II. iii. 36.

713 The snake-like Doom coiled underneath his throne
         —*Prom.* II. iii. 97.

714 And self-contempt, bitterer to drink than blood ;
         —*Prom.* II. iv. 25.

715 My soul is an enchanted boat,
  Which, like a sleeping swan, doth float
  Upon the silver waves of thy sweet singing ;
       —Prom. II. v. 72.

716 The soul of man, like unextinguished fire
  Yet burns towards heaven with fierce reproach,
       —Prom. III. i. 5.

717 And tho' my curses thro' the pendulous air,
  Like snow on herbless peaks, fall flake by flake,
  And cling to it ; tho' under my wrath's might
  It climb the crags of life, step after step,
718 Which wound it as ice wounds unsandalled feet.
       - -Prom. III. i. 11.

719   there the emulous youths
  Bore to thy honour thro' the divine gloom
  The lamp which was thine emblem ; even as those
  Who bear the untransmitted torch of hope
  Into the grave, across the night of life,
  As thou hast borne it most triumphantly
  To this far goal of time.   *--Prom.* III. iii. 168.

720 Till her heart thaw like flakes of April snow— *Prom.* III. iv. 89.

721 The painted veil, by those who were, called life,
  Which mimicked, as with colours idly spread,
  All men believed and hoped, is torn aside ;— *Prom.* III. iv. 190.

722 Once the hungry Hours were hounds
  Which chased the day like a bleeding deer,
  And it limped and stumbled with many wounds
  Through the nightly dells of the desert year.— *Prom.* IV. 73.

723 Wherever we fly we lead along
  In leashes like star-beams, soft yet strong,
  The clouds that are heavy with love's sweet rain.
       —Prom. IV. 177.

724   Yet its two eyes are heavens
  Of liquid darkness, which the Deity
  Within seems pouring, as a storm is poured
  From jaggèd clouds, out of their arrowy lashes,
  Tempering the cold and radiant air around
  With fire that is not brightness ; *—Prom.* IV. 225.

725   till the blue globe
  Wrapt deluge round it like a cloak. *— Prom.* IV. 315.

726 Borne beside thee by a power
  Like the polar Paradise
727 Magnet-like of lover's eyes ; *—Prom.* IV. 464.

728 Love, ...
 . . . . from the slippery steep
  And narrow verge of crag-like agony, springs
  And folds over the world its healing wings. *— Prom.* IV. 557.

729 And the wand-like lily, which lifted up,
  As a Mænad its moonlight-colored cup, *—Sens. P.* I. 33.

730 Thou art but the mind's first chamber
  Round which its young fancies clamber,
   Like weak insects in a cave,
  Lighted up by stalactites ;   *—Ode to Heav.* 28.

731 Thou on whose stream, 'mid the steep sky's commotion,
 Loose clouds like earth's decaying leaves are shed,
 Shook from the tangled boughs of Heaven and Ocean,

 Angels of rain and lightning : there are spread
 On the blue surface of thine airy surge,
732 Like the bright hair uplifted from the head

 Of some fierce Mænad, even from the dim verge
 Of the horizon to the zenith's height
 The locks of the approaching storm. *—Ode to West W.* II.

733 My soul spurned the chains of its dismay,
  And, in the rapid plumes of song,
   Clothed itself, sublime and strong ;
 As a young eagle soars the morning clouds among,
  Hovering in verse o'er its accustomed prey ; *—Ode to Lib.* I.

734 That multitudinous anarchy did sweep,
 And burst around their walls, like idle foam,
         —Ode to Lib. IX.

735 The eager hours and unreluctant years
  As on a dawn-illumined mountain stood,
 Trampling to silence their loud hopes and fears
        —Ode to Lib. XI.

736   as if day had cloven the skies
 At dreaming midnight o'er the western wave,
 Men started, staggering with a glad surprise,
 Under the lightnings of thine unfamiliar eyes.
        · Ode to Lib. XI.

737 How like Bacchanals of blood
  Round France, the ghastly vintage, stood
 Destruction's sceptred slaves, and Folly's mitred brood
        —Ode to Lib. XII.

 O, that the free would stamp the impious name
  Of King into the dust ! or write it there,
 So that this blot upon the page of fame
738 Were as a serpent's path, which the light air
 Erases, and the flat sands close behind !
    Ye the oracle have heard :
   Lift the victory-flashing sword,
 And cut the snaky knots of this foul gordian word,
739 Which, weak itself as stubble, yet can bind
        —Ode to Lib. XV.

740 Sweet Lamp ! my moth-like muse has burnt its wings ;
        —Epips. 53.

741 A well of sealed and secret happiness,
 Whose waters like blithe light and music are,
 Vanquishing dissonance and gloom ! *—Epips.* 56.

742 A Vision like incarnate April, warning,
With smiles and tears Frost the Anatomy
Into his summer grave.   —*Epips.* 121.

743 And in that best philosophy, whose taste
Makes this cold common hell, our life, a doom
As glorious as a fiery martyrdom ;   —*Epips.* 213.

744 And from her living cheeks and bosom flew
A killing air, which pierced like honey-dew
Into the core of my green heart, and lay
Upon its leaves :   —*Epips.* 261.

745 What storms then shook the ocean of my sleep,
Blotting that moon, whose pale and waning lips
Then shrank as in the sickness of eclipse ;—
746 And how my soul was as a lampless sea,
And who was then its Tempest ;   —*Epips.* 308.

747   Lady mine,
Scorn not these flowers of thought, the fading birth
Which from its heart of hearts that plant puts forth
Whose fruit, made perfect by thy sunny eyes,
Will be as of the trees of Paradise.   —*Epips.* 383.

748 Till the isle's beauty, like a naked bride,
Glowing at once with love and loveliness,
Blushes and trembles at its own excess :
749 Yet, like a buried lamp, a Soul no less
Burns in the heart of this delicious isle,   —*Epips.* 474.

750 Where some old cavern hoar seems yet to keep
The moonlight of the expired night asleep,

A veil for our seclusion, close as Night's   —*Epips.* 553

751   and when years heap
Their withered hours, like leaves, on our decay,   —*Epips.* 536

752 Or linger, where the pebble-paven shore,
Under the quick faint kisses of the sea,
Trembles and sparkles as with ecstasy,—   —*Epips.* 546.

753 It is a sweet thing, friendship,

A flower which, fresh as Lapland roses are,
Lifts its bold head into the world's frore air,
And blooms most radiantly when others die. —*Canc. Epips.* 62.

754   And barbèd tongues . . .
Rent the soft Form they never could repel,
Whose sacred blood, like the young tears of May
Paved with eternal flowers that undeserving way.
                                        —*Adon.* XXIV.

755 The monsters of life's waste had fled from thee like deer.
                                        —*Adon.* XXVII.

756 And cold hopes swarm like worms within our living clay.
                                        —*Adon.* XXXIX.

757   and thou Air
    Which like a mourning veil thy scarf hadst thrown
    O'er the abandoned Earth,   —*Adon.* XLI.

758 The splendours of the firmament of time
    May be eclipsed, but are extinguished not ;
    Like stars to their appointed height they climb,
    And death is a low mist which cannot blot
    The brightness it may veil.   —*Adon.* XLIV.

759   A Promethean conqueror came :
    Like a triumphal path he trod
      The thorns of death and shame   —*Hell.* 212

760   It has been sown
   And yet the harvest to the sickleman
     Is as a grain to each.   —*Hell.* 249.

761 Look, Hassan, on yon crescent moon, emblazoned
    Upon that shattered flag of fiery cloud
    Which leads the rear of the departing day ;
    Wan emblem of an empire fading now !
    See how it trembles in the blood-red air,
    And, like a mighty lamp whose oil is spent,
    Shrinks on the horizon's edge, while, from above,
    One star with insolent and victorious light
    Hovers above its fall, and with keen beams,
762 Like arrows through a fainting antelope,
    Strikes its weak form to death,   —*Hell.* 337.

763 The spirit that lifts the slave before his lord
    Stalks through the capitals of armed kings,
  .   .   .   .
    Exults in chains : and when the rebel falls,
    Cries like the blood of Abel from the dust :   —*Hell.* 351.

764 The coming age is shadowed on the past
    As on a glass   —*Hell.* 805.

765 The heavy fragments of the power which fell
    When I arose, like shapeless crags and clouds
    Hang round my throne on the abyss,   —*Hell.* 865.

766 The autumn of a greener faith has come,
    And wolfish change, like winter, howls to strip
    The foliage in which Fame, the eagle, built
    Her aerie, while Dominion whelped below.
    The storm is in its branches, and the frost
    Is on its leaves, and the blank deep expects
    Oblivion on oblivion, spoil on spoil,
    Ruin on ruin.   —*Hell.* 871.

767 Oh, bear me to those isles of jagged cloud
    Which float like mountains on the earthquake, mid
    The momentary oceans of the lightning,   —*Hell.* 957.

768 And weave into his shame, which like the dead
    Shrouds me, the hopes that from his glory fled   —*Napoleon,* 39.

769 And like that black and dreary bell, the soul,
Hung in a heaven-illumined tower, must toll
Our thoughts and our desires to meet below
Round the rent heart and pray—as madmen do
—Jul. & Madd. 123.

770   and those who try may find
How strong the chains are which our spirits bind ;
Brittle perchance as straw   .   .   *—Jul. & Madd.* 180.
   .   .   .   .

771 Month after month, he cried, to bear this load
And as a jade urged by the whip and goad
To drag life on, which like a heavy chain
Lengthens behind with many a link of pain.
—Jul. & Madd. 300.

772 And as slow years pass, a funereal train
Each with the ghost of some lost hope or friend
Following it like its shadow,—   *—Jul. & Madd.* 489.

773   but let the silent years
Be closed and sered over their memory
As you mute marble where their corpses lie.
—Jul. & Madd. 613.

774 Nor any could the restless griefs unravel
Which burned within him, withering up his prime,
And goading him like fiends, from land to land.
—Prince Ath. I. 3.

775 And others said that such mysterious grief
From God's displeasure, like a darkness, fell
On souls like his,   *—Prince Ath.* I. 93.

776   'Tis the shadow of a dream
Which the veiled eye of memory never saw,
But through the soul's abyss like some dark stream
Through shattered mines and caverns underground
Rolls, shaking its foundations   *—Prince Ath.* I. 98.

777 For like an eyeless nightmare grief did sit
Upon his being, a snake which fold by fold
Pressed out the life of life, a clinging fiend
Which clenched him if he stirred with deadlier hold –
—Prince Ath. I. 120.

778   who with the news of death
Struck body and soul as with a mortal blight,
—Prince Ath. II. 28.

779 The breath of night like death did flow
Beneath the sinking moon.   *- Lines* I.

780 And that slaughter to the nation
Shall steam up like inspiration   *—Mask.* LXXXIX.

781 Low-tide in soul, like a stagnant laguna   *—Peter B.* IV. xiv.

782 And wit, like ocean, rose and fell ?   *—Peter B.* IV. xxii.

783 He spoke of poetry   .   .   .
A spirit which like wind doth blow
As it listeth to and fro,   *—Peter B.* V. iv.

784 As troubled skies stain waters clear,
    The storm in Peter's heart and mind
    Now made his verses dark and queer :   *Peter B.* VI. xxxi.

785 The spider spreads her webs, whether she be
    In poet's tower, cellar, or barn, or tree ;
    The silk-worm in the dark green mulberry leaves
    His winding-sheet and cradle ever weaves ;
    So I, a thing whom moralists call worm,
    Sit spinning still round this decaying form,
    From the fine threads of rare and subtle thought
    No net of words in garish colours wrought
    To catch the idle buzzers of the day—
    But a soft cell, where when that fades away,
    Memory may clothe in wings my living name
    And feed it with the asphodels of fame,   — *Letter to M. G.* 1.

786 If living winds the rapid clouds pursue,
787 If hawks chase doves through the ætherial way,
788, 789 Huntsmen the innocent deer, and beasts their prey,
    Why should not we rouse with the spirit's blast
    Out of the forest of the pathless past
    These recollected pleasures ?   *Letter to M. G.* 187.

790 And there is he with his eternal puns,
    Which beat the dullest brains for similes, like duns
    Thundering for money at a poet's door ;   *—Letter to M. G.* 219.

790a Their spirits shook within them, as a flame
    Stirred by the air under a cavern gaunt :   — *Witch,* XI.

791 A haven beneath whose translucent floor
    The tremulous stars sparkled unfathomably,
    And around which the solid vapours hoar,
    Based on the level waters, to the sky
    Lifted their dreadful crags, and like a shore
    Of wintry mountains inaccessibly,
    Hemmed in with rifts and precipices grey,
    And hanging crags, many a cove and bay.   — *Witch,* XLIX.

792 And whilst the outer lake beneath the lash,
    Of the wind's scourge, foamed like a wounded thing
            — *Witch,* L.

793   There the meteor lay,
    Panting forth light among the leaves and flowers,
    As if it lived, and was outworn with speed :
794 Or that it loved, and passion made the pulse
795 Of its bright life throb like an anxious heart,
            —*Fragm. of Dram.* 130.

796 .   .   .   .   vigilant Fear,
    And open-eyed Conspiracy lie sleeping
    As on Hell's threshold ;   —*Chas. I.* I. 27.

797   Subdue thy actions
    Even to the disposition of thy purpose,
    And be that tempered as the Ebro's steel :
            —*Chas. I.* II. 126.

798   for on him
As on a keystone hangs the arch of life,
Whose safety is its strength.   —*Chas. I.* II. 155.

799 And whether life had been before that sleep
The heaven which I imagine, or a hell
Like this harsh world in which I wake to weep,
I know not.   —*Triumph*. 332.

800 And all the gazer's mind was strewn beneath
Her feet like embers ; and she, thought by thought,
Trampled its sparks into the dust of death :
As day. .   .   .   .   —*Triumph*, 386.

801 From every firmest limb and fairest face
The strength and freshness fell like dust,   —*Triumph*, 520.

802   Now is thy voice a tempest swift and strong,
On which like one in trance upborne,
    Secure o'er rocks and waves I sweep,
Rejoicing like a cloud of morn.   —*Const.* IV.

803 My spirit like a charmèd bark doth swim
    Upon the liquid waves of thy sweet singing,
Far away into the regions dim
804   Of rapture—as a boat with swift sails winging
Its way adown some many-winding river.
                 —*Fragm.* Vol. III., p. 394.

805   and every form
.   .   .   .
Was awed into delight, and by the charm
Girt as with an interminable zone.   —*Woodman*, 32.

806 O mighty mind, in whose deep stream the age
Shakes like a reed in the unheeding storm,
                 —*Fragm. to Byron.*

807   The nightingale's complaint,
        It dies upon her heart :
        As I must die on thine,
        Belovèd as thou art.   —*Ind. Ser.* II.

808 I have unlocked the golden melodies
Of his deep soul, as with a master-key,
And loosened them and bathed myself therein—
809 Even as an eagle in a thunder mist
Clothing his wings with lightning.   —*Fragm.* Vol. IV., p. 14.

810 When the chill wind, languid as with pain
Of its own heavy moisture,   —*Fragm. Fitful*, 2

811 And the pure stars in their eternal bowers
Are cinctured with my power as with a robe,   —*Apollo*, IV.

812 I went into the deserts of dim sleep
That world which, like an unknown wilderness,
Bounds this with its recesses wide and deep.
              —*Fragm.* Vol. IV. p. 64.

813 As an earthquake rocks a corse
    In its coffin in the clay,
So White Winter, that rough nurse,
    Rocks the death-cold year to-day.
Solemn hours ! wail aloud
For your mother in her shroud.

814 As the wild air stirs and sways
    The tree-swung cradle of a child,
So the breath of these rude days
    Rocks the year :   *—Dirge for the Year*, II. & III.

815 The heart which tender thought clothes like a dove
    With the wings of care   *—From Arabic*, II.

816 The sleepless billows on the ocean's breast
Break like a bursting heart, and die in foam
                —To Williams, VI.

817   from Tyranny which arms
Adverse miscreeds and emulous anarchies
To stamp, as on a wingèd serpent's seed,
Upon the name of Freedom ; from the storm
818 Of faction, which like earthquake shakes and sickens
The solid heart of enterprise :   *—Prol. to Hell.* 105.

819 The lamps which, half extinguished in their haste,
Gleamed few and faint o'er the abandoned feast,
Shewed as it were within the vaulted room
820 A cloud of sorrow hanging, as if gloom
Had passed out of men's minds into the air.   *—Giner.* 169.

821 We'll put a soul into her [*sc.* boat], and a heart
Which, like a dove chased by a dove, shall beat   *—Serchio*, 71.

822 Great spirit, whom the sea of boundless thought
    Nurtures within its unimagined caves,
In which thou sittest sole, as in my mind
    Giving a voice to its mysterious waves.
                —Fragm. Vol. IV. p. 122.

823   .   when I . .
  .   .   .   .
Wept o'er the beauty, which like sea retiring,
824 Had left the earth bare as the wave-worn sand
Of my lorn heart,   *—Zucca* I.

825 Like a cloud big with a May shower,
    My soul weeps healing rain,
On thee, thou withered flower ;   *—May. Lady*, IV.

826 The chains of earth's immurement
    Fell from Ianthe's spirit ; ·
They shrank and brake like bandages of straw.
                —Q. M. I. 188.

827   Monarchs and conquerors there
Proud o'er prostrate millions trod—
The earthquakes of the human race ;
Like them, forgotten when the ruin
    That marks their shock is past.   *—Q. M.* II. 121.

828 His slumbers are but varied agonies,
    They prey like scorpions on the springs of life.

                                  —*Q. M.* III. 77.

829   their influence darts
Like subtle poison through the bloodless veins
Of desolate society.   —*Q. M.* IV. 106.

830 Until pure health-drops, from the cup of joy,
    Fall like a dew of balm upon the world.   —*Q. M.* VI. 52.

831 And life. . . .

             Like hungry and unresting flame
    Curls round the eternal columns of its strength

                                —*Q. M.* VI. 235.

DOUBLE SIMILES.

832   His wan eyes
Gaze on the empty scene as vacantly
As ocean's moon looks on the moon in heaven   —*Alast.* 201.

833   and, as gamesome infants' eyes,
With gentle meanings, and most innocent wiles,
Fold their beams round the hearts of those that love,
These twine their tendrils with the wedded boughs
Uniting their close union :   —*Alast.* 438.

834 And I return to thee, mine own heart's home ;
As to his Queen some victor Knight of Faery,
Earning bright spoils for her enchanted dome :

                    —*Dedn.*, *L. & C.* I.

835 Thou Friend, whose presence on my wintry heart
Fell like bright Spring upon some herbless plain ;

                  —*Dedn. L. & C.* VII.

836 These things dwelt in me even as shadows keep
Their watch in some dim charnel's loneliness,

                    —*L. & C.* III. 22.

837   my scorched limbs he wound
In linen moist and balmy, and as cold
As dew to drooping leaves ;—   —*L. & C.* III. 29.

838 But Laon's name to the tumultuous throng
Were like the star whose beams the waves compel
And tempests,   '   —*L. & C.* IV. 17.

839 The tyrants send their armèd slaves to quell
Her power ;—they, even like a thunder gust
Caught by some forest, bend beneath the spell
Of that young maiden's speech,   —*L. & C.* IV. 20.

840   "and let the past
Be as a grave that gives not up its dead
To evil thoughts."   —*L. & C.* V. 12.

841   but his straight lips were bent,
Men said, into a smile which guile portended,
A sight with which that child like hope with fear was blended.
—*L. & C.* V. 36.

842   I could see

 .   .   .   .   .
The multitudes, the mountains and the sea;
As when eclipse hath passed, things sudden shine
To men's astonished eyes most clear and crystalline.
—*L. & C.* V. 46.

843   to each other
As when some parent fondly reconciles
Her warring children, she their wrath beguiles
With her own sustenance;   —*L. & C.* V. 55.

844   and over all
A mist was spread, the sickness of a deep
And speechless swoon of joy, as might befall
Two disunited spirits when they leap
In union from this earth's obscure and fading sleep
—*L. & C.* VI. 34.

845 Justice, or truth, or joy! those only can
From slavery and religion's labyrinth caves
Guide us, as one clear star the seaman saves,
—*L. & C.* VIII. 11.

Falsehood, and fear, and toil, like waves have worn
Channels upon her cheek, which smiles adorn,
846 As calm decks the false ocean:—   —*L. & C.* VIII. 15.

847 Yes—I must speak—my secret should have perished
Even with the heart it wasted, as a brand
Fades in the dying flame whose life it cherished,
—*L. & C.* VIII. 24.

848   a wide enthusiasm.
To cleanse the fevered world as with an earthquake's spasm!
—*L. & C.* IX. 5.

849 Those who were sent to bind me, wept and felt
Their minds outsoar the bounds which clasped them round,
Even as a waxen shape may waste and melt
In the white furnace;   —*L. & C.* IX. 11.

850 And Calumny meanwhile shall feed on us,
As worms devour the dead,   —*L. & C.* IX. 31.

851   those hosts of many a nation
Stood round that pile, as near one lover's tomb
Two gentle sisters mourn their desolation;   —*L. & C.* X. 43.

852   for many of those warriors young,
Had on his eloquent accents fed and hung
Like bees on mountain flowers   —*L. & C.* XI. 19.

853 Lo, that is mine own child, who in the guise
Of madness came, like day to one benighted
In lonesome woods: —*L. & C.* XII. 22.

854 Secure as one on a rock-built tower
   O'er the wrecks which the surge trails to and fro,
   'Mid the passions wild of human kind
   He stood, like a spirit calming them ;   —*R. & H.* 632.

855   All that others seek
   He casts away, like a vile weed
   Which the sea casts unreturningly.   —*R. & H.* 666.

856 Till, like an image in the lake
   Which rains disturb, my tears would break
   The shadow of that slumber deep :   —*R. & H.* 837.

857   but soon his gestures kindled
   New power, as by the moving wind
   The waves are lifted,   —*R. & H.* 1160.

858 Perish—let there only be
   Floating o'er thy heartless sea
   As the garment of thy sky
   Clothes the world immortally,
   One remembrance, more sublime
   Than the tattered pall of Time
   Which scarce hides thy visage wan :—   —*Eug. Hills*, 167.

   That incestuous pair [*sc.* Sin and Death] who follow
859 Tyrants as the sun the swallow,
860 As Repentance follows Crime,
861 And as changes follow Time   —*Eug. Hills*, 252.

862 Thou, that to human thought art nourishment,
   Like darkness to a dying flame   —*H. I. B.* 4.

863 I stood beside your dark and fiery youth
   Watching its bold and bad career, as men
   Watch meteors, but it vanished not—   —*Cenci*, I. i. 49.

864 Because I am a priest do you believe
   Your image, as the hunter some struck deer,
   Follows me not whether I wake or sleep ?   —*Cenci*, I. ii. 11.

865 I were a fool, not less than if a panther
   Were panic-stricken by the antelope's eye,
   If she escapes me.   —*Cenci*, I. ii. 89.

866 I see as from a tower, the end of all   —*Cenci*, II. ii. 147.

867   Consequence, to me,
   Is as the wind which strikes the solid rock
   But shakes it not.   —*Cenci*, IV. iv. 50.

868 She, who alone in this unnatural work,
   Stands like God's angel ministered upon
   By fiends ;   —*Cenci*, V. i. 42.

869   A word ? which those of this false world
   Employ against each other, not themselves ;
   As men wear daggers not for self-offence.   —*Cenci*, V. i. 99.

870 He shrinks from her regard like autumn's leaf
From the keen breath of the serenest north.

—*Cenci*, V. ii. 114.

871   Alas ! poor boy !
A wreck-devoted seaman thus might pray
To the deaf sea.   —*Cenci*, V. iv. 42.

872   she within whose stony veins
.   .   .   .
Joy ran, as blood within a living frame.   —*Prom.* I. 153.

873   so the revenge
Of the Supreme may sweep thro' vacant shades,
As rainy wind through the abandoned gate
Of a fallen palace.   —*Prom.* I. 215.

874 A spirit seizes me and speaks within :
It tears me as fire tears a thunder-cloud.   *Prom.* I. 254.

875 I see the curse on gestures cold and proud
.   .   .   .
Written as on a scroll.   —*Prom.* I. 258.

876 Pity the self-despising slaves of Heaven,
Not me, within whose mind sits peace serene,
As light in the sun, throned :   —*Prom.* I. 429.

877   and as lean dogs pursue
Thro' wood and lake some struck and sobbing fawn,
We track all things that weep, and bleed, and live,
                                             —*Prom.* I. 454.

878   and tho' we can obscure not
The soul that burns within, that we will dwell
Beside it, like a vain loud multitude
Vexing the self-content of wisest men :   —*Prom.* I. 484.

879   See a disenchanted nation
Springs like day from desolation ;   —*Prom.* I. 567.

880   I see
The wise, the mild, the lofty, and the just,
.   .   .   .
Some hunted by foul lies from their heart's home,
As hooded ounces cling to the driven hind ; —*Prom.* I. 604.

        And we breathe, and sicken not,
        The atmosphere of human thought :
.   .   .   .
881   As the birds within the wind,
882   As the fish within the wave,
883   As the thoughts of man's own mind
            Float through all above the grave ;
        We make these our liquid lair,
        Voyaging cloud-like and unpent
        Thro' the boundless element :   —*Prom.* I. 675.

7

884   Spirits ! how know ye this shall be ?
      (*Chorus.*) In the atmosphere we breathe,
        As buds grow red when the snowstorms flee
          From Spring gathering up beneath,   *—Prom.* I. 789.

885 Asia ! who, when my being overflowed,
      Wert like a golden chalice to bright wine
      Which else had sunk into the thirsty dust.   *—Prom.* I. 809.

886 But on each leaf was stamped, as the blue bells
      Of Hyacinth tell Apollo's written grief,
      O Follow, Follow !   *—Prom.* II. i. 139.

887 He taught to rule, as life directs the limbs,
      The tempest-wingèd chariots of the ocean,   *—Prom.* II. iv. 92.

888 We two will sink on the wide waves of ruin.
      Even as a vulture and a snake outspent
      Drop, twisted in inextricable fight,
      Into a shoreless sea.   *—Prom.* III. i. 71.

889 And I shall gaze not on the deeds which make
      My mind obscure with sorrow, as eclipse
      Darkens the sphere I guide ;   *—Prom.* III. ii. 35.

890 And death shall be the last embrace of her
      Who takes the life she gave, even as a mother,
      Folding her child, says, " Leave me not again."
                               —Prom. III. ii. 105.

891 Thrones, altars, judgment-seats, and prisons ; wherein
      And beside which by wretched men were borne
      Sceptres, tiaras, swords and chains, and tomes
      Of reasoned wrong, glozed on by ignorance,
      Were like those monstrous and barbaric shapes,
      The ghosts of a no more remembered fame,
      Which from their unworn obelisks, look forth
      In triumph o'er the palaces and tombs
      Of those who were their conquerors ; mouldering round
      Those imaged to the pride of kings and priests,
      A dark yet mighty faith, a power as wide
      As is the world it wasted, and are now
      But an astonishment ; even so the tools
892 And emblems of its last captivity,
      Amid the dwellings of the peopled earth,
      Stand, not o'erthrown but unregarded now.
                        —Prom. III. iv. 164.

893 The pale stars are gone !
    .   .   .   .   .
                and they flee
      Beyond his blue dwelling,
      As fawns flee the leopard.   *—Prom.* IV. 1.

894   We join the throng
        Of the dance and song
      By the whirlwind of gladness blown along :
        As the flying-fish leap
        From the Indian deep
      And mix with the sea-birds, half asleep.   *— Prom.* IV. 83.

895 And where two runnels of a rivulet,
 Between the close moss violet-inwoven,
 Have made their path of melody, like sisters
 Who part with sighs that they may meet in smiles,
 Turning their dear disunion to an isle
 Of lovely grief, a wood of sweet sad thoughts ;
          — *Prom.* IV. 196.

896 A sphere, which is as many thousand spheres,
 Solid as crystal, yet through all its mass
 Flow, as through empty space, music and light ;
          — *Prom.* IV. 238.

897   and over these
 The jagged alligator, and the might
 Of earth-convulsing behemoth, which once
 Were monarch beasts, and on the slimy shores.
 And weed-overgrown continents of earth,
 Increased and multiplied like summer worms
 On an abandoned corpse,   — *Prom.* IV. 308.

898 How art thou sunk, withdrawn, covered, drunk up
 By thirsty nothing, as the brackish cup
 Drained by a desert-troop, a little drop for all ;
          — *Prom.* IV. 350.

899 Man one harmonious soul of many a soul,
 Whose nature is its own divine control,
 Where all things flow to all, as rivers to the sea ;
          — *Prom.* IV. 400.

900 His will. . . .

 . . . . . .
 Is as a tempest-wingèd ship, whose helm
 Love rules, through waves which dare not overwhelm,
 Forcing life's wildest shores to own its sovereign sway.
          — *Prom.* IV. 406.

901 As the dissolving warmth of dawn may fold
 A half unfrozen dew-drop, green, and gold,

 . . . . . .
 Thou art folded, thou art lying
 In the light which is undying
 Of thine own joy, and heaven's smile divine ;
          — *Prom.* IV. 431.

902 I, a most enamoured maiden,

 . . . . .
      around thee move,
 Gazing, an insatiate bride,
 On thy form from every side
 Like a Mænad, round the cup,
 Which Agave lifted up
 In the weird Cadmæan forest   — *Prom.* IV. 467.

 Drinking from thy sense and sight
 Beauty, majesty and might,
903, 904 As a lover or chameleon
 Grows like what it looks upon,   — *Prom.* IV. 481.

L of C.

905 Thou, Moon, which gazest on the nightly Earth
　　With wonder, as it gazes upon thee ;　　*—Prom.* IV. 524.

906 The flowers . . .

　　When Heaven's blithe winds had unfolded them,
　　As mine-lamps enkindle a hidden gem,
　　Shone smiling to Heaven,　　*—Sens. P.* I. 63.

907 There was a power in this sweet place,
　　An Eve in this Eden ; a ruling grace
　　Which to the flowers did they waken or dream,
　　Was as God is to the starry scheme.　　*-Sens. P.* II. 1.

908 The water-blooms under the rivulet
　　Fell from the stalks on which they were set ;
　　And the eddies drove them here and there
　　As the winds did those of the upper air.　　*—Sens. P.* III. 42.

909 The sap shrank to the root through every pore
　　As blood to a heart that will beat no more　　*- Sens. P.* III. 88.

910　　　　　　　　　　　　then the cold sleep
　　Crept, like blight through the ears of a thick field of corn,
　　O'er the populous vessel.　　*—Vision of Sea,* 50.

911　　　　　　　　　　　　it rent them in twain,
　　As a flood rends its barriers of mountainous crag :
　　　　　　　　　　　　　　- Vision of Sea, 111.

912　　　　　　　　　　Like a sister and brother
　　The child and the ocean still smile on each other,
　　　　　　　　　　　　　—Vision of Sea, 167.

913　　　　　　　　　　　O thou
　　Who chariotest to their dark wintry bed
　　The wingèd seeds where they lie cold and low,
　　Each like a corpse within its grave,　　*—Ode to West W.* I.

914 Make me thy lyre, even as the forest is :　　*—Ode to West W.* V.

915 Scatter, as from an unextinguished hearth
　　Ashes and sparks, my words among mankind !
　　　　　　　　　　　　　—Ode to West W. V.

916 The sanguine sunrise with his meteor eyes,
　　　　And his burning plumes outspread,
　　Leaps on the back of my sailing rack,
　　　　When the morning star shines dead,
　　As on the jag of a mountain crag,
　　　　Which an earthquake rocks and swings,
　　An eagle alit one moment may sit
　　　　In the light of its golden wings.　　*—Cloud,* 31.

917　　　　　　　　　　　palace and pyramid,
　　Temple and prison, to many a swarming million
　　Were, as to mountain wolves their ragged caves.
　　.　　.　　.　　.　　.　　.　　.　　.　　.　　.

918　. . . but o'er the populous solitude
　　Like one fierce cloud over a waste of waves
　　Hung Tyranny ;　　*—Ode to Lib.* III.

919 And, like unfolded flowers beneath the sea,
920   Like the man's thought dark in the infant's brain,
921 Like aught that is which wraps what is to be,
   Art's deathless dream lay veiled by many a vein
   Of Parian stone ;   —*Ode to Lib.* IV.

922   one spirit vast
   With life and love makes chaos ever new,
   As Athens doth the world with thy delight renew.
923 Then Rome was, and from thy deep bosom fairest,
   Like a wolf-cub from a Cadmæan Mænad,
   She drew the milk of greatness,   —*Ode to Lib.* VI., VII.

924 O, that the words which make the thoughts obscure
   From which they spring, as clouds of glimmering dew
   From a white lake blot heaven's blue portraiture,
                   —*Ode to Lib.* XVI.

925 And power in thought be as the tree within the seed ?
                   —*Ode to Lib.* XVII.

926 Come, Thou, but lead out of the inmost cave
   Of man's deep spirit, as the morning star
   Beckons the Sun from the Eoan wave,
   Wisdom.   —*Ode to Lib.* XVIII.

927 For prophecies when once they get abroad,
   Like liars who tell the truth to serve their ends,
928 Or hypocrites who, from assuming virtue,
   Do the same actions that the virtuous do,
   Contrive their own fulfilment.   —*Œd. Tyr.* I. 131.

929 She met me Stranger, upon Life's rough way,
   And lured me towards sweet Death ; as Night by Day,
930,931 Winter by Spring, or Sorrow by swift Hope,
   Led into light, life, peace.   —*Epips.* 72.

932 A killing air, which pierced like honey-dew
   Into the core of my green heart, and lay
   Upon its leaves ; until, as hair grown grey
   O'er a young brow, they hid its unblown prime
   With ruins of unseasonable time.   —*Epips.* 262.

933 She hid me, as the Moon may hide the night
   From its own darkness, until all was bright
   Between the Heaven and Earth of my calm mind,
934 And, as a cloud charioted by the wind,
   She led me to a cave in that wild place,
   And sat beside me with her downward face
935 Illumining my slumber, like the Moon
   Waxing and waning o'er Endymion.   —*Epips.* 287.

936   and the dreaming clay
   Was lifted by the thing that dreamed below
   As smoke by fire,   —*Epips.* 338.

937 And, as those married lights, which from the towers
   Of Heaven look forth and fold the wandering globe
   In liquid sleep and splendour, as a robe ;
   And all their many-mingled influence bend

If equal, yet unlike, to one sweet end ;
So ye, bright regents, with alternate sway
Govern my sphere of being night and day !　　　—*Epips.* 355.

938　　　　　　　　adoring Even and Morn
Will worship thee with incense of calm breath
And lights and shadows ; as the star of Death
And Birth is worshipped by those sisters wild
Called Hope and Fear—　　　　　—*Epips.* 377.

939 The golden Day, which, on eternal wings
Even as a ghost abandoning a bier,
Had left the Earth a corpse　　　　—*Adon.* XXIII.

940 " Leave me not wild and drear and comfortless,
As silent lightning leaves the starless night ! "　—*Adon.* XXV.

941 And grey walls moulder round, on which dull Time
Feeds, like slow fire upon a hoary brand ;　　—*Adon.* L.

942 Life, like a dome of many-colored glass,
Stains the white radiance of Eternity　　—*Adon.* LII.

943 Whose soft smiles to his dark and night-like eyes
Were as the clear and ever-living brooks
Are to the obscure fountains whence they rise,
Showing how pure they are :　　　　—*Canc. Adon.*

944　　　　　　　　The wingèd glory
On Philippi half-alighted,
Like an eagle on a promontory.　　　　—*Hell.* 56

945 As an eagle fed with morning
Scorns the embattled tempest's warning,
When she seeks her aerie hanging
In the mountain-cedar's hair,
And her brood expect the clanging
Of her wings through the wild air,
Sick with famine—Freedom, so
To what of Greece remaineth now
Returns ;　　　　　　　—*Hell.* 76.

946 Thrice has a gloomy vision haunted me,
.　.　.　.　.　.　.　.　.
It shakes me as the tempest shakes the sea,
Leaving no figure upon memory's glass.　　—*Hell.* 128.

947 His cold pale limbs and pulseless arteries
Are like the fibres of a cloud instinct
With light, and to the soul that quickens them
Are as the atoms of the mountain-drift
To the winter wind.　　　　　—*Hell.* 142.

948　　　　　　　For thy sake cursèd be the hour
Even as a father by an evil child.　　—*Hell.* 264.

949 But recreant Austria loves thee as the grave
Loves Pestilence,　　　　　　—*Hell.* 312.

950　　　　　　　Even as that moon
Renews itself
Mahmud.　　　　Shall we be not renewed.　—*Hell.* 347.

951 The abhorred cross glimm'red .   .
   . . . and that fatal sign
Dried with its beams the strength in Moslem hearts,
As the sun drinks the dew.   - *Hell.* 501.

952   Go,
Where Thermæ and Asopus swallowed
Persia, as the sand does foam,   *Hell.* 687.

953   they know not, till the night of death,
As sunset, that strange vision, severeth
Our memory from itself, and us from all
We sought and yet were baffled.   —*Julian,* 127.

954 "Month after month," he cried, "to bear this load
And as a jade urged by the whip and goad
To drag life on   *Julian,* 299.

955 As the slow shadows of the pointed grass
Mark the eternal periods, his pangs pass
Slow, ever-moving,   —*Julian,* 416.

956 But me, whose heart a stranger's tear might wear
As water-drops the sandy fountain stone,   —*Julian,* 442.

957 The grave is yawning . . . as its roof shall cover
My limbs with dust and worms under and over,
So let Oblivion hide this grief .   .   .   —*Julian,* 506.

958 But I imagined, that if day by day

.   .   .   .
I studied all the beatings of his heart
With zeal, as men study some stubborn art
For their own good,   —*Julian,* 568.

959 As when day begins to thicken
   None knows a pigeon from a crow
So good and bad, sane and mad,
The oppressor and the oppressed ;
   All are damned.   —*Peter Bell,* III. xxi.

960 All things that Peter saw and felt
   Had a peculiar aspect to him ;
And when they came within the belt
Of his own nature, seemed to melt,
   Like cloud to cloud, into him.   —*Peter Bell,* IV. iii.

961 And men of learning, science, wit,
   Considered him as you and I
Think of some rotten tree, and sit
Lounging and dining under it,
   Exposed to the wide sky.   —*Peter Bell,* IV. xx.

962 And he made songs for all the land,
Sweet both to feel and understand,
   As pipkins late to mountain cotter.   —*Peter Bell,* V. xii.

963   Bohn's translation of Kant's book :
A world of words, tail foremost, where
Right-wrong-false-true and foul-and fair,
   As in a lottery wheel are shook.   —*Peter Bell,* VI. xiii.

964 When we shall be as we no longer are
    Like babbling gossips safe, who hear the war
    Of winds, and sigh, but tremble not :—   —*Letter to M. G.* 164.

965 As water does a sponge, so the moonlight
    Fills the void, hollow, universal air   —*Letter to M. G.* 255.

966   Or as on Vesta's sceptre a swift flame—
967 Or on blind Homer's heart a winged thought
    In joyous expectation lay the boat.   — *Witch*, XXXIV.

968 By Moeris and the Mareotid lakes,
    Strewn with faint blooms like bridal chamber floors,
               —*Witch*, LVIII.

969   He was so awful, yet
    So beautiful in mystery and terror,
    Calming me as the loveliness of heaven
    Soothes the unquiet sea :   —*Fragm. of Drama*, 103.

970   As adders cast their skins
    And keep their venom, so Kings often change ;
               —*Chas. I.* I. 126.

971   'Tis but
    The anti-masque, and serves as discords do
    In sweetest music.   —*Chas. I.* I. 173.

972 [It seems] now as the baser elements
      Had mutinied against the golden sun
    That kindles them to harmony, and quells
    Their self-destroying rapine. The wild million
973 Strikes at the eye that guides them : like as humours
    Of the distempered body that conspire
    Against the spirit of life throned in the heart.
               —*Chas. I.* II. 145.

974   Partly 'tis
    That our minds piece the vacant intervals
    Of his wild words with their own fashioning,
    As in the imagery of summer clouds,
975 Or coals of the winter fire, idlers find
    The perfect shadows of their teeming thoughts :
               —*Chas. I.* II. 465.

976 And of this stuff the ear's creative ray
    Wrought all the busy phantoms that were there,
    As the sun shapes the clouds ;   *Triumph*, 533.

977 There late was one within whose subtle being,
    As light and wind within some delicate cloud,
    That fades amid the blue noon's burning sky,
    Genius and death contended.   —*Sunset*, 1.

978 Two flames that each with quivering tongue
    Licked its high domes, and overhead
    Among those mighty towers and fanes
    Dropped fire, as a volcano rains
    Its sulphurous ruin on the plains.   —*Marianne's D.* XII.

979 The plank whereon that Lady sate
 Was driven through the chasms, about and about

 As the thistle-beard on a whirlwind sails —
 While the flood was filling those hollow vales.
        —*Marianne's D.* XVI.

980 By the false cant which on their innocent lips
 Must hang like poison on an opening bloom,
        —*To Lord C.* X.

981 Beware, O Man —for knowledge must to thee,
 Like the great flood to Egypt, ever be. — *To the Nile.*

982 Let us laugh, and make our mirth,
 At the shadows of the earth,
 As dogs bay the moonlight clouds —*To Misery,* XII.

983 As sunset to the sphered moon,
984 As twilight to the western star.
 Thou, beloved, art to me   --*To Mary,* 12.

985   As death to life,
986 As winter to fair flowers, (though some be poison).
 So Monarchy succeeds to Freedom's foison —*Marenghi,* III.

987   that band
 Of free and glorious brothers who had planted,
 Like a green isle 'mid Ethiopian sand,
 A nation amid slaveries.   —*Marenghi,* VI.

988 O foster-nurse [*sc.* Florence] of man's abandoned glory
  Since Athens, its great mother, sunk in splendour ;
 Thou shadowest forth that mighty shape in story,
  As ocean its wrecked fanes, severe yet tender : —
        —*Marenghi,* VII.

989 As the sunrise to the night,
990 As the north wind to the clouds,
991 As the earthquake's fiery flight,
  Ruining mountain solitudes,
 Everlasting . . . Italy.
 Be those hopes and fears on thee   — *To Italy.*

992 Alpheus rushed behind,—
  As an eagle pursuing
  A dove to its ruin
 Down the streams of the cloudy wind. —*Areth.*

993 Elysian City which to calm enchantest
  The mutinous air and sea : they, round thee, even
  As sleep round Love, are driven —*Ode to Naples,* 54.

994 The Anarchs of the North lead forth their legions
 Like chaos o'er creation, uncreating. —*Ode to Naples,* 137.

995 But, as Syrinx fled Pan, so night flies day, —*Orph.* 15.

996 My faint spirit was sitting in the light
  Of thy looks, my love ;
 It panted for thee like the hind at noon
  For the brooks, my love. —*From Arabic,* 1.

997 As a lizard with the shade
    Of a trembling leaf,
    Thou with sorrow art dismayed :   —*Song*, Vol. IV., p. 78,

998 As the wood when leaves are shed,
999 As the night when sleep is fled,
1000 As the heart when joy is dead
    I am left lone, alone.   —*Remembrance*, I.

1001 As the fruit is to the tree
    May their children ever be.   —*Epith.* 31.

1002 Then Hope approached . . .

    And Fear withdrew, as night when day
    Descends upon the orient ray,   —*Love*, 37.

1003 When, as summer lures the swallow,
    Pleasure lures the heart to follow—   —*Love*, 47.

1004   when Power and Pleasure,
    Glory, and science and security,
    On Freedom hung like fruit on the green tree, —*Prol. Hell.* 156.

1005 Till, as a spirit half arisen
    Shatters its charnel, it has rent
    In the rapture of its mirth
    The thin and painted garment of the earth,
          —*Frag.* Vol. IV. p. 102.

1006 Its leaves which had outlived the frost, the thaw
    Had blighted, like a heart which hatred's eye
    Can blast not, but which pity kills :   —*Zucca*, VI.

1007   As music and splendour
    Survive not the lamp and the lute,
    The heart's echoes render
    No song when the spirit is mute :—
          —*Lines*, Vol. iv., p. 132, ii.

1008   Its passions will rock thee
    As the storms rock the ravens on high :
          Bright reason will mock thee
1009 Like the sun from the wintry sky.   —*Lines*, IV.

1010   Fairer far than this fair Day,
    Which, like thee to those in sorrow,
    Comes to bid a sweet good-morrow
          To the rough year just awake
          In its cradle on the brake.   —*To June*, 2.

1011   Like one beloved the scene had lent
    To the dark water's breast,
    Its every leaf and lineament
          With more than truth exprest ;   —*To Jane, Recoll.* 77.

1012   The virtuous man,
    Who, great in his humility, as Kings
    Are little in their grandeur :   —*Q. M.* III. 150.

1013   Thine the tribunal which surpasseth
       The show of human justice,
        As God surpasses man.   --*Q. M.* III. 223.

1014   From his cabinet
      These puppets of his schemes he moves at will,
      Even as the slaves by force or famine driven,
      Beneath a vulgar master, to perform
      A task of cold and brutal drudgery ;   —*Q. M.* V. 70.

DOUBLE SIMILES.

HOMERIC.

1015   As an eagle grasped
      In folds of the green serpent, feels her breast
      Burn with the poison, and precipitates
      Through night and day, tempest, and calm, and cloud,
      Frantic with dizzying anguish, her blind flight
      O'er the wide aery wilderness : thus driven
      By the bright shadow of that lovely dream,
      Beneath the cold glare of the desolate night,
      Through tangled swamps, and deep precipitous dells,
      Startling with careless step the moonlight snake,
      He fled.   —*Alast.* 227.

1016   For, as fast years flow away,
      The smooth brow gathers, and the hair grows thin
      And white, and where irradiate dewy eyes
      Had shone, gleam stony orbs : – so from his steps
      Bright flowers departed, and the beautiful shade
      Of the green groves, with all their odorous winds
      And musical motions.   - *Alast.* 533.

1017 Then, like the forests of some pathless mountain,
      Which from remotest glens two warring winds
     Involve in fire, which not the loosened fountain
      Of broadest floods might quench, shall all the kinds
      Of evil catch from our uniting minds
     The spark which must consume them :—   —*L. & C.* II. 46.

1018   as whirlpools draw
      All wrecks of Ocean to their chasm, the sway
     Of thy strong genius, Laon, which foresaw
      This hope, compels all spirits to obey,   —*L. & C.* IV. 15.

1019   all mortal eyes were drawn,
      As famished mariners thro' strange seas gone
      Gaze on a burning watch-tower, by the light
      Of those divinest lineaments—   —*L. & C.* V. 44.

1020   as dead leaves wake
      Under the wave, in flowers and herbs which make
      Those green depths beautiful when skies are blue,
      The multitude so moveless did partake
      Such living change,   —*L. & C.* V. 53.

1021   as in the sacred grove
      Which shades the springs of Æthiopian Nile,
      That living tree, which, if the arrowy dove
      Strike with her shadow, shrinks in fear awhile,
      But its own kindred leaves clasps while the sunbeams smile :

      And clings to them, when darkness may dissever
      The close caresses of all duller plants
      Which bloom on the wide earth—thus we forever
      Were linked, for love had nursed us in the haunts
      Where Knowledge from its secret source inchants
      Young hearts with the fresh music of its springing,
      Ere yet its gathered flood feeds human wants
      As the great Nile feeds Egypt ;   —*L. & C.* VI. 40, 41.

1022   as an autumnal blossom
      Which spreads its shrunk leaves in the sunny air,
      After cold showers, like rainbows woven there,
      Thus in her lips and cheeks the vital spirit
      Mantled, and in her eyes, an atmosphere
      Of health and hope ;   —*L. & C.* VI. 55.

1023 As in its sleep some odorous violet,
      While yet its leaves with nightly dews are wet,
      Breathes in prophetic dreams of day's uprise,
      Or, as ere Scythian frost in fear has met
      Spring's messengers descending from the skies,
      The buds foreknow their life—this hope must ever rise.
                     —*L. & C.* VII. 37.

1024 My spirit moved upon the sea like wind
      Which round some thymy cape will lag and hover,
      Tho' it can wake the still cloud, and unbind
      The strength of Tempest :   —*L. & C.* VII. 40.

1025 Yes, it is Hate, that shapeless fiendly thing
      . . . .
      Which, when the heart its snaky folds intwine
      Is wasted quite, and when it doth repine
      To gorge such bitter prey, on all beside
      It turns with ninefold rage, as with its twine
      When Amphisbæna some fair bird has tied,
      Soon o'er the putrid mass he threats on every side,
                     —*L. & C.* VIII. 21.

1026   and as some most serene
      And lovely spot to a poor maniac's eye,
      After long years, some sweet and moving scene
      Of youthful hope returning suddenly,
      Quells his long madness—thus man shall remember thee.
                     —*L. & C.* IX. 30.

1027 Each of that multitude alone, and lost
 To sense of outward things, one hope yet knew ;
 As on a foam-girt crag some seaman tost,
1028 Stares at the rising tide, or like the crew
 Whilst now the ship is splitting thro' and thro';
 Each, if the tramp of a far steed was heard,
 Started from sick despair.   *—L. & C.* XI. 10.

1029   upon the mutes she smiled ;
 And with her eloquent gestures, and the hues
 Of her quick lips, even as a weary child
 Wins sleep from some fond nurse with its caresses mild,

 She won them, tho' unwilling her to bind
 Near me among the snakes.   *—L. & C.* XII. 14, 15.

1030 Two other babes, delightful more
 In my lost soul's abandoned night,
 Than their own country's ships may be
 Sailing towards wrecked mariners,
 Who cling to the rock of a wintry sea.   *—R. & H.* 391.

1031 For public hope grew pale and dim
 In an altered time and tide,
 And in its wasting withered him,
 As a summer flower that blows too soon
 Droops in the smile of the waning moon,
 When it scatters through an April night
 The frozen dews of wrinkling blight.   *—R. & H.* 692.

1032 Alas ! the unquiet life did tingle
 From mine own heart through every vein,
 Like a captive in dreams of liberty,
 Who beats the walls of his stony cell.   *—R. & H.* 1033.

1033 As the ghost of Homer clings
 Round Scamander's wasting springs :
1034 As divinest Shakespeare's might
 Fills Avon and the world with light
 Like omniscient power which he
 Imaged 'mid mortality ;
1035 As the love from Petrarch's urn,
 Yet amid yon hills doth burn,
 A quenchless lamp by which the heart
 Sees things unearthly ;—so thou art
 Mighty spirit—so shall be
 The City that did refuge thee.   *—Eug. Hills,* 194.

1036 As the Norway woodman quells
 In the depth of piny dells,
 One light flame amid the brakes,
 While the boundless forest shakes,
 And its mighty trunks are torn
 By the fire thus lowly born :
 The spark beneath his feet is dead,
 He starts to see the flames it fed
 Howling through the darkened sky
 With a myriad tongues victoriously,

And sinks down in fear : so thou,
O Tyranny, beholdest now
Light around thee, and thou hearest
The loud flames ascend, and fearest :   —*Eug. Hills*, 269.

1037   'Tis an awful thing
To touch such mischief as I now conceive :
So men sit shivering on the dewy bank,
And try the chill stream with their feet ; once in
How the delighted spirit pants for joy !   —*Cenci*, II. i. 124.

1038 In the atmosphere we breathe,
As buds grow red when the snowstorms flee,
From spring gathering up beneath,
Whose mild winds shake the elder brake,
And the wandering herdsmen know
That the white-thorn soon will blow :
Wisdom, Justice, Love and Peace,
When they struggle to increase,
1039 Are to us as soft winds be
To shepherd boys, the prophecy
Which begins and ends in thee.   —*Prom.* I. 790.

1040 Look how the gusty sea of mist is breaking
In crimson foam, even at our feet ! it rises
As Ocean at the enchantment of the moon
Round foodless men wrecked on some oozy isle.
                                                —*Prom.* II. iii. 43.

1041 He sunk to the abyss? to the dark void ?
Apollo. An eagle so caught in some bursting cloud
On Caucasus, his thunder-baffled wings
Entangled in the whirlwind, and his eyes
Which gazed on the undazzling sun, now blinded
By the white lightning, while the ponderous hail
Beats on his struggling form, which sinks at length
Prone, and the aerial ice clings over it.   —*Prom.* III. ii. 10.

1042 The flowers (as an infant's awakening eyes
Smile on its mother, whose singing sweet
Can first lull, and at last must awaken it),
When Heaven's blithe winds had unfolded them,
.   .   .   .
Shone smiling to heaven,   —*Sens. P.* I. 59.

1043 The hurricane came from the west, and passed on
By the path of the gate of the eastern sun,
Transversely dividing the stream of the storm ;
As an arrowy serpent, pursuing the form
Of an elephant, bursts through the brakes of the waste.
                                                —*Vision of Sea*, 100.

1044 Then, as a wild swan, when sublimely winging
Its path athwart the thunder-smoke of dawn,
Sinks headlong through the aerial golden light
On the heavy-sounding plain,
When the bolt has pierced its brain ;
.   .   .   .
My song, its pinions disarrayed of might,
Drooped ;   —*Ode to Lib.* XIX.

1045   The sun comes forth, and many reptiles spawn;
He sets, and each ephemeral insect then
Is gathered into death without a dawn,
And the immortal stars awake again ;
So is it in the world of living men :
A godlike mind soars forth, in its delight
Making earth bare and veiling heaven, and when
It sinks, the swarms that dimmed or shared its light
Leave to its kindred lamps the spirit's awful night.
                        —*Adon.* XXIX.

1046 Russia still hovers, as an eagle might
Within a cloud, near which a kite and crane
Hang tangled in inextricable fight,
To stoop upon the victor ;   —*Hell.* 307.

1047 From the surrounding hills, the batteries blazed,
Kneading them down with fire and iron rain :
. . . till, like a field of corn
Under the hook of the swart sickleman,
The band, entrenched in mounds of Turkish dead,
Grew weak and few.   —*Hell.* 380.

1048   Like one who finds
A fertile island in the barren sea,
One mariner who has survived his mates
Many a drear month in a great ship—so he
With soul sustaining songs, and sweet debate
Of ancient lore, there fed his lonely being :
                    —*Prince Ath.* II. i. 9.

1049 Such was Zonoras ; and as daylight finds
One amaranth glittering on the path of frost,
When autumn nights have nipped all weaker kinds,
Thus, through his age, dark, cold, and tempest-tost
Shone truth upon Zonoras ;   —*Prince Ath.* II. ii. 1.

1050 'Twas the season when the Earth upsprings
From slumber, as a sphered angel's child,
Shadowing its eyes with green and golden wings,
Stands up before its mother bright and mild,
Of whose soft voice the air expectant seems—
So stood before the sun, which shone and smiled
To see it rise thus joyous from its dreams,
The fresh and radiant Earth.   —*Prince Ath.* II. iii. 1.

1051   such seemed the jubilee
As when to greet some conqueror's advance
Imperial Rome poured forth her living sea
From the senate-house, and forum, and theatre,
                    —*Triumph,* 111.

1052 And her feet, ever to the ceaseless song
Of leaves, and winds, and waves, and birds, and bees
And falling drops, moved in a measure new
Yet sweet, as on the summer evening breeze
Up from the lake a shape of golden dew
Between two rocks, athwart the rising moon
Dances i' the wind, where never eagle flew ; —*Triumph,* 367.

1053   and she, thought by thought,
Trampled its sparks into the dust of death :
As day upon the threshold of the east
Treads out the lamp of night, until the breath
Of darkness re-illumine even the least
Of heaven's living eyes—   *—Triumph*, 387.

1054 And as the presence of that fairest planet,
Altho' unseen is felt by one who hopes
That his day's path may end as he began it,
In that star's smile, whose light, . . .
  .   .   .   .

1055 So know I in that light's severe excess
The presence of that shape which on the stream
Moved as I moved along the wilderness,
More dimly than a day-appearing dream,
The ghost of a forgotten form of sleep ;
A light of heaven whose half extinguished beam
Through the sick day in which we wake to weep,
Glimmers for ever sought, for ever lost :
So did that shape its obscure tenour keep
Beside my path, as silent as a ghost ;   *— Triumph*, 416.

1056 The earth was grey with phantoms and the air
Was peopled with dim forms, as when there hovers
A flock of vampire bats before the glare
Of the tropic sun, bringing, ere evening,
Strange night upon some Indian isle : thus were
Phantoms diffused around,   *— Triumph*, 482.

1057 But he who gains by base and arméd wrong,
Or guilty fraud, or base compliances,
May be despoiled, even as a stolen dress
Is stript from a convicted thief, and he
Left in the nakedness of infamy   *—Fragm.* Vol. 4, p. 8.

1058   As a poor hunted stag
A moment shudders on the fearful brink
Of a swift stream—the cruel hounds press on
With deafening yell, the arrows glance and wound,
He plunges in ; so Orpheus, seized and torn
By the sharp fangs of an insatiate grief,
Mænad-like waved his lyre in the bright air,
And wildly shrieked !   *—Orph.* 46.

1059 It never slackens, and through every change
Wisdom and beauty and the power divine
Of mighty poesy together dwell,
Mingling in sweet accord. As I have seen
A fierce south blast tear through the darkened sky,
Driving along a rack of wingéd clouds,
Which may not pause, but ever hurry on
As their wild shepherd wills them, while the stars,
Twinkling and dim, peep from between the plumes. *—Orph.* 84.

1060   so that the world is bare,
As if a spectre wrapt in shape'ess terror
Amid a company of ladies fair
Should glide and glow, till it became a mirror

Of all their beauty, and their hair and hue
The life of their sweet eyes, with all its error,
Should be absorbed, till they to marble grew.
—*Tower of Famine*, 16.

1061 As the world leaps before an earthquake's dawn,
And unprophetic of the coming hours,
The matin winds from the expanded flowers
Scatter their hoarded incense, and awaken
The earth, until the dewy sleep is shaken
From every living heart which it possesses,
Through seas and winds, cities and wildernesses,

. . . .
. . . . So Gherardis' hall
Laughed in the mirth of its lord's festivals, —*Ginev.* 123.

1062 Thus do the generations of the earth
Go to the grave, and issue from the womb,
Surviving still the imperishable change
That renovates the world ; even as the leaves
Which the keen frost-wind of the waning year
Has scattered on the forest soil, and heaped
For many seasons there, though long they choke,
Loading with loathsome rottenness the land,
All germs of promise. —*Q. M. V.* 1.

1063 Thus have I stood,—thro' a wild waste of years
Struggling with whirlwinds of mad agony,

. . . .
With stubborn and unalterable will,
Even as a giant oak, which heaven's fierce flame
Had scathed in the wilderness to stand
A monument of fadeless ruin there : —*Q. M.* VII. 254.

HUMAN TO NATURAL.

1064   serenely now
And moveless, as a long-forgotten lyre
Suspended in the solitary dome
Of some mysterious fane,
I wait thy breath, Great Parent —*Alast.* 41.

1065   and men
Go to their graves like flowers or creeping worms, —*Alast.* 621.

1066   But when Heaven remained
Utterly black, the murky shades involved
An image, silent, cold, and motionless
As their own voiceless earth and vacant air. —*Alast.* 659.

1067 Thou wert as a lone star, whose light did shine
On some frail bark in winter's midnight roar :
1068 Thou hast like to a rock-built refuge stood
Above the blind and battling multitude. —*To Wordsw.* 1.

1069 Thus solemnized and softened, death is mild
And terrorless as this serenest night :
—*Summ. Eve. Churchy.* 25.

8

1070 Her golden tresses shade
    The bosom's stainless pride,
  Twining like tendrils of the parasite
    Around a marble column   —*D. W.* 44.

1071 Hard hearts and cold, like weights of icy stone
   Which crushed and withered mine, —*Ded. L. & C.* VI.

1072   for one then left this earth
   Whose life was like a setting planet mild,
   Which clothed thee in the radiance undefiled
   Of its departing glory ;   —*Ded. L. & C.* XII.

1073   thou and I,
   Sweet friend ! can look from our tranquillity
   Like lamps into the world's tempestuous night,
        —*Ded. L. & C.* XIV.

1074 There was a woman, beautiful as morning,
   Sitting beneath the rocks, upon the sand
1075 Of the waste sea, fair as one flower adorning
   An icy wilderness—   —*L. & C.* I. 16.

1076 In the world's youth his empire was as firm
   As its foundations—   —*L. & C.* I. 31.

1077   and they [*sc.* impulses] were dear to memory
   Like tokens of the dead   —*L. & C.* II. 2.

1078   I will arise and waken
   The multitude, and like a sulphurous hill,
   Which on a sudden from its snows has shaken
   The swoon of ages, it shall burst and fill
   The world with cleansing fire : —*L. & C.* II. 14.

  79 As mine own shadow was that child to me, —*L. & C.* II. 24.

1080   thus subdued
   Like evening shades that o'er the mountain creep,
   We moved towards our home ; —*L. & C.* II. 49.

1081 Each heart was there a shield, and every tongue
   Was as a sword of truth—   —*L. & C.* IV. 10.

1082 And every bosom thus is rapt and shook,
   Like autumn's myriad leaves in one swoln mountain brook.
        —*L. & C.* IV. 13.

1083 And then my youth fell on me like a wind
   Descending on still waters—   —*L. & C.* IV. 29.

1084   To thy voice their hearts have trembled
   Like the thousand clouds which flow
   With one wide wind as it flies ! —*L. & C.* V. i.

1085   and the stain
   Of blood from mortal steel fell o'er the fields like rain
        —*L. & C.* VI. 6.

1086   in joy I found
Beside me then, firm as a giant pine
Among the mountain vapours driven around,
The old man whom I loved—   —*L. & C.* VI. 10.

1087 And there the living in the blood did welter
Of the dead and dying, which in that green glen
Like stifled torrents, made a plashy fen
Under the feet—   —*L. & C.* VI. 12.

1088   That friend so mild and good
Who like its shadow near my youth had stood,
Was stabbed !   —*L. & C.* VI. 15.

1089 She pressed the white moon on his front with pure
And rose-like lips,   —*L. & C.* VI. 26.

1090 Her marble brow, and eager lips, like roses
With their own fragrance pale, which Spring but half uncloses
        —*L. & C.* VI. 33.

1091   and then I felt the blood that burned
Within her frame, mingle with mine, and fall
Around my heart like fire ;   —*L. & C.* VI. 34.

1092 So we sat joyous as the morning ray
Which fed upon the wrecks of night and storm
Now lingering on the winds :   —*L. & C.* VII. 1.

1093   while tears pursued
Each other down her fair and listening cheek
Fast as the thoughts which fed them, like a flood
From sunbright dales :   —*L. & C.* VII. 2.

1094 Her madness was a beam of light, a power
Which dawned through the rent soul ; and words it gave
Gestures and looks, such as in whirlwinds bore
Which might not be withstood, where none could save
1095 All who approached their sphere, like some calm wave
Vexed into whirlpools by the chasms beneath ;
        —*L. & C.* VII. 7.

1096   the Æthiop there
Wound his long arms around her, and with knees
Like iron clasped her feet,   —*L. & C.* VII. 9.

1097   Ye shall be pure as dew   —*L. & C.* VIII. 18.

1098   years have come and gone
Since, like the ship which bears me, I have known
No thought . . . .   —*L. & C.* VIII. 25.

1099 Strange panic first, a deep and sickening dread
Within each heart, like ice, did sink and dwell,
        —*L. & C.* X. 16.

1100   Some shrouded in their long and golden hair,
    As if not dead, but slumbering quietly
Like forms which sculptors carve, then love to agony.
        —*L. & C.* X. 23.

1101 That monstrous faith wherewith they ruled mankind,
Fell, like a shaft loosed by the bowman's error,
On their own hearts :   —*L. & C.* X. 26.

1102   She trembled like one aspen pale
Among the gloomy pines of a Norwegian vale.
                                        —*L. & C.* XII. 6.

1103 The warm tears burst in spite of faith and fear,
From many a tremulous eye, but like soft dews
Which feed spring's earliest buds, hung gathered there,
Frozen by doubt,—   —*L. & C.* XII. 14.

1104 I was clammy cold like clay.   —*R. & H.* 309.

1105 Foul self-contempt, which drowns in sneers
Youth's starlight smile, and makes its tears
First like hot gall, then dry for ever !   —*R. & H.* 479.

1106 Many then wept, not tears but gall
Within their hearts, like drops which fall
Wasting the fountain-stone away.   —*R. & H.* 721.

1107   my hopes were once like fire :   —*R. & H.* 764.

1108 His motions, like the winds, were free,
Which bend the bright grass gracefully,
Then fade away in circlets faint :   —*R. & H.* 795.

1109 Yet o'er his talk, and looks, and mien,
Tempering their loveliness too keen,
Past woe its shadow backward threw,
Till like an exhalation, spread
From flowers half drunk with evening dew,
They did become infectious :   —*R. & H.* 803.

1110 And soon his deep and sunny hair,
In this alone less beautiful,
Like grass in tombs grew wild and rare.   —*R. & H.* 821.

1111 His breath was like inconstant flame,
As eagerly it went and came ;   —*R. & H.* 834.

1112 Like flowers, which on each other close
Their languid leaves when daylight's gone,
We lay   —*R. & H.* 975.

1113 But his [*sc.* life] it seemed already free,
Like the shadow of fire surrounding me ! —*R. & H.* 1037.

1114   and they fed
From the same flowers of thought, until each mind
Like springs which mingle in one flood became,
                                        —*R. & H.* 1287.

1115   Every little living nerve
That from bitter words did swerve
Round the tortured lips and brow,
Are like sapless leaflets now
Frozen upon December's bough   —*Eug. Hills*, 40.

1116 And the sickle to the sword
Lies unchanged, though many a lord,
Like a weed whose shade is poison,
Overgrows this region's foison,   *—Eng. Hills*, 225.

1117 I rarely kill the body, which preserves
Like a strong poison, the soul within my power,
         —Cenci, I. i. 114.

1118 So when I wake my blood seems liquid fire ;
         —Cenci, II. ii. 136.

1119 My tongue should like a knife tear out the secret
Which cankers my heart's core ; *—Cenci*, III. i. 156.

1120   May it be
A hideous likeness of herself, that as
From a distorting mirror, she may see
Her image mixed with what she most abhors,
Smiling upon her from her nursing breast. *--Cenci*, IV. i. 145.

1121 I am as universal as the light ;
1122 Free as the earth-surrounding air, as firm
1123 As the world's centre.   *—Cenci*, IV. iv. 48.

1124 What are a thousand lives ? A parricide
Had trampled them like dust ; *Cenci*, V. ii. 107.

1125 The Pope is stern, not to be moved or bent.
He looked as calm and keen as is the engine
Which tortures and which kills, exempt itself
From aught that it inflicts ; *—Cenci*, V. iv. 1.

1126 A pilot asleep on the howling sea
Leaped up from the deck in agony,

. . . .
And died as mad as the wild waves be *Prom.* I. 95.

1127 When thou didst from her bosom, like a cloud
Of glory, arise, a spirit of keen joy ! *—Prom.* I. 157.

1128 Blood like new wine bubbles within : *—Prom.* I. 575.

1129 And like the vapours when the sun sinks down,
Gathering again in drops upon the pines,
And tremulous as they, in the deep night
My being was condensed : *—Prom.* II. i. 83.

1130   Such the state
Of the earth's primal spirits beneath his [*sc.* Saturn's] sway
As the calm joy of flowers and living leaves
Before the wind or sun has withered them
And semi-vital worms ; *—Prom.* II. iv. 34.

1131 Yet if thou wilt, as 'tis the destiny
Of trodden worms to writhe till they are dead,
Put forth thy might   *—Prom.* III. i. 59.

1132   to me
Shall they [*sc.* human shapes] become like sister antelopes
By one fair dam. . . . . *—Prom.* III. iii. 90.

1133   hate, disdain, or fear,
Self-love or self-contempt, on human brows,
No more inscribed, as o'er the gate of hell,
" All hope abandon ye who enter here ; "   —*Prom*. III. iv. 133.

1134 A dark yet mighty faith, a power as wide
As is the world it wasted,   —*Prom*. III. iv. 174.

1135 A Lady, the wonder of her kind,
Whose form was upborne by a lovely mind
Which, dilating, had moulded her mien and motion
Like a sea-flower unfolded beneath the ocean   —*Sens. P*. II. 5.

1136   her child
Is yet smiling, and playing, and murmuring ; so smiled
The false deep ere the storm.   —*Vision of S*. 165.

1137
1138 } Oh ! lift me as a wave, a leaf, a cloud !   — *Ode to W. W*. IV.
1139

1140 Each heart was as a hell of storms.   —*Ode to Lib*. II.

1141   Athens diviner yet
Gleamed with its crest of columns, on the will
Of man, as on a mount of diamond, set ;   —*Ode to Lib*. V.

1142 Tomb of Arminius ! render up thy dead,
Till, like a standard from a watch-tower's staff,
His soul may stream over the tyrant's head.
                        Ode to Lib. XIV.

1143   and this Kingly paunch
Swells like a sail before a favouring breeze, —*Œd. Tyr* .I. i. 3.

1144   and these
Bœotian cheeks, like Egypt's pyramid
(Nor with less toil were their foundations laid),
Sustain the cone of my untroubled brain,
That point, the emblem of a pointless nothing
                        —*Œd. Tyr*. I. i. 6.

1145 We—are we not formed, as notes of music are,
For one another, though dissimilar .   —*Epips*. 142.

1146 Imagination ! which from earth and sky,
And from the depths of human phantasy,
As from a thousand prisms and mirrors, fills
The universe with glorious beams,   *Epips*. 164.

1147 Her touch was as electric poison,   *Epips*. 259.

1148 But now thy youngest, dearest one has perished,
The nursling of thy widowhood who grew,
Like a pale flower by some sad maiden cherished,
And fed with true love tears, instead of dew ;   —*Adon*. VI.

1149 See on the silken fringe of his faint eyes,
Like dew upon a sleeping flower, there lies
A tear some dream has loosened from his brain.   —*Adon*. X.

1150 Midst others of less note came one frail Form,
    A phantom among men ; companionless
    As the last cloud of an expiring storm
    Whose thunder is its knell ;   *—Adon.* XXXI.

1151 Kings are like stars—they rise and set, they have
    The worship of the world, but no repose.   *—Hell.* 195.

1152 Time has found ye light as foam.   *—Hell.* 442.

1153 And the quick spring like weeds out of the dead.
                         —Death of Nap. 24.

1154 Through the black bars in the tempestuous air
    I saw, like weeds on a wrecked palace growing,
    Long tangled locks flung wildly forth and flowing
                       —Julian, 223.

1155   though his lips did seem
    Like reeds which quiver in impetuous floods ;
                   —Prince Ath. I. 63.

1156   But we yet stand
       In a lone land,
    Like tombs to mark the memory
    Of hopes and fears,   *— Lines,* II.

1157 Yet now despair itself is mild,
    Even as the winds and waters are ;   *—Stanzas near Naples.*

1158   'tis to work and have such pay
    As just keeps life from day to day
    In your limbs as in a cell   *—Mask,* XL.

1159 Blood is on the grass like dew.   *—Mask.* XLVII.

1160 What if English toil and blood
    Was poured forth even as a flood ?   *—Mask,* LX.

1161 Stand ye calm and resolute,
    Like a forest close and mute,   *—Mask,* LXXIX.

1162   he who was
    Like the shadow in the glass
    Of the second.   *Prol. Peter B.* 13.

1163 He had as much imagination
    As a pint-pot ;—   *— Peter B.* IV. viii.

1164 For language was in Peter's hand
    Like clay,   *—Peter B.* V. xv.

1165 Is it my genius like the moon
    Sets those who stand her face inspecting

   .   .   .   .   .   .
1166 Like a crazed bell-chime, out of tune ?   *—Peter B.* VI. x.

1167 The language of a land which now is free,
    And winged with thoughts of truth and majesty
    Flits round the tyrant's sceptre like a cloud.
                —Letter to M. G. 176.

1168   till men should live and move
Harmonious as the sacred stars above. *—Witch*, XVIII.

1169   two lovers linkèd innocently
In their loose locks which over both did creep
Like ivy from one stem ;—   *— Witch,* LXI.

1170 And I wander and wane like the weary moon,
        - Fragm. of Drama, 4.

1171 He was as is the sun in his fierce youth,·
1172 As terrible and lovely as a tempest ; *—Fragm. of Drama,* 57.

1173 And weeps like a soft cloud in April's bosom
Upon the sleeping eyelids of the plant
       - Fragm. of Drama, 188.

1174 But I, whom thoughts which must remain untold
Had kept as wakeful as the stars that gem
The cone of night.   *--Triumph,* 21.

1175 And o'er what seemed the head a cloud-like crape
Was bent   *—Triumph,* 91.

1176 Till like two clouds into one vale impelled
That shake the mountains when their lightnings mingle
And die in rain--the fiery band which held
Their natures, snaps—while the shock still may tingle
       —Triumph, 155.

1177   till like a willow,
Her fair hair swept the bosom of the stream *— Triumph,* 364.

1178 And as a shut lily stricken by the wand
Of dewy morning's vital alchemy,
I rose ;   *—Triumph,* 401.

1179   and others made
Circles around it, like the clouds that swim
Round the high moon in a bright sea of air ; *— Triumph,* 453.

1180 For deaf as is a sea, which wrath makes hoary,
The world can hear not the sweet notes that move
The sphere whose light is melody to lovers— *--Triumph,* 477.

1181   and long before the day
Was old, the joy which waked like heaven's glance
The sleepers in the oblivious valley, died ; *— Triumph,* 537.

1182 Those marble shapes then seemed to quiver,
And their fair limbs to float in motion,
Like weeds unfolding in the ocean. *—M.'s Dream,* XXI.

1183 My heart is quivering like a flame ;
1184 As morning dew that in the sunbeam dies
I am dissolved in these consuming ecstasies. *—Const.* III.

1185 And thy tears upon my head
Burn like points of frozen lead. *—To Misery,* VIII.

1186 Clasp me till our hearts be grown
Like two shadows into one ; *—To Misery,* X.

1187 Her sons are as stones in the way. *—Lines,* II.

1188 An army, which liberticide and prey
   Makes as a two-edged sword to all who wield
   —Sonnet on Eng.

1189 As dew beneath the wind of morning,
1190 As the sea which whirlwinds waken,

   Is my heart when thine is near. *—Sophia,* IV.

1191 Their caresses were like the chaff
   In the tempest, *—Incantation.*

1192 One sung of thee who left the tale untold,
   Like the false dawns which perish in the bursting,
1193 Like empty cups of wrought and dædal gold,
   Which mock the lips with air, when they are thirsting
   —Fragm. Vol. 4, p. 19.

1194 And from its head as from one body grow,
   As grass out of a watery rock,
   Hairs which are vipers. *—Medusa,* IV.

1195 And so they grew together like two flowers
   Upon one stem, which the same beams and showers
   Lull or awaken in their purple prime.
   Which the same hand will gather—the same clime
   Shake with decay *—Fiord,* 15.

1196 But thou art as a planet, sphered above : *—Fiord,* 26.

1197 That withered woman, grey and white and brown —
   More like a trunk by lichens overgrown
   Than anything which once could have been human. *—Fiord,* 56.

1198 In my own heart I saw as in a glass
   The hearts of others— *—Hope.*

1199   In whom love ever made
   Health like a heap of embers soon to fade. *—To Emilia.*

1200 So that as if a frozen torrent
   The blood was curdled in its current ; *—Love,* 24.

1201 Like a herbless plain, for the gentle rain
   I gasp, I faint, till they wake again. *—Music,* I.

1202 When you die, the silent Moon
   In her interlunar swoon
   Is not sadder in her cell
   Than deserted Ariel.
   When you live again on earth,
1203 Like an unseen star of birth,
   Ariel guides you o'er the sea
   Of life from your nativity.

   And now, alas, the poor sprite is
   Imprisoned for some fault of his
1204 In a body like a grave— *— With a Guitar,* 23.

1205 Then like a useless and outworn machine
    Rots, perishes and passes.   —*Q. M.* I. 155.

1206   Man like these passive things
    Thy will unconsciously fulfilleth :
1207 Like theirs, his age of endless peace,
    Which time is fast maturing.
    Will swiftly, surely come :   —*Q. M.* III. **233.**

Human to Human.

1208 My powers revived within me, and I went
    As one whom winds waft o'er the bending grass,
    Through many a vale of that broad continent
                —*L. & C.* IV. **33.**

1209 I stood, as drifted on some cataract
    By irresistible streams, some wretch might strive
    Who hears its fateful roar :   —*L. & C.* VI. **6.**

1210 For with strong speech I tore the veil that hid
    Nature, and Truth, and Liberty, and Love—
    As one who from some mountain's pyramid
    Points to the unriseu sun.   —*L. & C.* IX. **7.**

1211 I am as one lost in a midnight wood,
    Who dares not ask some harmless passenger
    The path across the wilderness, lest he
    As my thoughts are, should be a murderer.   -*Cenci*, II. ii. **93.**

1212 Till, like one in slumber bound,
    Borne to the ocean, I float down, around
    Into a sea profound, of ever-spreading sound
            -*Prom.* II. v. **82.**

1213   all my being
    Like him whom the Numidian seps did thaw
    Into a dew with poison, is dissolved   —*Prom.* III. i. **39.**

1214   And then as one
    Whose sleeping face is stricken by the sun
    With light like a harsh voice, which bids him rise
            -*Giner.* **38.**

Human to Animal (or reverse).

1215   Two mighty Spirits now return,
    Like birds of calm, from the world's raging sea,
            —*L. & C.* I. **58.**

1216   fear with lust
    Strange fellowship through mutual hate had tied,
    Like two dark serpents tangled in the dust,
    Which on the paths of men their mingling poison thrust.
         —*L. & C.* II. **4.**

1217   Cythna then
. . . .
      and through the paths of men
Will pass, as the charmed bird that haunts the serpent's den
                        — *L. & C.* II. 46.

1218 Thirst raged within me, like a scorpion's nest
Built in my entrails :   — *L. & C.* III. 21.

1219 The tyrant's guards resistance yet maintain :
Fearless and fierce, and hard as beasts of blood,
                        L. & C. IV. 26.

1220 Those sanguine slaves. .   .
. . . .
Like rabid snakes, that sting some gentle child
Who brings them food, when winter false and fair
Allures them forth with its cold smiles, so wild
They rage among the camp :   — *L. & C.* V. 6, 7.

1221 But he (*sc.* the sceptred wretch)
. . . .
Glared on me as a toothless snake might glare
                        — *L. & C.* V. 25.

1222 Sorrow and shame, to see with their own kind
Our human brethren mix, like beasts of blood
To mutual ruin armed—   *L. & C.* VI. 15.

1223 And impotent their tongues they lolled into the air
Flaccid and foamy, like a mad dog's hanging,
                  — *L. & C.* VI. 16, 17.

1224   as a friend whose smile
Like light and rest at morn and even is sought,
That wild bird was to me,   — *L. & C.* VII. 14.

1225   obediently they came,
Like sheep whom from the fold the shepherd brings
To the stall, red with blood ;   *L. & C.* X. 5.

1226   and swore
1227   Like wolves and serpents, to their mutual wars
Strange truce,   — *L. & C.* X. 7.

1228 All night, the lean hyænas their sad case
Like starving infants wailed   — *L. & C.* X. 15.

1229   See ! See ! they fawn
Like dogs, and they will sleep with luxury spent,
When those detested hearts their iron fangs have rent !
                  — *L. & C.* X. 37.

1230   and with an inward fear possest,
They raged like homeless beasts whom burning woods invest
                  — *L. & C.* X. 40.

1231   So she scourged forth the maniac multitude
To rear this pyramid—tottering and slow,
Plague-stricken, foodless, like lean herds pursued
By gad-flies, they have piled the heath, and gums, and wood
                  — *L. & C.* X. 42.

1232   each girt by the hot atmosphere
Of his blind agony, like a scorpion stung
By his own rage upon his burning bier
Of circling coals of fire ;   *—L. & C.* XI. 8.

1233 When, like twin vultures, they hung feeding
On each heart's wound,   *—R. & H.* 932.

1234 I looked, and knew that he was dead,
And fell, as the eagle on the plain
Falls when life deserts her brain, *—R. & H.* 1183.

1235 Those who alone thy towers behold
Quivering through aerial gold

Would imagine not they were
Sepulchres, where human forms
Like pollution-nourished worms
To the corpse of greatness cling,
Murdered, and now mouldering : *—Eug. Hills,* 142.

1236 And we are left, as scorpions ringed with fire.*—Cenci,* II. ii. 70.

1237   I know two dull, fierce outlaws
Who think man's spirit as a worm's, *—Cenci,* III. i. 233.

1238 What ! can the everlasting elements
Feel with a worm, like man ? *—Cenci,* III. ii. 2.

1239   Heaven, rain upon her head
The blistering drops of the Maremm's dew,
Till she be speckled like a toad ; *—Cenci,* IV. i. 130.

1240 Until the subject of a tyrant's will
Became, worse fate, the abject of his own,
Which spurred him, like an outspent horse, to death.
       —Prom. III. iv. 139.

1241 And the sharks and the dog-fish their grave-clothes unbound
And were glutted like Jews with this manna rained down
From God on their wilderness. *—Vision of Sea,* 56.

1242 Chameleons feed on light and air ;
 Poet's food is love and fame ;
If in this wide world of care
Poets could but find the same
With as little toil as they,
 Would they ever change their hue
 As the light chameleons do,
Suiting it to every ray
Twenty times a day ?   *—Exhortation,* 1.

1243 Poets are on this cold earth,
 As chameleons might be,
Hidden from their early birth
 In a cave beneath the sea, *Exhortation,* 10.

1244   an antelope
In the suspended impulse of its lightness
Were less ætherially light. *—Epips.* 75.

1245 And towards the loadstar of my one desire
　　 I flitted, like a dizzy moth,　　　　　　　 *-Epips.* 219.

1246 Then as a hunted deer that could not flee,
　　 I turned upon my thoughts, and stood at bay,
　　 Wounded and weak and panting,　　　　　 *-Epips.* 272.

1247　　　　　 My muse has lost her wings,
　　 Or like a dying swan who soars and sings,
　　 I should describe you in heroic style,　　 *- Canc. Epips.* 84.

1248 Not so the eagle, who like thee could scale
1249 Heaven, and could nourish in the sun's domain
　　 Her mighty youth with morning, doth complain,
　　 Soaring and screaming round her empty nest
　　 As Albion wails for thee,　　　　　　　 *Adon.* XVII.

1250 A pardlike spirit beautiful and swift　　 *--Adon.* XXXII.

1251 And like a beaten hound tremble thou shalt　as now.
　　　　　　　　　　　　　　　　　 —Adon. XXXVII.

1252 In the great morning of the world,
　　 The Spirit of God unfurled
　　 The Flag of Freedom over Chaos,
　　　　 And all its banded anarchs fled,
　　 Like vultures frightened from Imaus,
　　　　 Before an earthquake's tread.—　　　 *Hell.* 46.

1253 Nor at thy bidding less exultingly
　　 Than birds rejoicing in the golden day,
　　 The Anarchies of Africa unleash
　　 Their tempest-wingèd cities of the sea,　　 *Hell.* 297.

1254 And the inheritors of the earth, like beasts
　　 When earthquake is unleashed, with idiot fear
　　 Cower in their dens--　　　　　　　　 *-Hell.* 356.

1255 The vultures and the dogs, your pensioners tame,
　　 Are overgorged ; but, like oppressors, still
　　 They crave the relic of Destruction's feast.　 *Hell.* 427.

1256　　　　　 Repulse is on the waters !
　　 They own no more the thunder-bearing banner
　　 Of Mahmud ; but like hounds of a base breed,
　　 Gorge from a stranger's hand, and rend their master.
　　　　　　　　　　　　　　　　　 —Hell. 466.

　　 They [*sc.* vultures]
　　 Stooped through the sulphurous battle-smoke, and perched
　　 Each on the weltering carcase that we loved
1257, 1258 Like its ill angel or its damned soul,　　 *—Hell.* 517.

1259　　　　　 The Greeks
　　 Are as a brood of lions in the net
　　 Round which the kingly hunters of the earth
　　 Stand smiling.　　　　　　　　　　 *—Hell.* 931.

1260 And as a jade urged by the whip and goad
　　 To drag life on,　　　　　　　　　 *—Julian,* 301.

1261 Nay, was it I who wooed thee to this breast
 Which, like a serpent thou envenomest
 As in repayment of the warmth it lent ?   *Julian*, 398.

1262 Even the instinctive worm on which we tread
 Turns, tho' it wound not, then with prostrate head
 Sinks in the dust and writhes like me.   —*Julian*, 412.

1263 Men of England, heirs of Glory

 .   .   .   .
 Rise like Lions after slumber
 In unvanquishable number,   —*Mask*, XXXVII., XXXVIII.

1264 There are mincing women, mewing,
 Like cats, who *amant misere*
 Of their own virtue,   —*Peter B*. III. viii.

1265 Each pursues what seems most fair,
 Mining like moles, through mind, and there
 Scoop palace-caverns vast,   —*Peter B*. III. xxiii.

1266 A toad-like lump of limb and feature,   —*Peter B*. IV. xvi.

1267 And so his soul would not be gay,
 But moaned within him, like a fawn
 Moaning within a cave,   —*Peter B*. VI. xxx.

1268   And the wood-gods in a crew
 Came, blithe, as in the olive copses thick
 Cicadæ are, drunk with the noon-day dew :   —*Witch*, VIII.

1269   like a sexless bee
 Tasting all blossoms, and confined to none,   —*Witch*, LXVIII.

1270 He lives in his own world, and like a parrot
 Hung in his golden prison from the window
 Of the queen's bower over the public way,
 Blasphemes with a bird's mind :   —*Chas. I.* II. 102.

1271 The slave of thine own slaves who tear like curs
 The fugitive, and flee from the pursuer ;   —*Chas. I.* II. 123.

1272 To which the eagle spirits of the free

 .   .   .   .
 Like eaglets floating in the heaven of time,
 They soar above their quarry, and shall stoop
 Through palaces and temples thunder-proof   —*Chas. I.* IV. 51.

1273   but as soon
 As they had touched the world with living flame,
 Fled back like eagles to their native noon,   —*Triumph*, 129.

1274 Maidens and youths flung their wild arms in air
 As their feet twinkle ; they recede, and now
 Bending within each other's atmosphere,
 Kindle invisibly—and as they glow
 Like moths by light attracted and repelled,
 Oft to their bright destruction come and go,   —*Triumph*, 149.

1275 Amid the mountains like a hunted beast
 He hid himself,   —*Marenghi*, XIII.

1276 Rulers who neither see nor feel nor know
    But leech-like to their fainting country cling,   *—Sonnet*, 4.

1277   As from an ancestral oak
        Two empty ravens sound their clarion
    Yell by yell and croak by croak
    When they scent the noon-day smoke
        Of fresh human carrion :—

1278   As two gibbering night-birds flit
        From their bowers of deadly yew
    Through the night to frighten it,
    When the moon is in a fit,
        And the stars are none or few :—

1279   As a shark and dog-fish wait
        Under an Atlantic isle,
    For the negro-ship, whose freight
    Is the theme of their debate,
        Wrinkling their red gills the while—

    Are ye, two vultures sick for battle,
                                  —Similes, Vol. 4, p. 6.

1280 As the birds at thunder's warning
.   .   .   .
Is my heart when thine is near it.   *—Sophia.*

1281 Her form was like a snake's—wrinkled and loose
And withered.   *—Fragm.*

1282 Like a blood-hound well-beaten,
The bridegroom stands,   *—Fugitive*, IV.

1283 The fair hand that wounded it,
    Seeking, like a panting hare,
    Refuge in the lynx's lair,   *—Love, etc.*

1284   and soon the priests arrived,
And finding death their penitent had shrived,
Returned like ravens from a corpse whereon
A vulture had just feasted to the bone.   *—Giner.* 191.

1285 The mind, which like a worm whose life may share
A portion of the unapproachable
Marks your creation's rise.   *—To Byron.*

1286   custom's force has made
His nature as the nature of a lamb.   *—Q. M.* VIII. 27.

Human Beings or Attributes to Personified Abstractions

(Spirits, Shapes, etc.)

1287   Nature's most secret steps
He like his shadow has pursued,   *—Alast.* 81.

1288 A Form most like the imagined habitant
Of silver exhalations sprung from dawn,
By winds which feed on sunrise woven,   *—L. & C.* V. 44.

1289 A liquid element, whereon
    Our Spirits, like delighted things
    That walk the air on subtle wings,
    Floated and mingled far away,
    'Mid the warm winds of the sunny day.   *—R. & H.* 963.

Natural Phenomena to Natural.

He wandered on
1290 Till vast Aornos seen from Petra's steep
    Hung o'er the low horizon like a cloud :   *—Alast.* 239.

1291   Spirit of Nature ! thou
    Imperishable as this glorious scene,
    Here is thy fitting temple.   *—D. W.* 186.

Its home
1292 The voiceless lightning in these solitudes
    Keeps innocently, and like vapour broods
    Over the snow.   *—Mont. B.* 136.

1293 For, from the encounter of those wondrous foes,
    A vapour like the sea's suspended spray
    Hung gathered :   *L. & C.* I. 11.

1294 A boat of rare device, which has no sail
    But its own curvèd prow of thin moonstone,
    Wrought like a web of texture fine and frail,
    To catch those gentlest winds   *—L. & C.* I. 23.

1295 This vital world, this home of happy spirits
    Was as a dungeon to my blasted kind,   *--L. & C.* II. 6.

1296 The islands and the mountains in the day,
    Like clouds reposed afar,   *—L. & C.* III. 15.

1297   a whirlwind keen as frost   *—L. & C.* III. 26.

1298 I led him forth from that which now might seem
    A gorgeous grave ;   *—L. & C.* V. 26.

1299 To see like some vast island from the ocean,
    TheAltar of the Federation rear
    Its pile in the midst ;   *—L. & C.* V. 40.

1300 Then : "Away ! away !" she cried, and stretched her sword
    As 'twere a scourge over the courser's head,   *—L. & C.* VI. 21.

that spacious cell
1301 Like an upaithric temple wide and high,
    Whose aëry dome is inaccessible,   *—L. & C.* VII. 12.

and on such bright floor did stand
1302 Columns, and shapes like statues,   *—L. & C.* VII. 13.

1303 The misery of a madness slow and creeping,
1304 Which made the earth seem fire, the sea seem air,
                              —L. & C. VII. 15.

And I became at last even as a shade,
A smoke, a cloud on which the winds have preyed,
1305 Till it be thin as air ;   —*L. & C.* VII. 26.

    Thither still the myriads came,
1306 Seeking to quench the agony of the flame,
 Which raged like poison through their bursting veins :
         —*L. & C.* X. 21.

1307 Steady and swift, where the waves rolled like mountains
 Within the vast ravine, whose rifts did pour
 Tumultuous floods from their ten thousand fountains,
 The thunder of whose earth-uplifting roar
 Made the air sweep in whirlwinds from the shore,
1308 Calm as a shade, the boat of that fair child
 Securely fled,   — *L. & C.* XII. 39.

1309 And in the midst, afar, even like a sphere
 Hung in one hollow sky, did there appear
 The Temple of the Spirit ; on the sound
 Which issued thence, drawn nearer and more near,
1310 Like the swift moon this glorious earth around,
 The charmèd boat approached, and there its haven found.
       —*L. & C.* XII. 41.

1311 O'er which the columned wood did frame
 A roofless temple, like the fane
 Where, ere new creeds could faith obtain,
 Man's early race once knelt beneath
 The overhanging deity.   —*R. & H.* 107.

1312 The next Spring shows leaves pale and rare
 But like flowers delicate and fair
 On its rent boughs   —*R. & H.* 789.

1313 And weeds like branching chrysolite,   *R. & H.* 1083.

1314 Save where many a palace gate
 With green sea-flowers overgrown
 Like a rock of ocean's own,
 Topples o'er the abandoned sea
 As the tides change sullenly.   *Eug. Hills*, 129.

1315 Oh, thou bright wine .   .   .
 .   .   .   .
 Could I believe thou wert their mingled blood,
 Then would I taste thee like a sacrament   —*Cenci*, I. iii. 77.

1316   Thou knowest
 This cell seems like a kind of paradise
 After our father's presence.   —*Cenci*, V. iii. 10.

1317 Brother, lie down with me upon the rack,
 .   .   .   .
 It soon will be as soft as any grave   —*Cenci*, V. iii. 48.

1318   and mighty realms
 Float by my feet, like sea-uprooted isles,   —*Prom.* I. 612.

1319 Mighty fleets were strewn like chaff   —*Prom.* I. 716.
 9

1320 Henceforth the fields of heaven-reflecting sea
Which are my realm, will heave, unstained with blood,
Beneath the uplifting winds, like plains of corn
Swayed by the summer air,   —*Prom.* III. ii. 18.

1321 Behold the Nereids under the green sea,
Their wavering limbs borne on the wind-like stream,
                                     —*Prom.* III. ii. 44.

1322 The dew-mists of my sunless sleep shall float
Under the stars like balm :   —*Prom.* III. iii. 100.

1323 The image of a temple, built above,
Distinct with column, arch, and architrave,
And palm-like capital   —*Prom.* III. iii. 161.

1324   and in the deep there lay
Those lovely forms imaged as in a sky ;   —*Prom.* III. iv. 82.

1325 I see a chariot like that thinnest boat,
In which the mother of the months is borne
By ebbing night into her western cave,
When she upsprings from interlunar dreams,
1326 O'er which is curved an orb-like canopy
Of gentle darkness, and the hills and woods
Distinctly seen through that dusk airy veil,
1327 Regard like shapes in an enchanted glass ;   —*Prom.* IV. 206.

1328 A sphere, which is as many thousand spheres,
Solid as crystal,   —*Prom.* IV. 238.

1329 Until each crag-like tower,   —*Prom.* IV. 344.

1330 My sea-like forests   —*Prom.* IV. 347.

1331 And it opened its fan-like leaves to the light   —*Sens. P.* I. 3.

1332 And the wand-like lily   —*Sens. P.* I. 33.

1333 And the sinuous paths of lawn and of moss,
. . . .
Were all paved with daisies and delicate bells
As fair as the fabulous asphodels,   —*Sens. P.* I. 49.

1334 The quivering vapours of dim noon-tide,
Which like a sea o'er the warm earth glide,   —*Sens. P.* I. 90.

1335 And agarics, and fungi, with mildew and mould,
Started like mist from the wet ground cold ;
                                     —*Sens. P.* III. 62.

1336 Their moss rotted off them, flake by flake,
Till the thick stalk stuck like a murderer's stake,
Where rags of loose flesh yet tremble on high,
Infecting the winds that wander by.   —*Sens. P.* III. 66.

1337 And at its outlet, flags huge as stakes
Dammed it up| —*Sens. P.* III. 72.

1338 And when lightning is loosed, like a deluge from heaven,
She sees the black trunks of the water-spouts spin
And bend as if Heaven was ruining in,   —*Vis. of Sea,* 4.

1339 The great ship seems splitting, it cracks as a tree,
　　　While an earthquake is splintering its root,　— *Vis. of Sea*, 26.

1340 One deck is burst up from the waters below,
　　　And it splits like the ice when the thaw-breezes blow
　　　O'er the lakes of the desert　　　— *Vis. of Sea*, 35.

　　　　　　　the screaming blast,
1341 Between ocean and heaven, like an ocean, past.
　　　　　　　　　　　　　　— *Vis. of Sea*, 105.

1342 Till it came to the clouds on the verge of the world
　　　Which, based on the sea and to heaven upcurled,
　　　Like columns and walls, did surround and sustain
　　　The dome of the tempest; it rent them in twain,
　　　As a flood rends its barriers of mountainous crag :
　　　And the dense clouds in many a ruin and ray,
1343 Like the stones of a temple ere earthquake has past,
1344 Like the dust of its fall, on the whirlwind are cast ;
　　　　　　　　　　　　　　— *Vis. of Sea*, 107.

1345 Glides glimmering o'er my fleece-like floor.　　　—*Cloud*, 47.

1346 When I widen the rent in my wind-built tent,
　　　　Till the calm rivers, lakes, and seas,
　　　Like strips of the sky fallen thro' me on high,
　　　Are each paved with the moon and these—　　—*Cloud*, 55.

1347 From cape to cape, with a bridge-like shape,
. . . .
1348 Sunbeam-proof I hang like a roof,
　　　The mountains its columns be.　　　　— *Cloud*, 63.

1349 And cloud-like mountains.　　　　—*Ode to Lib*. IV.

　　　　And many a warrior-peopled citadel,
1350 Like rocks which fire lifts out of the flat deep,
　　　　Arose in sacred Italy,　　　　—*Ode to Lib*. IX.

　　　　　　　Her petticoats streaming
　　　Streaming like—like—like
　　　　　　　Anything.

　　　Purganax.　　　Oh, no,
1351 But like a standard of an Admiral's ship,
1352 Or like the banner of a conquering host,
1353 Or water-fall from a dizzy precipice
　　　Scattered upon the wind.　　　　—*Œd. Tyr*. II. 95.

　　　　　　to whom this world of life
1354 Is as a garden ravaged　　　　—*Epips*. 186.

1355 When it would seek in Hesper's setting sphere
　　　A radiant death, a fiery sepulchre,
　　　As if it were a lamp of earthly flame.　　　—*Epips*. 222.

1356 It would have followed, tho' the grave between
　　　Yawned like a gulph whose spectres are unseen :　—*Epips*. 230.

1357 It is an isle under Ionian skies,
　　　Beautiful as a wreck of Paradise,　　　—*Epips*. 422.

1358 And level with the living winds, which flow
    Like waves above the living waves below.   *Epips.* 517.

1359 A veil for our seclusion, close as night,   *Epips.* 556.

1360 Of life which flows like a . . . dream
    Into the light of morning, to the grave
    As to an ocean.   —*Canc. Epips.* 151.

1361 Another clipt her profuse locks, and threw
    The wreath upon him like an anadem,
    Which frozen tears instead of pearls begem ;   —*Adon.* XI.

Go thou to Rome—

. . . .
1362 And where its wrecks like shattered mountains rise,
        —*Adon.* XLIX.

        and lofty ships even now
1363 Like vapours anchored to a mountain's edge,
    Freighted with fire and whirlwind, wait at Scala
    The convoy of the ever-veering wind.   —*Hell.* 283,

1364 The fleet which, like a flock of clouds
    Chased by the wind, flies the insurgent banner.   *Hell.* 460.

        Crete and Cyprus,
1365 Like mountain twins, that from each other's veins
    Catch the volcano-fire and earthquake spasm,
    Shake in the general fever.   *Hell.* 587.

        A chasm
1366 As of two mountains in the wall of Stamboul ;   *Hell.* 830.

1367 Between kingless continents sinless as Eden   —*Hell.* 1047.

1368 It [*sc.* earth] was cloudy, and sullen, and cold,
    Like a frozen chaos uprolled,   —*Death of Napoleon.*

1369 Those famous Euganean hills, which bear,
    As seen from Lido through the harbour-piles,
    The likeness of a clump of peaked isles—   —*Julian,* 77.

1370 I leaned and saw the city, and could mark
    How from their many isles in evening's gleam
    Its temples and its palaces did seem
    Like fabrics of enchantment piled to Heaven   *Julian,* 89.

1371 On its helm, seen far away
    A planet, like the Morning's lay ;   *Mask,* XXVI.

1372 Men of England, heirs of Glory,
. . . .
    Shake your chains to earth like dew
    Which in sleep had fallen on you,   —*Mask.* XXXVIII.

1373   A cloud, with lightning, wind and hail,
    It swept over the mountains like
    An ocean,   —*Peter Bell,* I. xii.

1374 And worse and worse, the drowsy curse
 Yawned in him, till it grew a pest—
 A wide contagious atmosphere,
 Creeping like cold through all things near ;
       --*Peter Bell*, VII. xvii.

1375   woven tracery ran
 Of light firm texture, ribbed and branching, o'er
  The solid rind, like a leaf's veined fan—
       — *Witch*, XXXIII.

1376 Where like a meadow which no scythe has shaven ;
  Which rain could never bend, or whirl-blast shake,
 With the Antarctic constellations paven,
  Canopus and his crew, lay the Austral lake—
       — *Witch*, XLVIII.

1377   this haven
 Was as a gem to copy heaven engraven.   — *Witch*, L.

1378 And where within the surface of the river
  The shadows of the massy temples lie,
 And never are erased—but tremble ever
  Like things which every cloud can doom to die,
       Witch, LIX.

1379 And as a veil in which I walk through Heaven
 I have wrought mountains, seas, and waves, and clouds,
 And lastly light, whose interfusion dawns
 In the dark space of interstellar air. --*Unfin. Drama*, 24.

1380 A soft hand issued from the veil of fire,
 Holding a cup like a Magnolia flower,
 And poured upon the earth within the vase
 The element with which it overflowed,
 Brighter than morning light, and purer than
 The waters of the springs of Himalah. —*Unfin. Drama*, 145.

1381 And thus it [*sc.* the fruit] lay in the Elysian calm
 Of its own beauty, floating on the line
 Which, like a film in purest space, divided
 The heaven beneath the waters from the heaven
 Above the clouds :   —*Unfin. Drama*, 228.

    See those thronging chariots
 Rolling, like painted clouds before the wind,
 Behind their solemn steeds : how some are shaped
1382 Like curvèd shells dyed by the azure depths
1383 Of Indian seas : some like the new-born moon,
1384 And some like cars in which the Romans climbed
 (Canopied by Victory's eagle wings outspread)
 The Capitolian.   — *Chas. I.* I. 136.

1385 This vaporous horizon, whose dim round
 Is bastioned by the circumfluous sea,
 Repelling invasion from the sacred towers,
 Presses upon me like a dungeon's grate,
 A low dark roof, a damp and narrow wall. —*Chas. I.* IV. 41.

1386 Isle, ocean and all things that in them wear
     The form and character of mortal mould,
     Rise as the Sun their father rose to bear
     Their portion of the toil which he of old
     Took as his own, and then imposed on them.   *—Triumph*, 16.

1387 And from it came a gentle rivulet,
     Whose water like clear air, in its calm sweep
     Bent the soft grass, and kept forever wet
     The stems of the sweet flowers,   *Triumph*, 314.

              yet contagion there

1388 Spread like a quenchless fire ;   *D. W. II.* 129.

1389   the flood
     Grew tranquil as a woodland river
     Winding through hills in solitude,   *Marianne's D.* XXI.

1390 And their swords and their sceptres I floating see,
     Like wrecks on the surge of eternity.   *—Wm. Shelley*, IV.

     They spread themselves into the loveliness
1391 Of fan-like leaves, and over pallid flowers
1392 Hang like moist clouds :—or where high branches kiss,
     Make a green space among the silent bowers
1393 Like a vast fane in a metropolis.   *Woodman*, 52.

1394 Surrounded by the columns and the towers
     All overwrought with branch-like traceries,   *—Woodman*, 57.

1395   which makes
     Even the mud and slime of the warm lakes
     A wrinkled clod as hard as brick ;   *—Summer and Winter.* 13.

1396 The wreaths of stony myrtle, ivy, and pine,
     Like winter leaves o'ergrown by moulded snow.
                                                   —To Naples, 17.

1397   And where the Baian ocean
             Welters with air-like motion,
     Within, above, around its bowers of starry green,
     Moving the sea flowers in those purple caves
     Even as the ever stormless atmosphere
             Floats o'er the Elysian realm,   *—To Naples*, 26.

1398   thy shield is as a mirror
     To make their blind slaves see, and with fierce gleam
     To turn his hungry sword upon the wearer ;   *—To Naples*, 78.

1399 The Earth is like Ocean,
     Wreck-strewn and in motion :   *—Fugitives*, I.

1400 While around the lashed Ocean,
     Like mountains in motion,
     Is withdrawn and uplifted,
     Sunk, shattered and shifted
             To and fro.   *—Fugitives*, III.

1401 Nourishing each tender gem
     Which like flowers will burst from them.   *—Epith.* 29.

1402 Through desert woods and tracts, which seem
    Like ocean, homeless, boundless, unconfined.
                    —Fragm. Wandering.

1403 The chasm in which the sun has sunk is shut
    By darkest barriers of cinereous cloud,
    Like mountains over mountains huddled—   *—Evening, IV.*

1404 Which the circumfluous plain waving below,
    Like a wide lake of green fertility,
    With streams and fields and marshes bare,
        Divides from the far Apennines—which lie
    Islanded in the immeasurable air.   *—Serchio, 41.*

1405   and its flowers fair,
    Full as a cup with the vine's burning dew,
    O'erflowed with golden colours.   *Zucca. IX.*

1406 Now all the tree tops lay asleep,
    Like green waves on the sea,
    As still as in the silent deep
        The ocean woods may be.   *—To Jane Recoll. III.*

1407 I sat and saw the vessels glide
    Over the ocean bright and wide,
    Like spirit-winged chariots sent
    O'er some serenest element
    For ministration strange and far ;
    As if to some Elysian star
    Sailed for drink to medicine
    Such sweet and bitter pain as mine.   *—Lines in Bay of L. 31.*

1408 Till from the breathing lawn a forest springs
    Of youth, integrity, and loveliness,
    Like that which gave it life, to spring and die.
                    —Q. M. V. 13.

Natural to Human Beings—Human Attributes—Natural Phenomena to Mental Phenomena—Spirits, etc.

1409   Now on the polished stones
    It [*sc.* rivulet] danced, like childhood laughing as it went
                        —Alast. 498.

1410 Watch the dim shades as like ghosts they come and go
                    —Stanzas 1814, 11.

1411   Calm as a slumbering babe
           Tremendous ocean lay.   *—D. W. I. 134.*

1412   and there the sea I found
    Calm as a cradled child in dreamless slumber bound
                     —L. & C. I. xv.

1413   The Morning Star
    Shone   .   .   .
    'Twas like an eye which seemed to smile on me
                     L. & C. I. xl.

1414 Sculptures like life and thought : immovable, deep-eyed.
—L. & C. I. li.

1415   what was this cave?
Its deep foundations no firm purpose knows
Immutable, resistless, strong to save,
Like mind while yet it mocks the all-devouring grave
—L. & C. VII. xxviii.

1416 Oh, thou bright wine whose purple splendour leaps
And bubbles gaily in this golden bowl
Under the lamplight, as my spirits do,   —<i>Cenci</i>. I. iii. 77.

1417   beneath this crag
Huge as despair, as if in weariness.
The melancholy mountain yawns,   —<i>Cenci</i>, III. i. 255.

1418   Thou small flame
Which, as a dying pulse rises and falls,
Still flickerest up and down,   —<i>Cenci</i>, III. ii. 11.

1419   the vain and senseless crowd,
Who, . . .
                   will leave
The churches and the theatres as void
As their own hearts?   —<i>Cenci</i>, V. iii. 36.

1420   made earth like heaven ;   —<i>Prom.</i> III. iv. 160.

1421   and water springs
Whence the great sea, even as a child, is fed   —<i>Prom.</i> IV. 284.

1422 And the Naiad-like lily of the vale   —<i>Sens. Plant</i>, I. 21.

1423 And the rose like a Nymph to the bath addressed,
Which unveiled the depth of her glowing breast
Till, fold after fold, to the fainting air,
The soul of her beauty and love lay bare :   —<i>Sens. Plant</i>, I. 29.

1424 The unseen clouds of the dew, which lie
Like fire in the flowers till the sun rides high,
Then wander like spirits among the spheres,
Each cloud faint with the fragrance it bears :
—Sens. Plant, I. 86.

1425 Each and all like ministering angels were
For the Sensitive Plant sweet joy to bear.   —<i>Sens. Plant</i>, I. 94.

1426 The garden, once fair, became cold and foul,
Like the corpse of her who had been its soul.
—Sens. Plant, III. 17.

1427 And the leaves .   .
 .   .   .   .   .
Like troops of ghosts on the dry wind past ;
—Sens. Plant. III. 34.

1428 And agarics and fungi
                       .
Pale, fleshly, as if the decaying dead
With a spirit of growth had been animated
—Sens. Plant, III. 62.

1429 The Sensitive Plant like one forbid
    Wept.   —*Sens. Plant*, III. 82.

1430 But the mandrakes, and toadstools, and docks and darnels
    Rose like the dead from their ruined charnels,
                            —*Sens. Plant*, III. 116.

1431 Whether the Sensitive Plant, or that
    Which within its boughs like a spirit sat

    Now felt this change, I cannot say.   —*Sens. Plant, Concl.* 1.

1432   The heavy dead hulk
    On the living sea rolls an inanimate bulk,
    Like a corpse on the clay which is hungering to fold
    Its corruption around it.   —*Vision of Sea*, 31.

1433 Thou, from whose unseen presence the leaves dead
    Are driven, like ghosts from an enchanter fleeing,
                        — *West Wind*, I.

1434 Like a child from the womb, like a ghost from the tomb,
1435 I arise and unbuild it again   .   -*Cloud*, 83.

1436   the odours deep
    Of flowers, which like lips murmuring in their sleep
    Of the sweet kisses that had lulled them there,
    Breathed but of her to the enamoured air ;   -*Epips.* 202.

1437   Let the fixèd bayonet
    Gleam with sharp desire to wet
    Its bright point in English blood
    Looking keen as one for food.   —*Mask*, LXXVII.

1438   like children chidden
    At her command they [*sc.* billows] ever came and went—
                     — *Witch*, IV.

1439 Couched on the fountain like . . .

    Or on blind Homer's heart a wingèd thought,
    In joyous expectation lay the boat   — *Witch*, XXXIV.

1440   till the car
    Of the late moon, like a sick matron wan,
    To journey from the misty east began.   - *Witch*, LI.

1441   the wave
    Which like a toil-worn labourer leaps to shore
    To meet the kisses of the flowrets there.   —*D. W.* II. 109.

1442 The works of faith and slavery, so vast,
    So sumptuous, yet withal so perishing !
    Even as the corpse that rests beneath their wall.
                        —*D. W.* II. 314.

1443   and earth,
    Even as a child beneath its mother's love
    Is strengthened in all excellence, and grows
    Fairer and nobler with each passing year.   —*D. W.* II. 326.

1444   and that tall flower that wets
  Like a child, half in tenderness and mirth -
  Its mother's face with heaven-collected tears,
  When the low wind, its playmate's voice, it hears.
            —*Question*, II.

1445 And like a dying lady, lean and pale,   •
  Who totters forth, wrapt in a gauzy veil,
  Out of her chamber, led by the insane
  And feeble wanderings of her fading brain,
  The moon arose up in the murky east,   — *Waning Moon.*

1446 A star has fallen upon the earth,
  .   .   .   .
  Like an angelic spirit pent
   In a form of mortal birth,   — *Prol. Hell.* 196.

1447   the dew
  Lay on its spotted leaves like tears too true   - *Zucca*, VI.

1448 Making the wintry world appear
  Like one on whom thou smilest, dear.   -- *To Jane, Invitation*, 19.

Natural Phenomena to Animals—Art Products to Animals, and Vice Versa.

1449   Higher and higher still
  Their [*sc.* waves] fierce necks writhed beneath the tempest's
   scourge,
  Like serpents struggling in a vulture's grasp.
            —*Alast.* 323.

1450   The glaciers creep
  Like snakes that watch their prey, from their far fountains
  Slow, rolling on :   —*Mont Blanc.*

1451 That land is like an eagle, whose young gaze
  Feeds on the noon-tide beam, whose golden plume
  Floats moveless on the storm, and in the blaze
  Of sun-rise gleams when Earth is wrapt in gloom :
            --*L. & C.* XI. xxiii.

1452 And he tamed fire which like some beast of prey
  Most terrible but lovely, played beneath
  The frown of man.   -- *Prom.* II. iv. 66.

1453   heaven's utmost deep
  Gives up her stars, and like a flock of sheep
  They pass before his eyes, are numbered, and roll on.
           —*Prom.* IV. 418.

1454 And none ever trembled and panted with bliss,
  In the garden, the field, or the wilderness,
  Like the doe in the noon-tide with love's sweet want
  As the companionless Sensitive Plant.   —*Sens. P.* I. 9.

1455 All loathliest weeds began to grow,
　　　Whose coarse leaves were splashed with many a speck,
　　　Like the water-snake's belly and the toad's back.
　　　　　　　　　　　　　　　　—*Sens. P.* III. 51.

1456 And at its outlet flags　.　.　.
　　　Dammed it up with roots knotted like water-snakes.
　　　　　　　　　　　　　　　　—*Sens. P.* III. 72.

1457 And a northern whirlwind, wandering about
　　　Like a wolf that had smelt a dead child out,
　　　　　　　　　　　　　　　　—*Sens. P.* III. 110.

1458 Who crowd [*sc.* tigers] side by side, and have driven, like a crank,
　　　The deep grip of their claws through the vibrating plank
　　　　　　　　　　　　　　　　-　*Vision of Sea.* 43.

1459 Thine azure sister of the Spring shall blow
　　　Her clarion　.　.　.
　　　(Driving sweet buds like flocks to feed in air)　—*West Wind*, I.

1460 With wings folded I rest on my airy nest
　　　As still as a brooding dove.　　　　　　　—*Cloud*, 43.

1461 And I laugh to see them [*sc.* stars] whirl and flee
　　　Like a swarm of golden bees.　　　　　　-*Cloud*, 53.

1462 Higher still and higher
　　　　　From the earth thou springest
　　　Like a cloud of fire,　　　　　　　　　—*Skylark*, 6.

ʰ1463　　　Like a star of heaven
　　　　　　In the broad day-light
　　　Thou art unseen,　　　　　　　　　　—*Skylark*, 18.

1464 How glorious it will be to see her Majesty
　　　　　　　.　.　.　her petticoats
　　　Streaming like　.　.　.
　　　　　　　　　or a war steed's mane.
　　　　　　　　　　　　　　　　—*Œd. Tyr.* II. i. 95.

1465 Streaming like　.　.　.
　　　　　　　　　or a cow's tail.　　　—*Œd. Tyr.* II. i. 95.

1466 And palisades of tusks, sharp as a bayonet.
　　　　　　　　　　　　　　　　—*Œd. Tyr.* II. i. 144.

1467 Our bark is as an albatross, whose nest
　　　Is a far Eden in the purple East;　　　—*Epips.* 416.

1468 The earth doth like a snake renew
　　　Her winter weeds outworn.　　　　　—*Hell.* 1062.

1469 When the exulting elements in scorn
　　　　　　　　.　.　.　lay
　　　Sleeping in beauty on their mangled prey
　　　As panthers sleep;　　　　　　　—*Letter to M. G.* 40.

1470 Couched on the fountain like a panther tame,
　　　One of the twain at Evan's feet that sat,
　　　.　.　.　.　.　.　.　.　.　.
　　　In joyous expectation lay the boat.　　—*Witch*, XXXIV.

1471 And there its fruit lay like a sleeping lizard
     Under the shadows   —*Unfin. Drama*, 205.

1472 The splendour-wingèd worlds disperse
     Like wild doves scattered.   —*Prol. Hell.* 54.

1473   but 'tis sleeping fast
     Like a beast unconscious of its tether.   —*Serchio*, 5.

1474 And the young and dewy dawn,
     Bold as an unhunted fawn,
     Up the windless heaven is gone—
     Laugh—for ambushed in the day
     Clouds and whirlwinds watch their prey.   —*Insecurity*.

1475 We paused amid the pines that stood
       .   .   .   .
     Tortured by storms to shapes as rude
     As serpents interlaced   —*To Jane, Recoll.* III.

1476 She left me at the silent time
     When the moon had ceased to climb
     The azure path of heaven's steep,
     And like an albatross asleep,
     Balanced on her wings of light
     Hovered in the purple night,
     Ere she sought her ocean nest
     In the chambers of the West.   —*Lines in Bay of Lerici*, I.

SIMILES OF SWIFTNESS, CHANGE AND
EVANESCENCE.

1477 And felt the boat speed o'er the tranquil sea
     Like a torn cloud before the hurricane.   —*Alast.* 314.

1478 As one that in a silver vision floats
     Obedient to the sweep of odorous winds
     Upon resplendent clouds, so rapidly
     Along the dark and ruffled waters fled
     The straining boat.   —*Alast.* 316.

1479   The little boat
     Still fled before the storm ; still fled, like foam
     Down the steep cataracts of a wintry river ;   —*Alast.* 344.

1480   the woven leaves
     Make net-work of the dark blue light of day,
     And the night's noon-tide clearness, mutable
     As shapes in the weird clouds.   —*Alast.* 445.

1481   But thou art fled
     Like some frail exhalation ; which the dawn
     Robes in its golden beams, --   —*Alast.* 686.

1482 We are as clouds that veil the midnight moon ;
How restlessly they speed, and gleam, and quiver,
Streaking the darkness radiantly ! yet soon—
Night closes round, and they are lost for ever.   —*Mutability*, 1.

1483 Or like forgotten lyres, whose dissonant strings
Give various response to each varying blast,
To whose frail frame no second motion brings
One mood or modulation like the last.   -- *Mutability*, 5.

1484 When all that we know, or feel, or see,
Shall pass like an unreal mystery   -*There is no work*, 17.

1485   For the very spirit fails,
Driven like a homeless cloud from steep to steep
That vanishes among the viewless gales.   - *Mont Blanc*, 57.

1486   The race
Of man flies far in dread ; his work and dwelling
Vanish, like smoke before the tempest's stream,
And their place is not known.   — *Mont Blanc*, 117.

1487   The vast clouds fled,
Countless and swift as leaves on autumn's tempest shed.
                    --*L. de C.* I. iv.

1488 The pallid semicircle of the moon
Past on in slow and moving majesty ;
Its upper horn arrayed in mists, which soon
But slowly fled, like dew beneath the beams of noon.
                    —*L. de C.* I. v.

1489 Even like a bark, which from a chasm of mountains,
Dark, vast, and overhanging, on a river
Which there collects the strength of all its fountains,
Comes forth, whilst with the speed its frame doth quiver,
Sails, oars, and stream, tending to one endeavour ;
So from that chasm of light a winged Form
On all the winds of heaven approaching ever
Floated, dilating as it came : the storm
Pursued it with fierce blasts, and lightnings swift and warm.
                    —*L. de C.* I. vii.

1490 Then soar—as swift as smoke from volcano springs.
                    —*L. de C.* I. xiii.

1491 I looked, and we were sailing pleasantly,
Swift as a cloud between the sea and sky,   —*L. de C.* I. xlvii.

1492 Even as a storm let down beneath the ray
Of the still moon, my spirit onward past,
Beneath truth's steady beams upon its tumult cast.
                    —*L. de C.* II. xii.

1493 In sudden panic those false murderers fled,
Like insect tribes before the northern gale :   —*L. de C.* V. viii.

1494 And all the shapes of this grand scenery shifted
Like restless clouds before the steadfast sun
                    —*L. de C.* V. xviii.

1495 The chains of earth like mist melted away,
—*L. & C.* V. xxxvii.

1496 Sudden, as when the moonrise makes appear
Strange clouds in the east ; —*L. & C.* V. xl.

1497 The third Image was drest
In white wings swift as clouds in winter skies, —*L. & C.* V. l.

1498 [*sc.* wisdom] swift and strong
As new-fledged Eagles, beautiful and young,
That float among the blinding beams of morning.
—*L. & C.* V. li. 1.

1499 The Fiend-God, when our charmèd name he hear,
Shall fade like shadow from his thousand fanes,
—*L. & C.* V. li. 6.

1500 the while,
Far overhead, ships from Propontis keep
A killing rain of fire ; when the waves smile
As sudden earthquakes light many a volcanic isle ;
Thus sudden, —*L. & C.* VI. vii.

1501 and ever
Our myriads, whom the swift bolt overthrew,
Or the red sword, failed like a mountain river
Which rushes forth in foam to sink in sands forever.
—*L. & C.* VI. xiv.

1502 We spake no word,
But like the vapour of the tempest fled
Over the plain ; her dark hair was dispread
Like the pine's locks upon the lingering blast :
—*L. & C.* VI. xxi.

1503 did seize a Tartar's sword, and spring
Upon his horse, and swift as on the whirlwind's wing
Have thou and I been borne beyond pursuer,
—*L. & C.* VI. xxvf.

1504 while tears pursued
Each other down her fair and listening cheek
Fast as the thoughts which fed them, —*L. & C.* VII. ii.

1505 Swift as an eagle stooping from the plain
Of morning light, into some shadowy wood,
He plunged through the green silence of the main
—*L. & C.* VII. x.

1506 And I became at last even as a shade,
1507 A smoke, a cloud on which the winds have preyed,
1508 Till it be thin as air ; —*L. & C.* VII. xxvi.

1509 Opinion is more frail
Than yon dim cloud now fading on the moon
Even while we gaze, tho' it awhile avail
To hide the orb of truth-- — *L. & C.* VIII. ix.

1510 High temples fade like vapour— —*L. & C.* VIII. xvi.

1511 She is my life,—I am but as the shade
1512 Of her,—a smoke sent up from ashes, soon to fade.
                                        —*L. & C.* VIII. xxv.

1513 This is the winter of the world ;—and here
     We die, even as the winds of Autumn fade,
     Expiring in the frore and foggy air.
     Behold, Spring comes, tho' we must pass, who made
     The promise of its birth,—even as the shade
1514 Which from our death, as from a mountain, flings
     The future, a broad sunrise ;   —*L. & C.* IX. xxv.

1515 Thy growth is swift as morn, when night must fade ;
                                        - *L. & C.* XI. xxii.

1516   Cythna sprung
     From her gigantic steed, who, like a shade
     Chased by the winds, those vacant streets among
     Fled tameless,   —*L. & C.* XII. xiii.

1517   like gossamer,
     On the swift breath of morn, the vessel flew

     . . . .

     Till down that mighty stream dark, calm, and fleet
     Between a chasm of cedarn mountains riven,
     Chased by the thronging winds whose viewless feet
1518 As swift as twinkling beams, had, under Heaven
     From woods and waves wild sounds and odours driven,
     The boat fled visibly— three nights and days,
1519 Borne like a cloud thro' morn, and noon, and even,
                                        —*L. & C.* XII. xxxii.

1520 Morn, noon, and even, that boat of pearl outran
     The streams which bore it, like the arrowy cloud
1521 Of tempest, or the speedier thought of man,
     Which flieth forth and cannot make abode,
                                        —*L. & C.* XII. xxxv.

1522 On the fourth day, wild as a wind-wrought sea
     The stream became, and fast and faster bare
     The spirit-wingèd boat,   —*L. & C.* XII. xxxviii.

1523 Like the swift moon . . . this glorious earth around,
     The charmèd boat approached, and there its haven found.
                                        —*L. & C.* XII. xli.

1524 For ever now his health declined,
     Like some frail bark which cannot bear
     The impulse of an altered wind,   —*R. & H.* 814.

1525 And swift and swifter the notes came
     From my touch, that wandered like quick flame,
                                        —*R. & H.* 1145.

1526   for human things
1527 Change even like the ocean and the wind,   —*R. & H.* 1279.

1528 Love, Hope, and Self-esteem, like clouds depart
     And come for some uncertain moments lent
                                        —*H. I. B.* IV.

1529 Thou unreplenished lamp, whose narrow fire
Is shaken by the wind, and on whose edge
Devouring darkness hovers. Thou small flame,
Which as a dying pulse rises and falls,
Still flickerest up and down, how very soon
Did not I feed thee, wouldst thou fail and be
1530 As thou hadst never been. So wastes and sinks
Even now, perhaps, the life that kindled mine,
But that no power can fill with vital oil
That broken lamp of flesh.   —*Cenci*, III. ii. 8.

1531 Both they and thou had vanished, like thin mist
Unrolled on the morning wind.   —*Prom*. I. 116.

1532 And the triumphant storm did flee
Like a conqueror swift and proud,
Between, with many a captive cloud,   —*Prom*. I. 710.

1533 It [*sc.* a Dream] has borne me here as fleet
As Desire's lightning feet.   —*Prom*. I. 733.

1534   As over wide dominions
I sped, like some swift cloud that wings the wide air's
       wildernesses,   —*Prom*. I. 763.

1535   As suddenly
Thou [*sc.* Spring] comest as the memory of a dream,
                                          —*Prom*. II. i. 7.

1536   Echoes, we : listen !
                We cannot stay :
                As dew-stars glisten
                Then fade away   —*Prom*. II. i. 166.

1537 That their flight must be swifter than fire   —*Prom*. II. iv. 4.

1538   like sister-antelopes
By one fair dam, snow-white and swift as wind,
Nursed among lilies near a brimming stream
                                          —*Prom*. III. iii. 97.

1539   Haste, oh, haste,
                As shades are chased,
Trembling by day, from heaven's blue waste.
                We melt away,
1540   Like dissolving spray.   —*Prom*. IV. 21.

1541 And your wings are soft and swift as Thought,
                                          —*Prom*. IV. 91.

1542   Death, Chaos, and Night
                From the sound of our flight,
Shall flee, like mist from a tempest's might. —*Prom*. IV. 144.

1543 Vast beams like spokes of some invisible wheel
Which whirl as the orb whirls, swifter than thought,
                                          —*Prom*. IV. 274.

1544   or some God
Whose home was in a comet, passed, and cried,
Be not ! And like my words they were no more.
                                          —*Prom*. IV. 316.

Ha ! ha ! the animation of delight
Which wraps me, like an atmosphere of light,
1545 And bears me as a cloud is borne by its own wind
Prom. IV. 322.

1546 The Earth.
I hear : I am as a drop of dew that dies. —*Prom*. IV. 523.

1547 Then the weeds . . .
Fled from the frost to the earth beneath.
Their decay and sudden flight from frost
Was but like the vanishing of a ghost. —*Sens. Plant*, III. 98.

1548 sweet spirit, which I day by day,
Have so long called my child, but which now fades away
Like a rainbow, and I the fallen shower ? —*Vision of Sea*, 88.

1549 Their unremaining gods and they
Like a river roll away. — *Ode to Heaven*, 25.

1550 Till from its station in the heaven of fame
The spirit's whirlwind rapt it, and the ray
Of the remotest sphere of living flame
Which paves the void was from behind it flung
As foam from a ship's swiftness. —*Ode to Lib*. I.

1551 Thou huntress swifter than the moon —*Ode to Lib*. X.

1552 When like heaven's sun girt by the exhalation
Of its own glorious light, thou didst arise,
Chasing thy foes from nation unto nation
Like shadows : —*Ode to Lib*. XI.

1553 As summer clouds dissolve unburthened of their rain ;
1554 As a far taper fades with fading night,
1555 As a brief insect dies with dying day,
My song, its pinions disarrayed of might,
Drooped. —*Ode to Lib*. XIX.

1556 Homeless she passed, like a cloud on the blast,
— *Œd. Tyr*. I. 246.

1557 my loyal pigs,
Now let your noses be as keen as beagles,
Your steps as swift as greyhounds. —*Œd. Tyr*. II. ii. 120.

1558 As with no stain
She faded, like a cloud which has outwept its rain
—*Adon*. X.

1559 Shall that alone which knows
Be as a sword consumed before the sheath
By sightless lightning —*Adon*. XX.

1560 Swift as a Thought by the snake Memory stung,
From her ambrosial rest the fading Splendour sprung.
—*Adon*. XXII.

1561 And like a sudden meteor, which outstrips
The splendour-wingèd chariot of the sun,
eclipse
The armies of the golden stars, each one, —*Canc. Adon*. 34.

10

1562   Worlds on worlds are rolling ever
       From creation to decay,
       Like the bubbles on a river
       Sparkling, bursting, borne away.   *Hell.* 197.

1563 Swift as the radiant shapes of sleep
    From one whose dreams are Paradise
Fly, when the fond wretch wakes to weep,
And day peers forth with her blank eyes ;
    So fleet, so faint, so fair,
    The powers of earth and air
Fled from the folding star of Bethlehem.   —*Hell.* 225.

1564 Like clouds, and like the shadows of the clouds,
1565 Over the hills of Anatolia,
    Swift in wild troops the Tartar chivalry
    Sweep :—   —*Hell.* 328.

1566   And thaw their frost-work diadems like dew ;   —*Hell.* 416.

1567   The fleet which like a flock of clouds
Chased by the wind, flies the insurgent banner.   —*Hell.* 460.

1568 And like loveliness panting with wild desire
      While it trembles with fear and delight ;
Hesperus flies from awakening night,   —*Hell.* 1036.

1569 Heaven smiles, and faiths and empires gleam
Like wrecks of a dissolving dream—   —*Hell.* 1064.

1570   Though his life, day after day,
Was failing like an unreplenished stream,   —*Prince Ath.* I. 58.

1571 The youth, as shadows on the grassy hill
Outrun the winds that chase them, soon outran
His teacher,   —*Prince Ath.* II. 13.

1572 How many a spirit then puts on the pinions
Of fancy, and outstrips the lagging blast,
And his own steps, and over wide dominions
Sweeps in his dream-drawn chariot, far and fast,
More fleet than storms—   —*Prince Ath.* III. 16.

1573 The Horse of Death tameless as wind
    Fled,   —*Mask*, XXXIII.

1574   tyrants would flee
Like a dream's dim imagery ;   —*Mask*, LII.

1575   and everything beside
Seemed like the fleeting image of a shade :   — *Witch*, XII.

1576 The boundless ocean like a drop of dew
    Will be consumed—the stubborn centre must
1577 Be scattered like a cloud of summer dust
                  —*Witch*, XXIII.

1578 And ever down the prone vale like a cloud
    Upon a stream of wind, the pinnace went :   —*Witch*, XLI.

1579   and the pale
     And heavy hue which slumber could extend
     Over its lips and eyes, as on the gale
     A rapid shadow from a slope of grass,
     Into the darkness of the stream did pass.   — *Witch*, XLIII.

1580 And then it winnowed the Elysian air
     Which ever hung about that lady bright,
        With its ætherial vans—and speeding there,
        Like a star up the torrent of the night,
1581 Or a swift eagle in the morning glare
        Breasting the whirlwind with impetuous flight,
     The pinnace oared by those enchanted wings
     Clove the fierce streams towards the upper springs.
                                          —— *Witch*, XLV.

1582   Circling the image of a shooting star,
     Even as a tiger on Hydaspe's banks
     Outspeeds the antelopes which speediest are,
        In her light boat :   *Witch*, LI.

1583 With motion like the spirit of that wind
        Whose soft step deepens slumber, her light feet
     Passed through the peopled haunts of human kind,
                              - - *Witch*, LX.

1584 He fled like a shadow before its noon :   —*Unfin. Drama*, 2.

1585   until my dream become
     Like a child's legend on the tideless sand,
     Which the first foam erases half, and half
     Leaves legible.   *Unfin. Drama*, 151.

1586 Swift as a spirit hastening to his task.
     Of glory and of good, the sun sprang forth
     Rejoicing in his splendour,   - -*Triumph*, 1.

1587   and those
     Who lead it—fleet as shadows on the green,
     Outspeed the chariot,   *Triumph*, 138.

1588   the chariot hath
     Passed over them—nor other trace I find
     But as of foam after the ocean's wrath
     Is spent upon the desert shore :   *Triumph*, 161.

1589 And suddenly my brain became as sand
     Where the first wave had more than half erased
     The track of deer on desert Labrador ;   *Triumph*, 405.

1590 And man, once fleeting o'er the transient scene
     Swift as an unremembered vision, stands
     Immortal upon earth :   — *D. W.* II. 150.

1591 The works of faith and slavery, so vast,
     So sumptuous, yet withal so perishing,
     Even as the corpse that rests beneath their wall
                               - *D. W.* II. 314.

1592   The shadows with swift wings
     Speeded like thought upon the light of Heaven.
                            - *D. W.* II. 322.

1593 The sweetness of the joy which made his breath
Fail like the trances of the summer air,   —*Sunset*, 5.

1594 My thoughts arise and fade in solitude,
The verse that would invest them melts away
Like moonlight in the heaven of spreading day :
                —*Fragm.* Vol. 3, p. 406.

1595   Till this dreadful transport may
Like a vapour fade away   —*Misery*, X.

1596 Then clouds from sunbeams, antelopes from leopards,
1597   And frowns and fears from thee
1598   Would not more swiftly flee
Then Celtic wolves from the Ausonian shepherds.
                —*Ode to Naples*, 170.

1599 And swifter thy step than the earthquake's tramp :
                —*Liberty*, III.

1600 And ever changing like a joyless eye
That finds no object worth its constancy ?   —*To the Moon*, 5.

1601 Ah, fleeter far than fleetest storm or steed,
1602   Or the death they bear,
1603 The heart which tender thought clothes like a dove
With the wings of care :   —*From Arabic*, 11.

1604   In whom love ever made
Health like a heap of embers soon to fade.   —*To Emilia*, II.

1605   I love Love—though he has wings,
And like light can flee,   —*Song*, VIII.

1606   Swifter far than summer's flight,
1607   Swifter far than youth's delight,
1608   Swifter far than happy night,
Art thou come and gone.   —*Remembrance*, I.

1609 Of that before whose breath the universe
Is as a print of dew.   —*Prol. Hell.* 5.

1610   A star has fallen upon the earth
    .   .   .   .
Swifter than the thunder fell
To the heart of earth,   —*Fragm. Hell.* III.

1611 The tempest of the   .   .   [incomplete]
.   .   .   doth come,
Swift as fire,   —*Serchio*, 96.

1612 Marks your creation rise as fast, as fair
As perfect worlds at the Creator's will.   —*To Byron*.

1613   I grow
Frail as a cloud whose (splendours) pale
Under the evening's ever-changing glow :
1614   I die like mist upon the gale,
1615 And like a wave under the calm I fail.
                —*Fragm.* Vol. 4, p. 119.

1616 Even whilst like a forgotten moon thou wanest ?
                —*Fragm.* Vol. 4, p. 121.

1617   That moment is gone forever,
       Like lightning that flashed and died,
1618   Like a snowflake upon the river,
       Like a sunbeam upon the tide
1619   Which the dark shadows hide.   —*Lines*, Vol. 4, p. 148.

1620   Man's brief and frail authority
       Is powerless as the wind
       That passeth idly by.   —*Q. M.* III. 220.

1621 Ahasuerus fled
    Fast as the shapes of mingled shade and mist,
      That lurk in glens of a twilight grove,
      Flee from the morning beam   —*Q. M.* VII. 268.

SIMILES OF LOVE.

1622 O Love! who to the hearts of wandering men
     Art as the calm to Ocean's weary waves.   —*L. & C.* VIII. xi.

1623 That love, which none may bind, be free to fill
     The world, like light;   —*L. & C.* VIII. xvi.

1624 Virtue, and Hope, and Love, like light and Heaven,
     Surround the world.—   —*L. & C.* IX. xxiii.

1625   and a light
    Of liquid tenderness like love, did rise
    From her whole frame, an atmosphere which quite
   Arrayed her in its beams, tremulous and soft and bright
                —*L. & C.* XI. v.

1626   The faintest stars are scarcely shorn
    Of their thin beams by that delusive morn
    Which sinks again in darkness, like the light
    Of early love, soon lost in total night

1627   Be it love, light, harmony,
     Odour or the soul of all
     Which from heaven like dew doth fall,
               —*Eug. Hills*, 315.
1628   And the love which heals all strife
     Circling, like the breath of life,
     All things in that sweet abode
     With its own mild brotherhood: —*Eug. Hills*, 366.

1629   the overpowering light
    Of that immortal shape was shadowed o'er
    By love; which, from his soft and flowing limbs,
    And passion-parted lips and keen, faint eyes,
    Steamed forth like vaporous fire; an atmosphere
    Which wrapt me in its all-dissolving power,
1630 As the warm æther of the morning sun
    Wraps ere it drinks some cloud of wandering dew.
                —*Prom.* II. i. 71.

1631   In the depth of the deep
     Down, down.

    Like the spark nurst in embers,
    The last look Love remembers,

    A spell is treasured.   —*Prom.* II. iii. 82.

1632   love like the atmosphere
  Of the sun's fire filling the living world,
   Burst from thee, and illumined, —*Prom.* II. v. 26.

1633   Common as light is love,
  And its familiar voice wearies not ever.
1634 Like the wide heaven, the all-sustaining air,
  It makes the reptile equal to the God : *Prom.* II. v. 40.

1635 With love which is as fire,   —*Prom.* III. iii. 151.

1636   the impalpable thin air
  And the all-circling sunlight were transformed,
  As if the sense of love dissolved in them
  Had folded itself around the sphered world.
        —*Prom.* III. iv. 100.

1637 And from beneath, around, within, above,
   Filling thy void annihilation, love
  Burst in like light on caves cloven by the thunder-ball.
        Prom. IV. 353.

1638 And like a storm bursting its cloudy prison
   With thunder, and with whirlwind, has arisen
  Out of the lampless caves of unimagined being :
       Prom. IV. 376.

1639 Which [*sc.* love] over all his kind, as the sun's heaven
   Gliding o'er ocean, smooth, serene, and even
  Darting from starry depths radiance and life, doth move.
       —*Prom.* IV. 385.

1640 Man, oh, not men ! a chain of linkèd thought,
   Of love and might to be divided not,
  Compelling the elements with adamantine stress
   As the sun rules, even with a tyrant's gaze
   The unquiet republic of the maze
  Of planets, struggling fierce towards heaven's free wilderness.
       Prom. IV. 394.

1641 *The Moon.* As in the soft and sweet eclipse
   When soul meets soul on lovers' lips,
  High hearts are calm, and brightest eyes are dull ;
   So, when thy shadow falls on me,
   Then am I mute and still, by thee
  Covered : of thy love, Orb most beautiful,
   Full, oh, too full.   *Prom.* IV. 450.

1642 Like the polar Paradise,
1643 Magnet-like of lovers' eyes : —*Prom.* IV. 465.

1644 And the spring arose in that garden fair,
  Like the Spirit of Love, felt everywhere ; —*Sens. P.* I. 5.

1645 For each one was interpenetrated
    With the light and odour its neighbour shed,
    Like young lovers whom youth and love make dear,
    Wrapped and filled by their mutual atmosphere.
                                  —Sens. P. 1. 56.

1646 Whether that lady's gentle mind,
    No longer with the form combined
    Which scattered love, as stars do light,   *—Sens. P. Concl. 5.*

1647   the heaped waves behold
    The deep calm of blue heaven dilating above,
    And, like passions made still by the presence of love,
    Beneath the clear surface reflecting it slide
    Tremulous with soft influence ;   *— Vision of Sea, 128.*

1648 Love is like understanding, that grows bright,
    Gazing on many truths ; 'tis like thy light,
    Imagination, which from earth and sky   *Epips.* 161.

1649 With flowers as soft as thoughts of budding love ; *—Epips.* 328.

                  but true love never yet
    Was thus constrained ; it overleaps all fence
1650 Like lightning, with invisible violence
1651 Piercing its continents ; like Heaven's free breath,
1652 Which he who grasps can hold not ; liker Death
    Who rides upon a thought, and makes his way
    Through temple, tower, and palace, and the array
    Of arms :   *—Epips.* 397.

1653 One passion in twin hearts, which grows and grew
    Till like two meteors of expanding flame,
    Those spheres instinct with it become the same,
    Touch, mingle, are transfigured ; ever still
    Burning, yet ever inconsumable :
    In one another's substance finding food,
1654 Like flames too pure and light and unimbued
    To nourish their bright lives with baser prey,
    Which point to Heaven and cannot pass away : *—Epips.* 575.

1655 Free love has this different from gold and clay,
    That to divide is not to take away
    Like ocean which the general north wind breaks
    Into ten thousand waves, and each one makes
1656 A mirror of the moon —like some great glass
    Which did distort whatever form might pass,
    Dashed into fragments by a playful child,
    Which then reflects its eyes and forehead mild ;
    Giving for one which it could not express,
    A thousand images of loveliness.   *—Canc. Epips.* 17.

1657 Untamable and fleet and fierce as fire,   *Canc. Epips.* 147.

1658   thou ever soarest
    Among the towers of men, and as soft air
    In spring, which moves the unawakened forest,
    Clothing with leaves its branches bare and bleak,
    Thou floatest among men   *Prince Ath.* II. iv. 1

1659   above
    One dream of Heaven smiles, like the eye of Love
    On the unquiet world :   —*Letter to M. G.* 126.

1660 And fed with love, like air and dew,
1661 Its growth—   —*To Const.* II.

1662 There is a warm and gentle atmosphere
      About the form of one we love, and thus
    As in a tender mist our spirits are
    Wrapt   —*Fragm.* Vol. 4, p. 20.

SIMILES OF DREAM.

1663   like mist on breezes curled
    From my dim sleep a shadow was unfurled   —*L. & C.* III. ii.

1664   Talk with me
    Of that our land, whose wilds and floods,
    Barren and dark although they be,
    Were dearer than these chestnut woods :
    Those heathy paths, that inland stream,
    And the blue mountains, shapes which seem
    Like wrecks of childhood's sunny dream :   —*R. & H.* 20.

1665 Athens arose : a city such as vision
    Builds from the purple crags and silver towers
    Of battlemented cloud, as in derision
    Of kingliest masonry :   —*Ode to Lib.* V.

1666 As one enamoured is upborne in dream
    O'er lily-paven lakes 'mid silver mist,
    To wondrous music, so this shape might seem
    Partly to tread the waves with feet which kissed
    The dancing foam :   —*Triumph,* 367.

1667 Along a shelving bank of turf, which lay
    Under a copse, and hardly dared to fling
    Its green arms round the bosom of the stream,
    But kissed it and then fled, as thou mightest in dream
                     —*Question.*

SIMILES OF THOUGHT.

1668 Soft and delightful thoughts did rest and hover
    Like shadows o'er my brain   —*L. & C.* I. xv.

1669 And this belovèd child then felt the sway
    Of my conceptions, gathering like a cloud
    The very wind on which it rolls away   *L. & C.* II. xxxi.

1670 Such are the thoughts which, like the fires that flare
In storm-encompassed isles, we cherish yet
In this dark ruin.   —*L. & C.* VII. xxxvii.

1671 What is this undistinguishable mist
Of thoughts, which rise, like shadow after shadow,
Darkening each other?   —*Cenci,* III. i. 170.

1672 Obscurely through my brain, like shadows dim,
Sweep awful thoughts, rapid and thick.   —*Prom.* I. 146.

1673   the thought
Which pierces this dim universe like light.   —*Prom.* II. iv. 40.

1674 Drive my dead thoughts over the universe
Like withered leaves to quicken a new birth   —*West Wind,* V.

1675 And his own thoughts, along that rugged way
Pursued, like raging hounds, their father and their prey.
                        Adon. XXXI.

1676   Earth and ocean,
Space, and the isles of life or light that gem
The sapphire floods of interstellar air,
This firmament pavilioned upon chaos,
With all its cressets of immortal fire,
Whose outwall, bastioned impregnably
Against the escape of boldest thoughts, repels them
As Calpe the Atlantic clouds.   —*Hell.* 769.

1677 Thoughts after thoughts, unresting multitudes,
1678 Were driven within him, by some secret power,
Which bade them blaze, and live, and roll afar,
Like lights and sounds from haunted tower to tower,
O'er castled mountains borne, when tempest's war
Is levied by the night-contending winds,
And the pale dalesmen watch with eager ear
                        —*Prince Ath.* I. 66.

1679 As flowers beneath May's footsteps waken,
1680 As stars from Night's loose hair are shaken,
1681 As waves arise when loud winds call,
Thoughts sprung where'er that step did fall.   —*Mask.* XXXI.

1682 How beautiful they were, how firm they stood
Flecking the starry sky like woven pearl.   —*Fragm. Thoughts.*

1683 Thy deep eyes, a double Planet
  Gaze the wisest into madness
With soft clear fire,—the winds that fan it
  Are those thoughts of tender gladness
Which, like zephyrs on the billow
Make thy gentle soul thy pillow—   —*Sophia,* II.

Ye gentle visitations of calm thought—
1684 Moods like the memories of happier earth,
Which come arrayed in thoughts of little worth,
1685 Like stars in clouds by the weak winds enwrought,
But that the clouds depart and stars remain,
While they remain, and ye, alas, depart.
                —*Fragm.* Vol. 4, p. 17.

1686   ye who sit
 Pavilioned on the radiance or the gloom
 Of mortal thought, which like an exhalation
 Steaming from earth, conceals the of heaven
 Which gave it birth   —*Prol. Hell.* 9.

1687 Until an envious wind crept by
 Like an unwelcome thought,
 Which from the mind's too faithful eye
 Blots one dear image out.   —*To June*, 81.

- - -

SIMILES OF NUMBER.

1688 '   the vast clouds fled
 Countless and swift as leaves on autumn's tempest shed'.
         —*L. & C.* I. iv.

1689 Wingèd and wan diseases, an array
 Numerous as leaves that strew the autumnal gale ;
         —*L. & C.* I. xxix.

1690 And multitudinous as the desert sand
 Borne on the storm, its millions shall advance,
         L. & C. II. xlv.

1691   those millions swept
 Like waves before the tempest— —*L. & C.* VII. iii.

1692   their throngs did make
 Behind the steed, a chasm like waves in a ship's wake
         —*L. & C.* X. iii.

1693 Great people, as the sands shalt thou become,
         L. & C. XI. xxiii.

1694 Look, sister, where a troop of spirits gather,
 Like flocks of clouds in spring's delightful weather,
 Thronging in the blue air !   —*Prom.* I. 664.

1695   And see ! more come,
 Like fountain-vapours when the winds are dumb,
 That climb up the ravine in scattered lines.
         —*Prom.* I. 666.

 Four hundred thousand Moslems from the limits
 Of utmost Asia, irresistibly
1696 Throng like full clouds at the Sirocco's cry ;
1697 But not like them to weep their strength in tears.
         Hell. 275.

1698   The Grecian fleet
      . . . hung
 As multitudinous on the ocean line
 As cranes upon the cloudless Thracian wind —*Hell.* 477.

1699 And when the windless snow descended thicker
 Than autumn leaves   —*Witch*, XXX.

1700 And o'er its gentle countenance did play
The busy dreams as thick as summer flies.   *Witch*, XL.

1701 And as the day grew hot, methought I saw
A glassy vapour dancing on the pool,
And on it little quaint and filmy shapes,
With dizzy motion, wheel and rise and fall,
Like clouds of gnats with perfect lineaments
                                  —*Unfin. Drama*, 234.

1702   and the crowd divided
Like waves before an admiral's prow.   —*Chas. I.* I. 133.

1703   and a great stream
Of people there was hurrying to and fro,
Numerous as gnats upon the evening gleam.   —*Triumph*, 44.

1704 He made one of the multitude, and so
Was borne amid the crowd, as through the sky
One of the million leaves of summer's bier ;   —*Triumph*, 49.

1705 And as I gazed, methought that in the way
The throng grew wilder, as the woods of June
When the south wind shakes the extinguished day,
                                  —*Triumph*, 74.

1706 And saw like clouds upon the thunder blast
The million with fierce song and maniac dance
Raging around—   —*Triumph*, 109.

1707 But all like bubbles on an eddying flood
Fell into the same track at last, and were
Borne onward—   —*Triumph*, 458.

1708 ⎫
1709 ⎬ Or like small gnats or flies, as thick as mist
1710 ⎭ On evening marshes,   —*Triumph*, 508.

1711   each one
Of that great crowd sent forth incessantly
These shadows, numerous as the dead leaves blown
In autumn evening from a poplar tree.   —*Triumph*, 528.

1712 The thronging thousands, to a passing view
Seemed like an ant-hill's citizens.   —*Q. M.* II. 101.

LIFE.

I was born in Toronto, Canada, on March 17, 1871. I received my early education at Upper Canada College, and matriculated at the University of Toronto in 1887, where, with the intermission of a year, I remained until the spring of 1892. In that year I graduated with the Governor-General's medal in Modern Languages. For the three following years I taught Modern Languages at Upper Canada College, at the same time working under the general direction of Dr. Bright. In the autumn of 1895 I entered the Johns Hopkins University, where I followed courses in English, German and French. In January, 1896, I was appointed Scholar in the Department of English, and Fellow in June of the same year. I have studied under Dr. Bright, Dr. Brown, Dr. Wood, Dr. Menger and Dr. de Hahn, to all of whom I desire to express my gratitude.

To Dr. Bright, especially, I wish to convey my warm appreciation of the benefit I have received from his stimulating and sympathetic direction of my work.

PELHAM EDGAR.

www.ingramcontent.com/pod-product-compliance
Lightning Source LLC
Chambersburg PA
CBHW021110020726
47500CB00003B/690